Jay Carp
Fish Tales

Books by
Award Winning Author Jay Carp

The Gift of Ruth 2003

The Gift of Ruth—Large print 2008

Cold War Confessions 2007
USA Best Books of 2007 Award Winner

The Patriots of Foxboro 2009

Loneliness 2011

Jay Carp Fish Tales 2011

Jay Carp
Fish Tales

Tall and Short Stories
by Humorist Jay Carp . . .
A Modern Day Mark Twain

River Pointe Publications
Milan, Michigan, USA

Jay Carp Fish Tales
© 2011 by Jay Carp, first edition

Published by
River Pointe Publications
Milan, Michigan 48160
734-439-8031

ISBN: 978-0-9817258-6-4

This is a work of the author's memories and observations.
Any resemblance to persons, living or dead,
events or locales are entirely coincidental.

Interior design and composition by Sans Serif Inc.
Cover design by Barb Gunia
Cover art by Gay Kerry Halseth

Printed in USA

Dedication

Strictly speaking, *FISH TALES* are not considered an exact, specific category within the realm of biological classifications.

However, *FISH TALES* does have an interesting background and, as the author, I would be remiss if I failed to reveal the identities of the scoundrels responsible for making these stories available to an unsuspecting public.

The spawning pond where *FISH TALES* were first hatched was the writing class of Helen Hill. Ms. Hill had retired after a career of teaching as an English professor at Eastern Michigan University; however, feeling the urge to do something useful, she offered to moderate a writing group for the Turner Senior Resource Center, part of the University of Michigan Health System outreach program. This was the class that I joined in the early 1990's. That writing group, with almost all of its original members, was close knit for years and, even to this date, they remain loyal to each other and Helen. She did an excellent job of teaching us how to enhance our work and guiding us into becoming more precise writers. Helen Hill has a gift for making us all better and wiser people without hurting our pride or our feelings. Being in her class brought out the best in each of us; she made us proud of who we were and what we had done with our lives. Her love of life was an inspirational candle of light that she passed on to each of her students.

I subsequently dropped out of the class in the early 2000's but, by that time, the damage had been done. I had written dozens and dozens and dozens of short stories, reminiscences, and two autobiographical books. All of these shorter works might have remained under a rock except for a series of incidents that took place this last summer.

First, I got sick from a gall bladder infection that flared up and threatened my life. For a few weeks, I was critically ill. During that period, my wife made herself a promise that she only revealed to me after I began to recover.

She, Hazel Proctor Carp, told me that, while I was sick, she had made a vow to publish my short stories. Hazel meant them to stand either as a tribute to my memory or as an explanation of why the world is off kilter. Secretly, I hope it is for the latter reason.

There are two other groups that deserve some of the blame for keeping these stories alive. The first group are the ladies that play bridge with Hazel every week. The three of them, Alice Allsetter, Isabelle Schultz, and Maribeth Bramlage, listened to Hazel's problems and, as a group, they helped plan my fate. As a matter of fact, it was Isabelle who suggested to Hazel the title, "*FISH TALES—Tall and Short Stories by Humorist Jay Carp . . . Our Modern Day Mark Twain*".

My thanks also go to Barbara Gunia and Susan Kenyon of Sans Serif. They worked with Hazel to assemble the manuscript and get it to the printer. Barbara also took Gay Kerry Halseth's painting of a carp fish and designed it into our cover.

Savor the taste of life. No person ever gets too much and it lasts such a short time.

Contents

Contents

Ebb Tide

Memories are like the flow of the ocean. Both of them can surge in strongly or recede slowly and we have no control over either of them.

As I look back at past events in my life, a lot of my memories are surrounded in a fog of forgetfulness. Sometimes the fog is only a mist and I remember the details quite well and sometimes it is pea soup thick and I have to use my imagination. And, when that happens, the truth sometimes gets squeezed into a slightly different shape, like toothpaste out of the tube.

I was reminded of this after a visit with my older brother. We were talking about our childhood when he remarked that I used to disappear for long stretches at a time without anyone knowing where I had gone. He was correct; I did vanish. For me, there is no mist around where I went and what I did. I have to admit though, that there is pea soup fog concerning some of the minor details.

When I was close to sixteen years old, I developed a desire, almost an obsession, to watch the ocean. Whenever I could, I would drive from Malden, Massachusetts, where I lived, to Cape Ann and spend hours enchanted with the area and the ever changing beauty of the Atlantic Ocean.

I would drive through the salt marshes of Lynn with the window down just to inhale the heavy, earthy smell that is common to stagnant ocean water. Some people think that the strong odor is not pleasant; however, I enjoyed it as a harbinger of things to come because Lynn was the last city before I got to the edge of the Atlantic.

When I first began ocean watching, I would make a right turn when I got to the water and drive down a small peninsula that jutted out towards Boston Harbor. The whole peninsula was the town of Nahant. After a few trips, I decided that Nahant was not as interesting as the rest of the trip so I stopped turning right. As a result, I would turn left and that would bring me into Swampscott and Fisherman's Beach.

Fisherman's Beach was long, semicircular beach that had a high sea wall behind it and a massive rock formation that divided it into two sections. The entire rock formation was called Red Rock and its fissures trapped the incoming tides and threw huge sprays of water into the air. Between the spray and the shorebirds, the seagulls, the terns, the ospreys, there was always a show at Red Rock. I would stay to watch the many performances and time would completely slip away from me.

Eventually, I would drive down every back road along the ocean as I traveled through the towns of Marblehead, Salem, Beverly, Manchester, Gloucester, Rockport, Essex, and, finally, Ipswich. There were stops to make at each of these old seaport towns and sights unique to Cape Ann. In addition to the rocky shores and thundering ocean there were cemeteries dating back to the 1600's, castles built by wealthy people, fishermen working on their tiny boats and nets, a statue of a deep sea fisherman, and an intersection which was called Prides Crossing. I have always wondered how that junction got its name. There was no set pattern; I would just meander and each trip I planned new nuggets of beauty for me to discover.

It was at Ipswich that I would stop for either clam chowder or a pail of steamed clams. My trip around Cape Ann, although it was no longer than thirty miles, always lasted for many, many hours. I would eat my meal with gusto and make plans for my next trip.

However, I am having trouble recalling the pea soup details. First of all, World War II was on and gasoline was rationed and I now wonder where I got coupons to buy the gas to go roaming around? I know it wasn't black market gas because, by then, my brother was in the army and my family was too patriotic to buy anything on the black market.

Another detail that puzzles me was what was I doing driving the family car without a license? The age for obtaining a license in Massachusetts has always been sixteen and I know I was driving a truck into the produce market in Boston for my father's business a little before license time. But that was necessary; driving around Cape Ann was not. I must have been extremely careful not to speed or get stopped for a traffic infraction.

On the other hand, my trips to the ocean were usually at odd times because I was still in high school and working in my father's store when it was open. I went whenever I was free which meant any time, any season, and any weather. Rarely did my travels occur during any busy times. Because of my hankering, I went whenever I was able to.

I made these pilgrimages by myself as often as I could until I was drafted. When I came back from the Army, I continued to ocean watch whenever there was an opportunity.

Occasionally, I would bring a date with me but that actually didn't work out too well. The young ladies didn't want to linger as long as I wanted and the weather stopped them from enjoying themselves as much as I did. So, for their sake's as well as my own, I went back to going by myself.

I came to Michigan to go to college, and then got married, raised a family, and, by sheer coincidence, returned to Massachusetts to work. Over the course of time, I took my three daughters many, many times to Cape Ann. They loved to jump over the cracks in Red Rock just as the waves sprayed upwards and they looked forward to exploring the wonders and beauty of Cape Ann before we got to the chowder and steamers at Ipswich.

I have been inland for many years now and I do miss the ocean. Whenever I went to Boston, I would drive the same route on Cape Ann that I used to drive as a young man. But it is not the same. Construction has brought a surge of people and buildings along the ocean front. Access and solitude are much harder to come by. Even the chowder and steamers are different, having been affected by the Red Tide pollutants.

However, even though modern day changes may prevent me from seeing what used to be, they can't stop me from recalling the past. I can shut my eyes and ocean watch as I did when I was sixteen. I open my memory box and recall the sights, the smells, and the sounds I so enjoyed as a youngster. The pleasantness of those details infuses me with warmth and I can smile.

It is on the pea soup details that I can't recall.

A Grave Injustice

I was eating lunch at the mess hall, during my last week of basic training, when I was told that sergeant Donnelly wanted to see me immediately. It was Thursday. Thinking that he had information about my request to transfer into the paratroops, I went to the orderly room. Donnelly was sitting with his feet on his desk, his hands behind his head, and he was smoking a cigar.

"Carp, after roll call tomorrow morning, you will be excused from regular duties. You and several others are going on a special assignment with Sergeant Wexler. Go see him for the details."

"What is this special assignment, Sergeant Donnelly?"

Donnelly brushed me off very quickly. "I don't have all day to chit chat with you. I am very busy. Wexler is in his barracks waiting for you, so go see him."

Wexler's barracks was next to mine. I did not know him but I had learned a lot about him in the last few months. He was a platoon sergeant who had been in the army for over thirty years. He was born in Alabama and joined the army when he was fifteen. Some of my friends, who were in his platoon, called him "The Bonehead from Birmingham" because they thought that he was dumb. At first, I had no opinion one way or the other, but, almost every night, he would show up at the BX, drink beer, and loudly tell stories about all the women who were attracted to him. Then, he would detail all his sexual escapades that resulted from his irresistible attraction. After hearing him for a while, I began to believe my friends.

When I entered his barrack, I saw six or seven men of our company sitting around Wexler. He said, "Where the Hell have you been? I have had to wait until you got here so I can explain our assignment for tomorrow."

"Sergeant Wexler, I wasn't told about any assignment until less then five minutes ago."

"Well, dammit, that's no excuse. Next time find out faster. Now listen up. Tomorrow, you soldiers, under my direct supervision, are going to be honor guards at a funeral that will be performed near Baltimore. Some guy from World War I died and his family wants him to have a military funeral. I have all the details in my head. We will leave early in the morning. You will wear your class A dress uniforms, your helmets, and bring your rifles. I will supply you with blank cartridges. I want you to look sharp because there may be some young chicks at this funeral. If there are, when I meet them, I will ask them if they have any girl friends for you.

"That is all that you recruits need to know. There should be no questions. If you do exactly as I say, this will be an easy assignment, especially if there are any chicks. I will see you in the morning."

I returned to my own barrack shaking my head. I had no idea why any of us, especially me, had been selected for this detail, and more puzzling to me, why Wexler had been picked as the non commissioned officer in charge. I was a little concerned about how this was going to turn out, but it wasn't my problem so I stopped thinking about it.

The next morning was cloudy and bitterly cold. The temperature hovered around freezing. It was February and in the DC area the cold can be humid and penetrating. That, plus a steady wind, chilled us as we stood and waited for Sergeant Wexler. There were eight of us; six riflemen, one bugler, and one man to help fold the flag with Wexler. We were wearing our dress uniforms, with Ike jackets, and our steel helmets. When Wexler arrived, he was wearing his Ike jacket and he had rows of ribbons on his chest. If you stay in the military for thirty years you can't avoid picking up some kinds of ribbons. The rest of us, since we were not even out of basic training, had no ribbons at all.

One of our group asked Wexler, "Sarge, it is cold. Can't we wear our overcoats and gloves?"

"No," he replied. "We look more military wearing just our uniforms. No overcoat or gloves. If there are any chicks there, I want them to see my ribbons."

I just shook my head. I could not believe him. By now, I was convinced that, as long as his hands were free and he could see both of them, Sergeant Wexler could count to ten. Anything more would be a risk. We got in the back of an army truck that had a tarpaulin to protect us from the wind but there was no heat. Wexler got in the cab with the driver and he had heat. We froze on the trip from Fort Belvoir to the outskirts of Baltimore. When we got to the gate of the cemetery where the funeral was to be held, Wexler got out and made a phone call from a telephone booth down the street. He came back and told us that the funeral was going to be delayed for a while so we would have to wait. He ordered the driver to park the truck off the road just inside the gate.

There was no sun, it was cold, and the wind made us huddle just to try to keep warm. After twenty minutes Wexler said, "Jesus Christ, it's cold. I don't intend to just hang around and wait for this guy to show up. Here's what we are going to do. See that bar across the street? We are going in there to keep warm. We can watch out the window and see when this guy arrives. Each man has to pay for himself."

Our driver declined to go with us because he did not want to drive a government vehicle with alcohol on his breath. He stayed in the heated cab and he guarded our rifles and our equipment. We all went across the street to the neighborhood bar. With the exception of Wexler, none of us was over nineteen but the bartender never checked our ages. With the exception of Wexler, none of us had drunk much hard liquor before. However, since we were cold, miserable, and furious with Wexler, we tried to overcome this deficiency. We started to drink straight shots of liquor. Shortly, we not only got over our chills, we took on enough antifreeze to protect us against Arctic temperatures. All of us, including Sergeant Wexler, were feeling no pain.

Suddenly, someone yelled, "Hey, a hearse is pulling into the cemetery." We all dashed out of the bar room, ran back to the truck, got our gear, got into formation, and marched down the road to where the hearse had stopped. As we got close, I could see that on one side of the open grave was a mound of dirt about two feet high. On the other side, closest to the road, was a casket covered with an American flag, a minister wearing a black hat and a stole, and two individuals. One was a frail elderly woman, the other was an elderly man who held the woman's arm. They looked forlorn in this dreary setting.

Sergeant Wexler could have marched us behind the man and woman or he could have marched us to the foot of the grave. Instead he marched us over to the side where the mound of earth was. He maneuvered us so close to the edge of the grave that we marched over the mound. There we stood at parade rest, two riflemen at the head, two riflemen on top of the mound of dirt, and two riflemen at the foot. We certainly did not resemble any honor guard I had ever seen.

When the time came for the bugler to play taps, considering the weather and the whiskey, he did a fairly good job of hitting the notes. Sergeant Wexler gave us our orders. "Detail Tenhut, Ready, Aim, Fire." There was not one crisp salvo. There was just the ragged sound of individual shots. The other two salvos were just as bad. What was worse was the fact that the funeral party was less than six feet away from us on the other side of the grave. The smoke from the burnt powder completely enveloped them. At first I thought we had shot them. The wind blew the smoke away and I felt better when I saw that they were still standing. Wexler folded the flag, gave it to the woman, and we marched back to the truck.

On the drive back to base, I didn't say a word. The only person who chattered away was Sergeant Wexler. I was so cold that I was shaking and I also had one hell of a hangover. What depressed me even more was the fiasco that I had not only just witnessed but that I had been a party to. All of us, with the exception of Wexler, knew that we had made a travesty of a solemn occasion.

When a person dies, his life deserves more attention and celebration than just two elderly mourners. And he certainly deserves more honor and respect than we provided. My mood was black. I did not feel well and I felt guilty. The only minor consolation I had was that, at least, there were no chicks at the funeral.

A Plea to Homo Sapiens

Can a rhinoceros sing? Can a panda speak in three different languages? Can a rabbit dance a tango? Of course the answers to all three questions are "no." The questions were framed that way. However, they do serve the purpose of showing just how versatile human beings can be. As a species, we are capable of magnificent accomplishments.

We have evolved from creatures that smashed clams with rocks to survive into people who can slice steel with lasers. We have populated the entire planet adapting to climate and geographical differences by changing racial characteristics. Humans have developed different languages, cultures, and alphabets to suit their needs. We use the knowledge obtained from our predecessors to teach ourselves even more. And, within this category of Homo sapiens, there are individuals who have reached sublime heights.

Writers, from centuries past, have written poems, plays, and books that stir our emotions today. The same can be said of musicians and painters. Every one of us can name an author, composer, or painter who has stirred his or her feelings. The point is that we can be moved by the creativity of human beings who have lived long before we were born.

And this capacity, the ability to look backwards for ideas and ideals, is probably the biggest difference between Homo sapiens and every other species on earth. Our science shows that other species can communicate with each other in a limited capacity and that some species can even handle basic abstract thought. But no other species can reach back in history and touch the wellsprings of emotion as we humans can.

As a result of our unique potential, humans have reached marvelous heights and done wondrous things. Besides stirring our souls and our consciences with the arts, we have unlocked many of the mysteries of the universe that we live in. Our capability for abstract reasoning has put us on the moon, shown us how to eradicate deadly diseases, and even lengthened our own life span.

We do indeed possess all the potential necessary to be a majestic species. Because of our amazing gifts some humans are convinced that Homo Sapiens is the most intelligent species of animal on the face of this earth.

We may, or may not be, the most intelligent. However, I am convinced that those people who believe this are missing a very important point. We are also the most irrational animals on the face of this earth. No other species behave as perversely as we do. There is no other species that has destroyed as much of its own kind as have human beings.

We have base feelings, emotions, and motives that can swell as deeply and as fiercely as our positive attributes. As a group, whether under the guise of religion, patriotism, or race, humans have attacked each other's civilizations and cultures since history has been recorded. And the aggressors, when they detail their stories, have been proud of their deeds and have boasted of their accomplishments.

None of these appalling transgressions are a new phenomenon for humans. Historians, from time immemorial, have recorded detailed journals of cultures and religions attacking each other. As we cluster together, either as a religion, a country, or a race, we become fearful of different religions, countries, and races. Although rational reasons are always given as justification for what we humans do, the driving forces behind our group actions are usually irrational, either fear, or greed, or hatred.

Because of our group irrationality, humans are putting themselves in danger of ruining our planet and making their own species extinct. We are also endangering the existence of many other species, as well as the earth itself. We have polluted the air, fouled the water, and littered the land. So much damage has been done to our environment that future generations will soon be living in a different climate and in an altered landscape.

We are close to the point of no return primarily because the human race has been unwittingly stripping the planet for its personal wants and needs. In so doing, we have unwittingly tipped over Earth's natural rhythms and cycles. After thousands of years of warfare against other humans and two hundred years of plundering the planet, the bills are beginning to come due.

There are many reasons that a doomsday scenario is beginning to appear at this time. One of the major problems is the number of Homo sapiens on this Earth. It is at an all time high. A billion in China, a billion in India, four hundred million in America, the total number of humans is almost seven billion, and counting. Because of the population surge, we are overusing every resource on the face of the earth. Feeding this mass of humanity is not the only concern. Whether the population is in the developed countries, the developing countries, or the underdeveloped countries, as a species we are ripping asunder our environment.

In the developed countries we are gorging energy, producing green house gasses, polluting streams and waterways, and ruining our natural habitat. With absolutely no concern for the consequences we build where we shouldn't. In the United States we are turning our backs on our own history in order to sell newly developed properties. We have become so productive that child obesity is becoming a problem.

In the under developed countries, many of which are dominated by the developed countries, they strip their forests and grow illicit drugs in order to keep alive. Famine, disease, and tribal warfare are rife on all of our continents while genocide is a fact of life in Africa. Infant mortality is extremely high and diseases such as AIDS are rampant.

In the developing countries, we have the worst of both worlds. China and India, for example, are building power plants without regard to emissions, and driving more and more automobiles with absolutely no thought of pollution control.

And in all countries, no matter what their economic status, a large part of their budgets are being spent on both armaments and building nuclear weapons.

These facts and attitudes do not follow each other sequentially. They arise out of past events over the centuries and are all jumbled together and are like the "chicken and the egg controversy." What is important is the fact that we are facing an imminent danger from our behavior. We lump all of our problems together and give it the name of "global warming."

Fortunately, political leaders are finally beginning to understand what the scientists have been predicting for decades. Even business executives, who in the past were driven only by profits, are becoming concerned about what is happening to our environment. There has finally been a stirring to discover what can be done to mitigate the results of mankind's excesses.

This newly found awareness raises many questions. Is it too late to prevent major changes to our biosphere? Can scientists, politicians, and businessmen agree on what needs to be done? Considering the economic, political, racial, religious, and cultural differences of Homo sapiens, will we be able to work together to solve our problems? Can we react in time to stabilize our bruised and battered planet?

I don't believe anyone really knows the answers to any of these questions yet. The scientists are wrestling with imprecise data and each estimate depends on how the particular scientist evaluates his individual mathematical model. Some renowned scientists are pessimistic and other renowned scientists are optimistic. However, all of them are in agreement that more changes are coming but they are not sure when the changes will occur or how severe they will be.

The scientists can only make recommendations. Unfortunately, for the rest of humanity, it will be the heads of state and the elected politicians who will make the decisions that will affect our future. Those leaders run the gamut of intelligence, vested interests, and willingness to compromise and, without unanimous agreement, there is little chance of making any change. For example, the Kyoto Treaty available since 1997, and signed by the United States in that year, is languishing because the United States has not ratified it. Both the Clinton administration and the Bush administration have refused to bring the treaty up for ratification, each citing different problems with the treaty. Surely, if mankind is going to make any progress, we are going to have to overcome all obstacles. If a path away from global warming is to be followed, our differences, whether real or imagined or irrational, are going to have to be resolved. I'm not sure that we can resolve differences.

As for me, I am concerned about global warming. I want the world clean and shiny for all species. But I don't know if Homo Sapiens, all seven billion of us, can react in concert to avoid a catastrophe. Some days I hear global warming news and I feel good and some days I hear global warming news and I feel bad. And what can one individual do against a problem that is world wide in scope?

Hopeless or not, I am fighting a one-person war to help stave off global warming. I recycle everything I can, I conserve as much energy as I can, and I try not to waste precious resources such as water and gasoline. That isn't much but it is about the best that I can do. I do wonder, though, what the world would be like if my seven billion brothers and sisters were also doing their best to fight global warming?

Abigail Flunks Out of Obedience School

Last Thursday night I was watching television and a panel of experts was discussing this new wave of school age killers who were shooting their teachers and classmates. As I heard them explain all of the social and psychological reasons for this terrible phenomenon, a question popped into my mind. Did any of these troubled and disturbed children ever have a pet? I don't know the answer to that question, but I don't think that they did have pets. That's because taking care of a pet means having compassion and love; and obviously these self centered, disturbed creatures have absolutely no joyous emotions.

That question, though, started me thinking about all of the cats and dogs that have owned me over the years. There were many pets and I want to tell you about one dog in particular, whose name was Abigail.

However, to fully appreciate Abigail, you should know a little about her predecessor, Ludwig Von Beethoven. Beethoven, as he allowed me to call him, was a Dachshund. He was a purebred and we got him while he was a puppy from a kennel in Plymouth. As he grew he developed a bad back and epilepsy. Our veterinarian said that his blood line had been inbred too much and that the people who sold him were only interested in producing and selling dogs. The health of their dogs was not important to them. His problems made Ginny love him all the more. I will say Beethoven did look helpless and pitiful when he had his epileptic fits. However much Ginny loved him, my three young daughters and I never really warmed up to Beethoven.

First, Beethoven was not a friendly dog. He would only respond to Ginny. When she wasn't home he would follow any of the rest of us around, barking and yipping constantly. Worse, when nobody was around he would chew. His preference was the wood trim near the floorboards; but he also liked the girl's shoes and clothes. He just had to chew. Our house was slowly being reduced by a dog who must have had termites and goats somewhere in his ancestry. This was annoying because he could not be punished or disciplined or he might have an epileptic seizure. I used to dream that someone would recognize him as a former war criminal and he would be deported back to Germany.

Beethoven lived to be fourteen before he joined his ancestors Tristan and Isolde in Valhalla. Ginny was devastated by his death; the three girls and I were what I would best define as semi sad. It was with this history as a background that we went out and purchased an Old English Sheep dog. I wanted to name her perfume because she cost more than thirty dollars an ounce, but I was outvoted four to one. The name selected was Abigail.

She had one brown eye and one blue eye. The girls were constantly pushing her hair away from her face, looking into her eyes and asking, "Is that you in there, Abigail?" By the time she was eight months old she weighed seventy pounds and with her long white, gray and black hair she took up plenty of room. I thought of her as a haystack on the move. She was happy and playful and she never barked. That pleased us except when one night a burglar broke the latch on the door of our screened-in porch. He stepped over Abigail, picked up a television set, stepped over Abigail again, and was gone. I heard the noise of the latch breaking and I got to the porch as the thief restepped over Abigail. I yelled, he ran, Abigail heard my voice and got up, ready to play. That was when I decided that maybe Abigail ought to go to obedience school.

After making several phone calls I located a trainer in Walpole who was starting an obedience class. We talked about Abigail for a while and he told me that he thought she would do just fine, so, unbeknown to Abigail, she was enrolled.

The evening of her first class, Julie, my middle daughter, asked me if she could come along. Julie would not let Beethoven into her room, but she would not let Abigail out of her sight. I said sure she could join us but she was not to wave at Abigail, or talk to Abigail, or distract Abigail in any way. Julie promised to behave like an angel, and that would have been a first. So, off we went, Abigail, Julie, me and a hefty check for the tuition. When we arrived, the trainer, Mr. Daugherty, took the check, asked Julie to sit in a chair about ten feet behind us and lined up all the dogs in front of him. There were nine owners thirsting for knowledge on how to make their dog's obey. The dogs were placed according to size, and Abigail and I found ourselves in the center of the student body. Mr. Daugherty told us not to worry about our dogs for a while as he wanted to talk to us the masters. The eight other dogs laid down when they got this news. Abigail kept straining on her leash, trying to go visit Julie, who, much to my surprise, was behaving like an angel.

Mr. Daugherty said that our dogs loved us and would do anything to please us. However, it was necessary for us to tell the dogs in clear, unmistakable language what we wanted. As he was speaking the eight other dogs were lolling and listing, Abigail was straining to go to Julie. I was telling her clearly and unmistakable, by yanking her leash, that I did not want her pulling. I wondered why she wasn't paying attention to Mr. Daugherty or me. Mr. Daugherty went on to say that our first meeting would cover the most important basic commands, sit and heel. The five other meetings would take the rest of the commands and hand signals; when we finished we would have dogs that would obey us under any condition. During his entire discussion he kept watching Abigail but he did not say a word.

He told us to walk our dogs around for a few minutes and then come back in line, in the same order, and have the dogs on our left side. He wanted the dogs to be sitting beside our left legs. Abigail was delighted at the chance to walk around with me and when I swung back into line she quickly sat at my left leg. The only problem was that, while all the other dogs were facing Mr. Daugherty, Abigail was sitting backwards, facing Julie.

Mr. Daugherty said to me, "Walk her around again and when you come back into line, slide your hand down the leash near her collar and pull up so she can't put any weight on her front paws." I did as he said and after two more tries Abigail was facing the front of the class.

I asked him, "Do you think that my daughter should wait in the car instead of being in here?" "No," answered Mr. Daugherty. "Your daughter is behaving quite nicely. It has nothing to do with her. Your dog is a big lovable young dog. She is the one that is lacking the training, not your daughter."

That time, Abigail must have been listening to Mr. Daugherty because she obeyed and did what she was supposed to do for the next few minutes. Then her mind wandered and she got interested in her classmates. She wanted to wander over to them and sniff. By the time her classmates were sitting, when commanded to, almost one hundred percent of the time, Abigail was up to thirty percent. Her mind was just not on her schoolwork. Next, Mr. Daugherty showed us how to make our dogs heel. We would walk them around, come back into line, and pull their shoulders close to our left legs. Abigail did this difficult maneuver two or three times when tragedy struck.

I had just wheeled Abigail back into line when I smelled the reeking stink of dog shit. "Oh, Oh," I thought, "Some poor owner has a dog that just made a mess." I looked to my left to see if I could tell which dog it was; all I saw were four guys looking to their right. I then looked to my right; all I saw was four guys looking to their left. I got the picture. I looked down and Abigail was the dog. I guess she decided to critique the class even before it was finished. Mr. Daugherty took this unscheduled event in stride. Without stopping his talking, he took a long handled, square ended shovel, marched over to the pile and with a deft sure motion scooped up all of the dog shit. He put it into a metal barrel, put the lid on the barrel and kept giving us our instructions.

After that Abigail paid even less attention to me, Mr. Daugherty, or her classmates. She was intent on getting over to visit Julie. Even when Mr. Daugherty took her leash to demonstrate how to handle her, Abigail was not too cooperative. She spent more time licking his hand than she did obeying his command. Since the rest of the class was waiting for him, he finally shook his head and gave her leash back to me.

At the end of the class Mr. Daugherty came over to where Julie, Abigail, and I were standing, and he said, "Mr. Carp, I am sorry to say this but I am going to have to ask you to withdraw Abigail from this class." Somehow I was not surprised. I asked, "Does that mean that you think that Abigail is untrainable?" "Oh no, not at all," Mr. Daugherty replied. "No dog is untrainable. But she still acts like a puppy and she is disruptive. Give her a few months and she might be less exuberant and more prepared for discipline. Of course, I shall refund you your money." And he returned my check. We rode home with Julie kissing Abigail, scratching her ears, and crooning over and over. "Naughty, naughty Abigail."

When we got home, Abigail bounded out of the car, jumped up on Cynthia, Elizabeth and Ginny and tried to lick them clean. Then she raced around the yard for a few minutes and tried to give all of us seconds in lickings. Ginny asked, "How did she do?" Julie piped up, "Mommy, Mommy, Abigail pooped in class." Ginny looked at me; "Did she? Really?" I answered, "She did. Not only that, she has been invited not to return to obedience school." Ginny said in surprise, "For pooping in class? I can't believe that. You have to be kidding me." "No, it wasn't for that," I replied. And then I told Ginny what had happened giving her all the details. Ginny was not happy. "Couldn't the trainer, Mr. Daugherty give Abigail more time?" "I don't think so Ginny," I said to her "He has eight other dogs he has to train. Abigail acts like a wild puppy. Besides, there are some dogs, like there are some people, who are just not college material. Maybe Abigail, being an Old English Sheep Dog, feels that it is not right for her to own a sheepskin."

Abigail lived for fifteen years and she never went back to obedience school. Every moment of those fifteen years she gave us devotion, boundless energy and love. There is nothing more important or satisfying than what she gave us. Rest in Peace Abigail.

AWOL

When I graduated from Malden High School early in June of 1945, I was seventeen years old. I immediately went to work for my father who owned two produce stores, one in Somerville and one in Malden. My workday started about two in the morning when I drove my father into the Fanuel Hall area of Boston. This is the same area that is now known as the Quincy Market. He would get out of the truck and then I would park our vehicle, a half-ton pickup truck, blocks away from Fanuel Hall.

I would catch up with my father somewhere in those crowded blocks of wholesale produce companies. He was an excellent judge of produce and, a few of the large chains, such as A&P, frequently hired him to buy their produce. He would examine the quality of the fruits and vegetables as well as their price before he decided to purchase any merchandise. He was very selective. I accompanied him to learn what he was buying and where he was buying his goods. He would give me a list of what to deliver to each store and I would go get the truck, load it, and leave for the stores as fast as I could. And that was a problem.

Fanuel Hall, early in the morning, was absolute chaos. Farmers from all over New England came to Fanuel Hall to unload quickly. At the same time, stores from all over New England came to Fanuel Hall to load quickly. Boston did not own enough streets to accommodate even bicycles never mind truck traffic. Each night was total gridlock with truck drivers moving only a few feet after sitting in their cabs for hours. And since there were no females around, there was a lot of swearing that accompanied the continuous honking of horns. The air was blue from these angry expletives. By the start of summer, in three different languages, I could name every male and female body part, every sexual activity, and every religious blasphemy there was. My friends were impressed with my linguistic capabilities. My father certainly was not.

Something else I learned was how to load a truck. Our half-ton pickup was always overloaded, as much as a ton and a half of produce would usually be packed on it. The distribution of the weight was the problem. The load would be stacked almost seven feet high and lashed down tightly. I would put the heaviest items on the truck bed or else I would have a problem trying to steer the truck. Several times the truck almost tipped over because of a side wind.

I would drive to the Somerville store first, unload, repack the truck, and leave for the Malden store. I would work in the store until three or four in the afternoon and then go on home to get ready for the next day. This was my routine six days a week, although, sometimes on Saturday, I would leave early and go out on a date. Sunday, I would sleep past noon and then go to the movies with my friends.

That was my routine from the time I graduated until December of 1945. I didn't mind the work; I guess I thought everyone worked hard. But, because of what was happening in the world around me, I was apprehensive about the future. I knew we were at war and I wanted to avenge Pearl Harbor as much as any other American. Germany had surrendered and, until Hiroshima, we were slogging it out in the Pacific, island by island.

When I went to the movies I saw Cary Grant, coolly and methodically torpedo Japanese battleships, I witnessed Tyrone Power calmly shoot down most of the German Luftwaffe, and I watched John Wayne rally his outnumbered Marines against banzai attacks.

"Damn," I thought, "they are not saving any of the enemy for me." I wanted desperately to be in the paratroopers and see combat. That was my ambition, to do something daring and dangerous against our enemies. I had this crazy vision of a seventeen-year-old. In my vision, I would be standing at attention while Rita Hayworth put the Medal of Honor around my neck. And that could never happen while I was driving my fruit and vegetable truck. So, I watched the movie screens and felt that Hollywood was not saving any of the war for me. I honestly wanted America to win, but not so quickly.

Finally, on December 24th, I turned eighteen and within two weeks I was drafted. About thirty other draftees and I traveled by train, from Boston to Fort Devens, which is located about thirty miles west and slightly north, of Boston. In truth, we could have marched to Fort Devens and gotten there faster. The problem was that the army was totally disorganized and they continually misplaced us. As we draftees came into the army by platoons, there were veterans of the Europe Theatre of Operation entering Boston by the boatload. And Boston was not alone. Every eastern seaboard port was overwhelmed with the influx of veterans. The army wanted to discharge them and transport them home as rapidly as possible. The numbers of returning veterans was staggering.

As a result, the railroads did not have enough locomotives and railroad cars to handle this volume. Even worse was a breakdown in the communications between the army and the railroads. The army was so overloaded it could not give the railroads accurate estimates of either manpower or destinations. It took a while to make the system work smoothly.

When we left North Station, heading for Fort Devens, we were the only railroad car that our engine was pulling. The other draftees started to whoop it up and shout that the army was so anxious to start training us that they cleared all traffic just for us. However, when we got to Newton, maybe ten miles down the track, our car was shunted onto a sidetrack, the engine was decoupled and it headed back to Boston. We were left alone. About three hours later, a train heading into Boston stopped and attached us at the end of a string of empties.

We returned to North Station and, after another long wait, our car was placed in a long train of cars filled with veterans and we eventually arrived at Fort Devens. We draftees were put into different barracks than the other soldiers and the army promptly forgot we were there. For two entire days we sat around and did nothing. We found that there were mess halls opened twenty-four hours a day and, even though we were wearing civilian clothes, no one stopped us from entering any of them any time we wanted. That was because many of the veterans were also wearing civvies.

The third morning a private first class came into our barracks at Reveille and announced, "OK, it's time you civilian bastards went to war." We got into trucks and were driven to a warehouse where we were issued GI clothing and uniforms. The next two days we scoured Fort Devens picking up cigarette butts, coffee cups, and trash. Early in the evening of the second day, without eating dinner, we were loaded on another train. When we asked the PFC where we were going he said that he couldn't tell us because it was a military secret. Someone in our group said that we were going to Camp Lejeune. Another draftee spoke up and said, "You're a stupid dumbass. Camp Lejeune is a marine camp." The first draftee replied, "Well, maybe we've been traded to them because they need our help."

At any rate, the train made frequent long stops and we rode for over eighteen hours. Finally, at one stop the PFC yelled at us to grab our duffel bags and get off the train. We did and we found ourselves inside a huge train station. We were at Union Station in Washington, D.C. Our PFC leader, whom we referred to as "General Grant" behind his back, told us to settle down and stay together because we would be there for a couple of hours. When we complained that we hadn't been fed since noontime yesterday, he told us we were now earning money as soldiers and for us to spend some of it on candy bars.

This was the first time I had ever been out of New England, and I wanted to see what Washington, D.C. looked like. I left my duffel bag with a couple of the other draftees and went outside the station. The weather was freezing cold as I walked over to the White House and stood there looking at it. Going from a hot, crowded, waiting room into the cold air soon had me shivering, and I made my way back to my group. We were spread out on benches in one area and after a few hours of sitting and waiting, I dozed off.

The next thing I remember was a gentle tapping on my helmet liner. All troops in transit wore their helmet liners instead of soft caps because that made it easier to see who was in transit. I woke up to see two MP's standing in front of me. One of them had used his nightstick to wake me up. "Soldier, can I see your orders?" It was not really a question.

"I don't have any orders."

"Well, what are you doing here?"

"I was with a group of draftees from Fort Devens. We were waiting here for transportation and I fell asleep. I don't know what happened to the others."

"Where were you headed?"

"I don't know. General Gr, er, the PFC in charged refused to tell us."

"Soldier, you had better come with us."

I knew an order when I heard one, so I picked up my duffel bag and walked, between the two MP's, out of the station. They put me in the back seat of a staff car that was like a steel grilled cage. They drove for about ten minutes and then the staff car went down a concrete ramp, two floors below a large government building.

When the car stopped, they opened the back door and I got out and walked between them into a room that had a counter on one end. They pointed to me and the sergeant behind the counter told me to put my duffel bag, my helmet liner, and my overcoat on the counter. He tagged them and then told me to take off my necktie, my belt, and both of my shoelaces and put them on the counter. He told me that everything would be returned to me when I left. The two MP's then brought me into a small room that had a desk in the middle with two chairs on one side and one chair on the other. They told me to sit in the single chair and then they left.

I sat there about ten minutes wondering what was going on and, finally, a lieutenant and a sergeant came in and sat down. "Why did you leave your unit?" the lieutenant asked. "I didn't, Sir. I fell asleep and when the two MP's woke me up they were gone."

"Where were you headed?"

"I don't know, Sir."

"How the Hell long have you been in the Army?"

"About six days, Sir."

"Oh, Jesus Christ. All right, I'll find you a home. We'll start at the beginning." He took my name and my serial number and asked questions about where I was going and who was in charge of the detail and then he and the sergeant left. Another soldier came in and escorted me to a jail cell that was small and clean and had a single mattress on a bunk that was welded to the wall. In the back of my new home was a toilet and a sink. I was the only person in the cellblock and I wondered why the two dozen or more cells were not bigger and more occupied. I fell asleep immediately.

Some of my questions were answered that evening. The cellblock was slowly filled with drunk, aggressive soldiers and the individual cells prohibited them from fighting with each other. They also had their belts, ties, and shoelaces removed. The guards later told me that removing them was standard operating procedure to prevent a drunk from committing suicide. Each morning the hung over soldiers either were returned to their units or went in front of a military tribunal and the cellblock became quiet again, ready for the next night's batch.

I was in jail for two days while they checked my story. The third morning the Lieutenant who had interviewed me came and got me out of my cell. We went to the counter where my duffel bag, my overcoat, my hard had, my belt, necktie, and shoelaces, were returned to me and I signed a paper that I had received all my worldly possessions in good shape. Then, I was put into a staff car, except that, this time, I was in the front and not in the cage. I was driven to Fort Belvoir, Virginia. After we got on base I was taken to a building which was Headquarters for the Basic Training Center located at Fort Belvoir.

I met with a Captain who asked me how I got separated from everyone else. I said that I had been in the middle of the group and that we were told to stay together because we would be picked up in a few hours. I fell asleep and when the MP's woke me up I was alone. The Captain had me repeat my story twice and then he told me that everyone he had talked to had reported the same thing; I was where I had been told to be. Based on our discussion, he was going to recommend that no AWOL charges be filed against me and that my record would be clean. However, for all the trouble I had caused the Training Center to locate me, I would be on KP detail the next three weekends. With that, he dismissed me and I joined the rest of the draftees I had started with so long ago.

They welcomed me with hoots and jeers and told me that they were now experienced troopers while I was nothing but a raw recruit. After the hazing they said that they had asked General Grant to look around because I was not the only one missing, there were two others. He refused, but some of them sneaked back and found the other two. When they appeared before a board looking into my going AWOL they explained what had happened and General Grant was reduced in rank from Private First Class to Private. They were kind of hoping that I was permanently lost so that General Grant would be court martialed. I thanked them for their devoted support and told them that when they passed through the chow lines on the next three weekends I would try to serve them extra desserts.

Thus ended the first phase of my illustrious military career.

Beer Drinking Bombardiers

Of all the shortcomings in my character, and I do have a few, the one that I have enjoyed the most is my total inability to resist temptation. It is such a delicious flaw that I have never seriously tried to correct it, no matter how much trouble I got into. I willingly went along with any plan that my irresponsible friends would come up with and we would dance until we had to pay the piper. Sadly though, as I grew older, the people I met seemed to be less and less irresponsible and the chances to exercise my incapacity to restrain myself are not as frequent as I would like.

One Wednesday night, many years ago when I was attending the University of Michigan, I was in my room studying, when three of the most disreputable students on campus came into my room. Like me, they were going to school courtesy of the GI Bill, but they were always busy and didn't have much time for classwork.

Jeff, their leader, closed the book that I was reading and said, "Jay, quit reading. How many times have I told you that reading, along with one or two other things, will make you go blind. If you keep disregarding what I tell you, you will probably graduate and have to get a job. Is that what you want?"

"Sure," I answered, "and then I'll hire the three of you turkeys and bust your gonads. Why are you invading my privacy, anyhow?"

"Listen, you won't believe me, but we were almost getting ready to study when we began talking about the football team. We are not at all sure that they are going to win next Saturday. They are playing Illinois at Champaign-Urbana and it is Illinois' homecoming game. That is a terrible place to play football. One of those towns is wet and one is dry and they have a time zone change right in the middle of their campus. They are trying to take advantage of our Maize and Blue."

I could see what was coming, but I still asked, "And what do you intend to do about all this unsportsman like conduct?"

Jeff was quick to reply, "I propose that the four of us drive down Friday and go the game on Saturday. It is about a seven hour drive. We can leave after we get our government checks and we cash them. We will split the expenses; we can sleep at our fraternity, and we will be able to pick up some student tickets when we get there. We will insure that our team wins and we will be able to see what the Illinois coeds look like and we can drink Illinois beer at whichever town serves it. How does that sound for a weekend?"

I had to think for a second. My finances were already stretched thin. I had no steady income outside of the money I got from the government. As it was, I needed extra money. To earn it, I had a part time job scrubbing pots and pans at a fraternity and I was selling my blood, alternating every two weeks, between St. Joe's and the University hospitals. I decided that if I scrimped when I got back, I could afford to go and make sure that the Michigan football team was treated honorably; so I agreed.

That Friday, the four of us skipped our afternoon classes and we started out just before noon for Champaign-Urbana. When we arrived, we went to the fraternity house that my three companions belonged to and made arrangements for sleeping and eating at the frat house and obtaining tickets for the game. By early evening we were ready to go out and scout the opposition. We decided we would do that by watching how they disported themselves in their bars and taverns. So as not to be taken as spies and shot at dawn, we each wore apparel that showed we were Michigan rooters. Jeff and I had on Michigan sweatshirts and our other two companions had on varsity jackets with a block M on the front.

When we made our rounds, we avoided the dry town, Urbana, as if it had an epidemic of foot and mouth disease. Upon entering each establishment, we were greeted with jeers and hoots. Patiently, we tried to explain to these poor, misguided natives the fate that was awaiting their beloved football team on the morrow. It was to no avail; they were so set in their ways that our warnings fell on deaf ears. So, we toasted them, and they toasted us, and then we would move on.

By the end of the evening, we were awash with good feelings and good spirits. The last place we visited was a beer cellar. Literally. We had to go down a flight of cement stairs and we entered a smoky, noisy, room, that had whitewashed cement walls. The floor was a cement slab. The round tables were packed with people drinking beer, and, when we were noticed, they seemed to rise, en masse, to tell us how sorry they felt for us. We tried to forgive them their sins and bless them, but they were an unruly flock that rejected our ministrations. So we sat at a table with some of them and, when the waitress came over, we ordered beer. She brought back some large bottles of beer; they may have been two quart bottles. Certainly they were bigger than a quart size. We shared our beer with our wayward flock and we continued drinking.

Shortly, I heard the noise of glass breaking and I looked around and saw a bottle that had hit the cement floor and had broken. I thought nothing about it, but in a few minutes I heard the noise of other bottles breaking. I started looking and soon I saw someone hold an empty bottle away from his body, at arm's length, and let it drop. While I watched, I saw two more patrons hold their beer bottles out, say "bombs away", and drop them on the cement floor. I saw and heard this happened two or three times and I couldn't believe it. Was this their custom? Nobody seemed to either care or to pay attention. I thought it was odd.

Eventually, the waitress made her way back to our table to pick up our empty bottles and find out if we wanted any more to drink. When she returned with more beer bottles, I asked her, "Don't you get upset with all the glass that is lying on the floor?"

She reared back, put both hands on her hips, and answered in a very haughty tone, "You guys from Michigan are a pain in the ass, and you make me sick. What the Hell do you think? Do you think that we have bare foot waitresses or bare foot customers?" She took her money and her tip and she bolted away.

I did not know what to think, and since I had shoes on, I did not care. I willingly joined the bottle breaking bunch. I too became a bombardier.

Bill Jackson Fell Asleep

When Bill Jackson came into my office, I thought that a professional football player had taken a wrong turn. He was huge; he stood 6'6" and weighed about 300 pounds. "Hi" he said extending his right hand that was as big as a catcher's mitt, "I am Bill Jackson. You are our new test supervisor. You just came back from North Dakota and your job is to make our tests run smoothly. Isn't that correct?"

I shook his hand and replied, "Not quite but it will do for starters. My name is Jay. If you are the Bill Jackson listed on this organizational chart, your job is handling test equipment. Isn't that correct?"

He smiled and replied, "Yes, it is and I do a darn good job. Does the fact that I am big and black bother you?"

"Does the fact that I am big and white bother you?"

He looked startled, and then he chuckled. "Fair question. No, I don't think that that is going to bother me a bit."

"Well then, you have just answered your own question. You will have no problem with me as long as you are doing your job. All I expect is that, if you have problems, you come see me and let me know. If you do that you are in a safe harbor. I do not like surprises in my territory."

We chatted for a few more minutes and then he left. Over the course of the next few months, I had the opportunity to watch him do his job, and to find out about him personally. Both were pleasant surprises. General Telephone & Electronics (GTE) had constructed three segments of the Minuteman Missile System in Massachusetts. Two were in Waltham, in the building I worked in and the third was in Needham. All three were connected by complex telephone and radio links. They were exact duplicates of the missile system buried underground in North Dakota and Montana. The only major difference was that our test sites did not have missiles or nuclear warheads; we did not need them. Our charter was to solve field problems and evaluate the safety of the total missile system. Bill's job was to have the necessary test equipment available for each test. That was not an easy job. We had a store room in Waltham with over a thousand meters, recorders, special test equipment, and instruments. Any other equipment that was necessary was either borrowed from Needham or rented from an outside company. Each piece of test equipment needed to have a valid calibration or certification sticker on it before a test began. It was a massive task requiring him to spend hours doing the calibrations or making sure the laboratories did. In addition, he had to keep track of all the test equipment, their location, and when they needed to be checked. Any error could stop a test. Bill did his job so well that there were few complaints.

On a personal basis, the longer I worked with him, the more I liked and admired him. He was married and had three daughters. He held this job and, on the side, had a TV repair business to bring in extra income. He went to school nights, at Northeastern University, working towards an Engineering degree. He was an elder in his church and a leader in his community. Bill was an amazing decent person.

For over two years I had no problems with Bill and then all hell broke loose. GTE was hosting a technical interchange meeting in our building. At a technical interchange meeting all of the Minuteman prime contractors meet with the Air Force to discuss problems, schedules, milestones, and differences. Boeing, Martin Marietta, Rockwell, TRW, and GTE were the contractors. The Strategic Air Command, the Ballistic Missile Organization, Minuteman Maintenance Management, and Nuclear Safety were the Air Force representatives. Monday and Friday were travel days so the meeting was scheduled Tuesday through Thursday. It was late Thursday when the trouble began.

Sometime close to 5:00 PM, a major from SAC went into the men's room and, as he was walking towards a urinal, he heard snoring. He stopped and looked at the four toilet stalls, only one door was shut, and all he could see was a pair of huge black legs with trousers and underwear draped on the floor. He listened to the snoring for a few seconds and then he yelled and ran out of the men's room screaming to see the manager.

When I came in early Friday, I followed my normal routine; I went and had coffee with Tom Kerby. Kerby was the maintenance supervisor and I was the test supervisor. Between us, we were responsible for the conduct of everything that took place in the test facility. He was as glum as I was.

We discussed what Bill Jackson had done, what was likely to happen, and what we each thought about it. Later that morning, Bill Jackson's wife called to say that Bill was sick and would not be coming to work. Just before quitting time Tom and I were informed that Monday at 7:00 AM we were to attend a special meeting to discuss an Air Force complaint against GTE's work practices. Attendance was mandatory.

At the meeting, there was Tom and me, our boss George Hoover, our department manager, Bob Schultz, and our personnel representative, Norm Fenton. We met in Bob's office.

We had no sooner sat down around the table when Bob said, "This is one hell of an embarrassment." He looked directly at Tom and me because Bill Jackson worked for us.

Before any one else could say anything Fenton spoke out, "I am going to fire his black ass!"

I talked directly to Bob Schultz. In all the years that I had known him and worked for him I always had considered him fair and honest. "Bob, you are absolutely correct. This is a mess. We look dumb. We have egg all over our corporate face. Despite that, you cannot fire Bill Jackson."

Fenton slapped his open palm on the table and almost yelled, "The hell I can't fire him. See, Bob, didn't I tell you these two would defend that lazy black." He pointed to Tom and me. "They will tell you about years of working for us, they will tell you about his going to school. They will do anything to tug on your heart strings. Fire his black ass!"

I took a deep breath. As much as I wanted to get into it with Fenton I couldn't. I was trying to help Bill Jackson. "Bob, heartstrings or no heartstrings, you will have a difficult time if you try to fire Bill Jackson."

Bob was listening to me. Even before the meeting, he knew what Fenton would say. What he wanted to know was what we would say. "And just why can't we fire Bill Jackson? He surely screwed up."

I answered his question with one of my own. "Did you read the complaint yourself?"

"Why no, Norm gave me all the particulars. What is your point?"

"If you look at the complaint you will see that the major said he found a black man sleeping on the toilet at 4:55 PM." Fenton broke in again. "Who cares about the time? That black bastard was sleeping in a government facility. I say make an example of him. Fire his black ass."

I waited until he had finished his tirade. My temper was beginning to rise, but I continued, "Bill is on first shift; the posted hours for the first shift are 7:30 AM to 4:00 PM with a half hour for lunch. When Bill was caught sleeping on the toilet he was sleeping on his own time."

Fenton said, "So what? I am sure he was sleeping on our time too. I say make an example of him and fire his black ass." I had had enough. I took in a breath of air and I was going to tangle with Fenton, when Schultz, who had been watching me, raised his hand like a traffic cop. I held back what I was going to say. Schultz looked at Fenton and said, "Just cool it Norm. You seem determined to do just one thing, 'Fire his black ass.' How come you did not notice the time? It makes all the difference in the world. If I had fired him, and by the way that is not your decision to make Norm, we would have a major lawsuit on our hands. How can you fire a man for sleeping on his own time? To the media we would look as bad as we now look stupid to the Air Force. We seem to have two problems on our hands."

Fenton sat quietly. He would not say much more during the rest of the meeting. However, he would not take his mistake or his reprimand personally; he was much too egotistical for that. Rather, he would be quiet because his idea had been dismissed and he would not speak until he got another idea. And that would take a long time. Nor did I say much more. As part of our bad cop, good cop routine, Tom would now carry the conversation.

"Bob," Tom said, "Bill did a stupid irresponsible thing that hurt our image. It is a given that he should not go unpunished. However, our big problem is regaining the trust of the Air Force along with the rest of the test community. GTE/Sylvania really looks bad."

Schultz said, "Tom, I am sure that between you and Jay you have what you think will solve our problem. I am concerned with our image, so give me your opinion, I'm anxious to hear it."

Tom was a little nervous; he was timid and he felt uneasy giving his opinions to his boss's boss. "This is such a bad professional breach that going through normal channels is not enough. A phone call or letter won't convey how badly our pride has been hurt. We think that you and maybe Krownberg fly out to Offutt Air Force Base and personally carry your concerns and apologies to SAC. That kind of action the Air Force will understand."

Krownberg was the senior GTE manager in charge of the entire Minuteman program.

Bob said, "That just might be the best way to handle this. Have Lew stand up and take his medicine. That's why they pay him the big bucks. Let me discuss this with Lew. In the meantime what about Bill Jackson?"

"Well, he deserves a reprimand and a good ass chewing,"

Bob laughed for the first time since the meeting started. "The two of you are really something else. Don't do anything about Bill yet. Let me talk to Lew and find out what he has by way of suggestions. I will get back to you as soon as I can."

Tom and I heard from Bob by noon time. A reprimand would be given to Bill Jackson and a copy would be put into his personnel file. Krownberg and Schultz would be on a plane tomorrow flying to Offutt Air Force Base. Tom and I flipped a coin and I won the honor of talking to Bill.

He came into my office and sat down and for once he was very quiet. I did not know where to begin. Finally, I asked, "Bill just what the hell happened last Thursday?"

"I don't know, Jay. I went into the john and I felt so tired and it was so quiet, I just shut my eyes and fell asleep. I woke up when I heard a yell and I got out in a hurry. I knew I got caught so I stayed out Friday. When I came back to work this morning, I found out how bad I did get caught. How bad is it? Are you going to fire me?"

I knew that his activities and his lack of sleep had finally brought him to a standstill in a toilet stall. He was wrong but he looked so scared and pathetic, I wanted to answer his questions quickly. "It is bad and no, you are not going to be fired. But just between you and me, how long were you sleeping on the toilet?"

"I figure almost two hours"

I burst out laughing. Lord knows what Fenton would have said if he knew that.

"Bill this is what is happening. Tom and I were at a meeting this morning arguing that GTE should not fire you. We succeeded but this incident is being written up as a reprimand and will be in your personnel file. What you did has hurt you, it has caught Tom and me in the middle of an internal squabble, and it has put this company in a bad light. Krownberg and Schultz are flying out to Omaha to Offutt Air Force Base to personally apologize to SAC. How soon all of this is going to settle down I do not know. I do know that Schultz is going to write the reprimand, which means that Fenton will probably draft it for him. Your mistake is going to be costly."

"Listen, I thought I was going to be fired. I'll bet you and Tom helped me. I can't afford to be fired and lose my security clearance. I owe you and Tom. Thank you, thank you, thank you, all I can say to both of you is thank you."

"You're talking too much. I kind of enjoy scrimmaging against Fenton. You have always given your best, so Tom and I owed you one good fight. But that is all we can afford. If there is another goof-up it will blow you away and neither Tom nor I will be able to stop it."

"I understand, but I surely do thank you," Bill said. He got up, shook my hand and left.

Actually the incident died fairly quickly. The fact that our senior management went to meet and mollify the Air Force helped. So we all returned to work.

About two years after the fall asleep incident, Bill Jackson told me that he was finally going to graduate. I was pleased and in the next day or two, Tom and I discussed having a party for him. We had Bill pick the day for the party. I also asked Schultz about getting Bill a classification change from senior technician to engineer. Schultz said he would look into the possibility.

As the day neared for the party Tom informed me that he would take care of the money collections; I was to take care of the gift selection. We decided the party would be held in the "Bull Pen" which was a large room used for shift change over meetings. It was to be at lunch time with no brass invited at all . . . only worker bees. Bill mentioned to me that he was having his picture taken, right after the party, for the company newspaper. Tom got the easier job. The amount of money that poured in was surprising, until you realized how popular Bill was. I ordered pizzas, soft drinks, a huge graduation cake and a handsome pen and pencil set and the money continued to pour in. I then ordered flowers and appetizers and still lost ground to the cash flow. Tom and I decided to give him the extra money, as that was something he didn't have much of all these years.

The day of the party I still had some money left over, so, on an impulse I sent someone out to the Waltham supermarket to buy the biggest watermelon they had. Bill Jackson absolutely loved to eat watermelon, so I thought "why not?"

The party was one of the happiest and most sincere graduation parties I have ever attended. Bill's coworkers came with plates of food, home baked cookies and cakes and graduation cards just to show Bill how pleased they were for him. When Tom presented him with his pen and pencil set, his cash, his watermelon, and his cake, Bill cried; I guess we all did.

At one o'clock we all went back to work. At one thirty, I got a phone call from Norm Fenton. He was furious. "Son of a bitch, Jay. Why is it the only problems I have around here are from your people?"

Since I did not know what he was talking about I played it straight. "Norm, would you be kind enough to tell me what you are talking about?"

"Talking about? Talking about? I'm talking about that black bastard that's what I'm talking about. Don LeGrande is here in my office. He is trying to take a picture of that black bastard and he is not cooperating."

"Norm, would you please put Don on the phone."

The next voice I heard was that of Don saying tentatively "Jay?"

"Yes, Don, this is Jay. What kind of problems are you having?"

"Well, it sounds kind of funny but it really isn't. I have Bill posed in his cap and gown and on his lap is a big watermelon. He wants his picture taken with that thing and I can't get him to put it down."

I just shook my head. This business surely does take some strange twists and turns. I asked Don where he was posing Bill and his watermelon and I told him that I would meet him there. When I got there Don was looking flustered and Bill was seated, capped, gowned, and watermeloned.

In a not too friendly tone, I said "Bill, you are acting like a horse's ass."

"Listen, my friends, including you, gave me this watermelon. I am proud of this watermelon. I am proud of that friendship. Why can't I have some pictures with it?"

"You can have pictures of your watermelon. I am not saying a word to you about that. But you also know damn well that if GTE publishes a picture of you in your cap and gown holding a watermelon, the NAACP, along with all the TV networks, will be screaming that GTE is a racist employer."

Bill said, "To hell with the NAACP."

"That's easy enough for you to say Bill, but you are going to have to be reasonable. I'll tell you what. Don take as many pictures as Bill wants with that watermelon on his lap. Bill, you sit through as many pictures as Don wants without the watermelon. And, Don, I want Bill to have a copy of every picture you take. Unless either of you guys can think of anything, I am out of here. Oh, there is one more thing; Bill, you make sure Don gets some of your cake and cookies before he leaves the building."

The next edition of the GTE paper carried a nice picture of Bill without watermelon, and the following week he got his degree. Not having heard from Bob Schultz I went to see him and ask about Bill's classification change.

"Come in and sit down, Jay", Bob said.

From his tone of voice, I knew that there were problems. I sat down and decided not to say anything until he did.

After a moment he said, "For some odd reason, the bean counters in GTE do not like to change anyone's classification from technician to engineer. I have looked into it and I can assure you that that has been their attitude for years. Under even the best of conditions it would take months to get a classification change. Now that would be for anyone. Bill's case is even more complicated. Because of the 'sleep' episode Norm Fenton is fighting any classification change. He sure has it in for Bill. Now if you and Tom want a classification change, I probably can get it done in spite of Fenton. However, because of that incident Fenton surely has a case and can get a change delayed for a long time. I damn well do not like it. Bill has earned his chance to better himself. And, just who is Fenton to sit in judgment of anyone?"

I replied, "I know some of the past history of Colonel Norm Fenton and I also know that you do too. He has done things much worse than whatever Bill Jackson did and he has been forgiven. That is not fair or right. And, what am I going to tell Bill?"

Bob looked at me sharply. "I didn't know you knew about Fenton. I guess I should have known you would find out. I rarely pay attention to Fenton, but he can stir the pot on this one.

"I am truly sorry. I know what you and Tom think of Bill as a worker and as a person. My guess is that GTE is going to lose a good man."

I left his office and went to find Tom. He was as disappointed as I was. I began to feel that Tom, Bill, and I were not going to win. Not without a fight though, I resolved.

The next day I spoke privately with Bill. "Getting a classification change from technician to engineer is neither easy nor automatic. I think the bean counters delay as long as they can just to keep someone at the lower salary. It takes months. Your case is even more difficult because of your 'sleep in'. If we push hard enough, I guess we can get a change. It just depends on how long the change can be delayed."

Bill asked, "What should I do?"

"Believe it or not, let's start by following procedures."

I hand him an envelope. "This is a request for a change of work classification. I have filled in my portion. You fill in yours. Take it and a copy of your degree to Needham personnel; the guy's name and phone number is inside the envelope. Make an appointment to see him and give him the paperwork personally. Do not leave it with his secretary or drop it off on his desk. Leave them no opportunity to claim they can't find your paperwork."

"Then what do we do?" Bill asked.

"I want you to call him every three weeks and ask for a progress report. Let's see if we can't force them to stand up and be counted."

"And, what do I do if they won't?"

"Bill, you have worked for this company for years. It is your choice what to do. I can't tell you what is best for you. I will tell you what I would do if I had the same problem. Let's say I have a wife and three children and that I finally earned a degree. Now this degree entitles me to make a lot more money than I am presently making. If GTE isn't smart enough to recognize my value, then shame on them. I would wait four months for GTE to wise up. If they didn't, I would go to a company that would give me a job offer based on my degree."

"Is that what you would really do, Jay?"

"Yes"

"Can I use you as a reference?"

"If you wait the four months to give us a chance to come to our senses, you can certainly use both Tom and me as references."

Bill took the paperwork and left my office. Five months later he was working for Sandrews Electronics in New Hampshire designing test equipment. He worked for them 31 years until he retired.

Christmas in Merida

When Hazel and I left Detroit Metro Airport on December 19th, the plane had to be deiced before we could take off. When we landed at Cancun the temperature was eighty- five degrees. The temperature differential did not make us feel sad that we had left Michigan. We rented a car at the airport and drove two hundred miles across the Yucatan Peninsula to the city of Merida. Since the airport is south of Cancun we didn't see much damage to the buildings from Hurricane Wilma. However, after a few miles of driving inland, all signs of uprooted trees were gone. We got to Merida after dark and driving at night caused a lot of trouble.

The Spanish founded Merida in 1540. The streets are narrow and they are all one way streets. They barely accommodate two lanes of traffic and many of the intersections are dark and do not have street signs. Drivers switch lanes constantly. The sidewalks are narrow, not even wide enough for two people to walk abreast. And, what's worse, they are uneven, they slope, and the cement is cracked.

The result is that, whenever cars stop, people dash from one side of the road to the other between the cars. It is a completely stop or a completely go flow of traffic and, when it is going, cars rush and weave and pedestrians jump and leap out of the way. It is a city of over a million people and, for strangers, it is hard to get where you want to go, even in daylight.

To make matters worse, the theory is that almost all the streets are numbered with even numbers going north and south and odd numbers going east and west. But the practice isn't quite that clean. First of all, numbers, both even and odd, are skipped or appear out of order. And, sometimes the same number is repeated endlessly. For example, the city can have a Calle 36, Calle 36a, Calle 36b, etcetera up to Calle 36h or 36j. When you are driving, making four consecutive left hand turns or four consecutive right hand turns will not bring you back to where you started, not even close.

We knew the location of our hotel but it was maddening trying to find it. I would dodge traffic, circle a block, and find myself three streets away instead of being in front of the hotel. We must have done this dance of the dunces for over an hour and a half and still were not where we wanted to be. I ruled out asking the pedestrians because, for the most part, they didn't speak English and I didn't understand Spanish.

I was running a fever and saying naughty words when I noticed that the car behind me was a police car and that it had its red and blue lights flashing. We were dead in traffic so I suggested to Hazel that she ask the police if they could direct us to our hotel. She was a little hesitant but, since she was as frustrated as I, she got out and walked back to their car.

She was gone a long four or five minutes and, meanwhile, the traffic started to flow. Drivers began honking their horns because of the tie up until one of the officers got out of the police car and directed traffic around us. Finally, Hazel came back and she said that she was going to get into the police car and that one of the officers would get into our car. She said that she had had a difficult time explaining that we wanted to get to the Hotel Del Gobernador but, when they finally understood, they indicated that they would take us over there. She returned to their car and an officer got in beside me. He did not speak English but he motioned to me that I should follow the police car that had darted ahead of me. I did and, within five blocks with a lot of left and right turns, they deposited us in front of the hotel. That evening, Hazel and I walked to a restaurant around the corner from our hotel and ate a late dinner. It was an excellent meal and we had no trouble finding our way back.

The next morning, before breakfast, I encountered a plumbing problem. Hazel had taken a shower the night before and she had told me that there was hardly any water coming out of the showerhead. Her statement was an understatement. There wasn't enough moisture to dampen a postage stamp and the water was cold no matter how long you let it drip. I went to the front desk and tried to explain to them that there was a problem with the shower.

There were three people on duty at the desk but none of them spoke English well enough to understand what I was trying to tell them. Each took a turn talking to me and then he or she would huddle with the other two and speak rapidly in Spanish. Finally, one of them made a phone call and spoke to someone in Spanish. In a few minutes one of the waiters in their restaurant came over and spoke to me in English, "Can I be of service to you, Senor?"

When I explained the problem to him he spoke to the people behind the desk. Through him, they told me that they would fix the shower. I crossed my fingers and hoped that they could.

Over breakfast, we decided not to take our car out of the hotel garage that day. We would take in the sights of Merida and thus avoid a police escort. Hazel stopped by the front desk and found a flyer saying that there was a daily English speaking tour of downtown Merida every morning. The City of Merida sponsored the tour and it was free. Our hotel was close by the center of Merida so we decided to go on that tour before we did anything else.

Many government buildings and the oldest active Catholic

Cathedral in this hemisphere surround the Central Park of Merida. A crew that never seems to go home keeps the park beautifully maintained taking care of the flowers, shrubs, and trees, and there is absolutely no litter. Centro, as it is called, is always crowded with tourists, onlookers, and people meeting at the park. It is a vibrant and energetic scene that invigorates everyone who is there.

Hazel and I waited in front of the cathedral for the tour to materialize. It never did but waves of tourists, led by guides speaking many other languages besides English, passed us constantly. And, because we both looked like tourists standing there wearing shorts, holding a flyer and a map in our hands, and constantly looking around, a host of Mexican people tried to sell us things. A man, with a wooden paddle that had carved chickens pecking and peeping when he moved the paddle in a horizontal circle, wanted us to buy it for our grandchildren. Another man wanted to sell us Panama hats from the warehouse of them that he had sitting on his head. An old woman just came up to us and held out her cupped hands to us. Ten pesos disappeared when that happened. The exchange rate is ten pesos to the dollar.

Two or three times different men came up to us and asked, "Where do you live in America?"

When we would answer by saying we lived in Michigan, they would ask, "Where in Michigan?"

When we replied Ann Arbor, the response was always the same. "I have a cousin that lives in Ann Arbor." I got the impression that more Mexicans live in Ann Arbor than reside in Mexico. These overtures were invariably followed by an offer to guide us around for fifty or sixty pesos. We invariably declined the offer.

After waiting more than a half-hour past the starting time of our tour, we left the front of the church, crossed the street, and wandered into the park. After carefully searching for a bench that was clean of bird droppings, we sat down to discuss what else to do. As we were talking, an elderly man passed us, stopped, turned around and came back to where we were sitting. He asked, "Are you from the USA?"

When we looked up, he put both his hands up beside his shoulders with the palms facing us. "I am not trying to sell you anything. I moved here from Florida two years ago and I just wanted to speak in English with someone."

Hazel, who is one of the most trusting people in the world, responded immediately, "We are from Ann Arbor and we really like this city of Merida."

The man replied, "I do, too. I retired to Florida and came here on a visit and found that living here is much cheaper than it is in Florida."

I asked, "But isn't it hotter here in the summer?"

"Oh my, yes. The temperature rises to 120 degrees with 100% humidity, but I have air conditioning."

We had a lively fifteen or twenty-minute conversation and then the man excused himself and went on his way. Just as Hazel said, "What a nice man," another man came up to us. He was younger, good looking, and was clean and neat. His loafers were shined and his blue jeans were pressed and creased. He asked, "Are you enjoying our Centro?"

Hazel replied, "Yes, Merida is a lovely city."

"The Spanish took it over from the Mayans in 1540 and that cathedral across the street was completed in 1560. It is the oldest cathedral on any continent in the New World. There may be an older church on an island in Guatemala but it is much smaller than our cathedral."

Our unknown speaker spoke English perfectly with no accent at all. He continued, "Mayan civilization had been here for two thousand years before the Spanish arrived. When they got here, looking for gold, the Spanish decided that the Mayans were worshipping devils and that they were backward. So, they subjugated and enslaved them in an effort to enlighten them and teach them Catholicism."

"HAH," I thought to myself, "Their motto must have been 'No Mayan left behind.'"

He continued, "You can see that in the cathedral. The seven huge pillars that hold the roof up are anchored on stones from Mayan temples. The Spaniards made the Mayans dismantle their places of worship and forced them to use the stones as the foundation of the cathedral. I will show these stones to you.

"But first, I would like to show you the original furnishings of the first Spanish governor of this province. They are just across the street, if you will come this way."

He was an engaging person and Hazel rose immediately without question. I was more reluctant because I knew that there would be a charge and I didn't know what it would be."

I asked, "And how much is this going to cost us?"

"Oh, Senor, I do not know. We will discuss that later."

There followed two hours of a very detailed history and tour of the area around Centro. Our guide was very knowledgeable about the Spaniards and the Mayans. His wife was an archeologist who worked for the Mexican government. He elaborated on the life of the Mayans before the Spaniards arrived. It was a fascinating tour.

It came to an end at the side door of that magnificent cathedral when our guide told us that he usually got one thousand pesos for his time. Hazel immediately protested, "But senor, we don't have that much money with us."

I finally settled with our guide for four hundred pesos. He had earned his money by being entertaining and interesting. After I paid him, he walked us across the alleyway into a store that he owned. His merchandise was of good quality as was his prices. Hazel suggested that he write a book about his touring experiences and that we would publish it for him. With that we left and went back to Centro.

We meandered around looking at the city and got back to our hotel in mid afternoon. When we entered the lobby the people at the desk told us that they could not fix the shower and that they would move us to another room. We moved, rested for a while, and then returned to the same restaurant that we had been to the night before.

(Hazel's note:) This restaurant was in the walled garden of an old traditional Mexican home. The tables were scattered around the garden among the statutory, flowers, vines and fountains. The tables were covered with heavy white linen cloths with large linen napkins and highly polished silverware. All very elegant . . . and the food was excellent. The owner showed me around all the garden and the first floor of the house. He said the family still lived in the home.

As we were eating our dinner we heard distance music but couldn't make out where it was coming from. After we finished our meal and were walking back to the hotel we passed what looked like another walled garden which was occupied with a fairly large group of men and women practicing the Hallelujah Chorus. They were attempting to sing in English and were having trouble getting the words correct but their voices were beautiful. We were deeply touched. As we stood in the shadows and listened to that special music we rejoiced at our being together to celebrate Christmas in Mexico.

Club 23

All kinds of people have all kinds of reasons for eating out at all kinds of restaurants. Whatever the reasons people have for not dining at home, they never entertain the hope of being served a disappointing meal in a disappointing restaurant. I say that because Hazel and I came close to both of those negative possibilities one Saturday night at a Milan landmark.

We were busy all day Saturday and when it came time to have dinner we suddenly decided to eat out. Because neither one of us wanted to change the clothes we were wearing we thought that we would go to a low-key restaurant. Since both of us consider franchises like McDonald's or Burger King as only low-taste not low-key, eating at them was not even considered. Usually, whenever the low-key mood is upon us, we go to downtown Milan and dine sumptuously at Roy's, a hamburger emporium that serves delicious, greasy, hamburgers and French fries.

In the past, we had talked about trying Club 23 since it was a local bistro and, because Saturday was such a pretty day, we decided to give it a try. It was located about seven miles from our front door, about 200 yards off of Interstate Highway 23. Our mistake was in thinking that our choice was low-key. It is but it is also much more low brow than low-key.

Club 23 was a large wood frame structure at the corner of Willis and Carpenter roads. There wasn't a large sign to identify Club 23 as an eating place and it more resembled a farm shed that needed painting than a five star restaurant. Behind the restaurant was what we thought was a small golf course and then there is nothing but farmland. However, the parking lot at Club 23 always seemed to be filled with cars. We had never eaten there but we had wondered about it whenever we drove by.

We drove over to Club 23 early, not for their Early Bird Specials, which they never heard of, but because Saturday was when Ohio State was playing Villanova in basketball. We didn't want to get stuck in a loud, noisy crowd while we were eating. As it turned out, a large crowd was not one of our problems, no customers ever came in after us. We got over to Club 23 about 5:30. The parking lot held eight vehicles, four were motorcycles the other four were pickup trucks. As I parked our Schultz Motor's red van I thought that it looked out of place. "What the Hell," I thought, "This was supposed to be an adventure."

The entrance was at the corner of the building closest to the parking lot. Club 23 was a cavernous, dimly lit, room with the bar along one side and small tables and chairs randomly located around the middle of the room. In the opposite corner from the entrance were two empty pool tables. Over the bar was a normal sized television, in the middle of the room, near the ceiling, was a gigantic, flat screen television. Both were tuned to different stations and both were blaringly loud. The other customers, all men, were clustered at the bar, watching the smaller television.

Hazel picked out a table against a wall about halfway down the room. She sat on a bench that ran the length of the wall and I sat opposite her. The walls were covered with pictures of old racecars and over Hazel's head was hung a large American flag. We sat for a while, listening to the loud televisions and enjoying the ambience of Club 23. Shortly, the bartender came over to our table. She was a lady in her mid thirties with a pleasant face. We ordered two light Miller beers and she returned with two bottles that she placed in front of us. After she left, Hazel asked whether or not we were going to get glasses for our beers. When I suggested that a drinking glass might cost extra, Hazel shrugged her shoulders and drank from the bottle.

I swiveled around to see what program was being shown on the huge screen television and I saw something I had never seen before. The program was coming from Florida and they were auctioning off classic automobiles. When I first looked, they were flashing the sign $300,000.00. I never found out what had been sold for that price. However, while I was watching, a 1958 Chevrolet that had been completely restored was rolled out. They televised that car from every angle, even showing the underside, clean and shining. The auctioneer started the bidding at $65,000.00. That's the price that flashed across the screen.

And that's when it got even odder for me. The auctioneer, who was chanting the numbers so quickly I couldn't understand what he was saying, was wearing a bright orange necktie. That didn't register until I noticed that he had two or three helpers, I call them shills, in the stands talking to the bidders. They were wearing orange ties also. I guess they wore them so that the auctioneer could spot them quickly. As soon as a bid was received the shills would start talking to the other bidders trying to get them to up the bid. It looked almost comical. The bidder would stand there stonefaced, looking as if he were not paying a bit of attention to the shill, until the auctioneer was ready to shout, "SOLD". Then he would up the bid by $5,000.00. That Chevrolet sold for $350,000.00. As I watched the auction, I wondered about two things. The first thing I wondered was if they could sell their automobiles at a lower volume of sound and then I wondered who would dare to drive those cars.

Anyhow, as we worked our way through our bottles of beer, it was getting time for the basketball game, so when the bartender/waitress took our orders I asked if she couldn't switch the channel from the car auction to the basketball game. It took a while but, with the help of the men at the bar, she finally got the correct station. One of the patrons at the bar said that he never watches any sport where there is only one ball used in the game. He switched the small television to the car auction and turned up the volume. Another patron put a dollar in the jukebox and had country music played by the Milan Symphony Orchestra.

Club 23 had a rather restricted menu if you want something other than finger foods or fried foods. Hazel and I ordered deep fried mushrooms as an appetizer and then she had a bacon cheeseburger while I had a plain hamburger. Every thing was served in plastic baskets. I assume that plates were in as much demand as were glasses. We both had another round of bottled beer and we were preparing to watch the beginning of the game when a man came in and started unloading some large speakers.

I asked the waitress if they were going to have live music and she told me quite proudly that they were and that they had a band every Saturday night. That's when I suggested to Hazel that we should flee the premises as soon as possible. Which we did. We went home and watched the game, with much less sound volume, in the comfort of our living room.

If any of you are planning a wedding, a birthday party, a Bar Mitzvah, or any other private function, and are looking for an inexpensive place to have the event, I highly recommend Club 23. My only suggestions would be to have them turn off the jukebox and lower the volume on the television sets.

However, Club 23 was razed a couple of years ago and the vacant space has been left idle in anticipation of some other restaurant or business. I don't know what. However, Milan lost a true Honky-Tonk Heaven, which I'm not sure is at all bad.

Debbie Does Doughnuts

It was just after midnight when Bill Whitman returned with two fresh cups of coffee. He handed me one and then sat down at the table where we had our paperwork scattered around. Bill was a thin man of medium height. He wore big horned rim glasses and had a perpetual scowl on his face, and he possessed so much nervous energy that some of him was always in motion. He was either smoking, or tapping his fingers, or beating a rhythm with a pen or pencil.

We were in the electronics lab at Warren Air Force Base in Cheyenne, Wyoming. This was the second day we had started at nine in the morning and worked more than fifteen hours. Both of us were tired and frustrated and circling each other like pit bulls ready to attack.

Bill lit a cigarette, took a drag, and then said, "Damn, this whole thing is irritating and stupid. And where is your fellow worker, Mike Andrews? Is he out looking for doughnut places again?"

I looked at Bill and let my mind wander. I first met him in the early sixties, over twenty years ago, when I went to Grand Forks to work on Minuteman. He was in the Air Force then, the youngest man to ever achieve the rank of Chief Master Sergeant. He had a mind like a junkyard magnet; when he turned his mind on he pulled every thought and idea into it and there they stayed, locked up until he turned off the power. He was intense and intelligent, but he was also hard to get along with. He would argue with anyone and the only way you could get his attention was to subtly smash him on the head with a baseball bat. Almost every contractor hated and feared him. I didn't. I respected his dedication and his honesty, and I liked him. Right now, though, I felt like strangling him.

In all these years he himself had not changed, but his job had. He now worked, as a civilian, for the Ballistic Missile Office. BMO was the Air Force unit that designed Minuteman. They watched over all six wings of Minuteman Missiles looking for flaws or problems.

I finally answered, "I guess he is, Bill. Mike is young and the idea of seeing a bare chested female has grabbed his attention."

I was unhappy with Mike Andrews. He was a technical writer who had come with me in case we had to correct any of the Air Force technical orders. This evening he had borrowed our car about 9:00 PM to run an errand and he had not yet returned. Previously on our way from Boston to Cheyenne, when we landed in Denver he had disappeared for a few minutes. He had returned clutching a handful of yellow pages.

Ed Bannon, the third member of our trio, asked him what he was doing. Mike was excited. "Listen, Ed. I have a friend who told me that in either Denver, or Fort Collins, or Cheyenne there is a place that makes and sells donuts on their premises. They only hire girls and they are all topless. I didn't have a chance to go through all the donut shops in the phone book so I just ripped out the listings. "I think I'm looking for the name Debbie Does Donuts."

I got mad. "Mike, I am telling you right now that you had better be careful. I don't give a damn what you do when we are not working. If you can order plain donuts in an A cup size or honey dipped in a C size, good luck to you. I think it is a pipe dream. However, if you slack off Whitman will notice and he is a devil; not much gets by him."

"Oh, this won't interfere with my work, Jay. You know my habits by now."

I did and that was why I had spoken to him. Bill had a deep bass voice which interrupted my thoughts. He said, "I don't like him chasing babes and boobies on my time."

"Neither do I, Bill, and I will take care of it. But right now let's stick to the problems at hand," I replied. "Namely, what are we going to do about this mess you have gotten us into?"

Bill smiled for the first time in two days. His smile was wide and so in contrast with his normal dour look. "Well, you kind of suggested this problem before we got here, but I, of course, didn't listen. You got lucky, I got unlucky, that's all I can say.

"Let's look at what you call a mess. Right now we are sitting in the E. Lab. We are trying to check out a piece of equipment and it is not passing some tests. And, we can't tell whether the equipment is bad or the test that we are using is bad. So far that is correct, is it not?"

"Not quite, Bill. Our test set can not check out the equipment the way it is presently configured. Face it, Bill, Technical Orders were not followed and this equipment has an operational P plug in it that should have been removed; and that is our real problem," I said to him.

Air Force technical orders are manuals that minutely define every activity involved with Minuteman. There are thousands of these T.O.'s and any violation is a court martial offense. In our case the problem of not following tech orders was made worse by the P plug itself. The Permutation Plug, or P Plug, is a cryptographic device designed so that no one can monitor the missile system. The P Plug is controlled and coded by the National Security Agency, a huge Government Agency independent of the Air Force. The NSA takes any compromise of their equipment very seriously.

I continued, "So far, Bill, we have inherited an operational problem. If we break the quality control seal on the equipment and replace the operational P plug with a dummy P plug we can check the equipment, but we will have a crypto compromise. If we don't break the seal we can show NSA that there has been no compromise. A crypto compromise investigation takes months and it is a pain in the ass. You have to make a decision, Bill. Either check out the equipment, or don't check out the equipment. It is your call."

Bill thought for a few minutes. "You know as soon as NSA hears of this incident they are going to force code change, and that is what I have been trying to avoid. Damn, it will happen, so let's go the easier way; a code change without a crypto compromise.

"Let's go get some sleep and meet back here at 10:00 AM. I have a lot of phone calls to make and I will have to brief the Wing Commander, who ain't going to be a happy camper."

Whitman drove me back to the motel.

A code change is the removal of all the crypto devices, and there are a lot more in addition to the P plug at each site in the entire wing. They are immediately replaced with other crypto devices that are coded differently. Doing a code change involves hundreds of Air Force Personnel driving thousands of miles to 165 separate underground facilities. It takes hours to configure the equipment and check out each site using T.O.'s. It is a frenzied hectic activity.

As we drove, Bill said, "I have got to tell you, Jay, that Andrews is annoying me. I could put up with his humming hormones but for the last two days he has been bothering the personnel in the E Lab. He has done nothing but tie up the phone calling bakeries and donut shops looking for Debbie Does Donuts. He looks stupid and so do you."

I was not going to contest the point with Bill. All I wanted was a hot shower and sleep. And that is what I did. Before I went to breakfast I called Mike Andrews' room and told him to come to my room immediately. He rapped on my door and when I let him in he handed me the keys to the car and said, "I didn't go back to the E Lab last night because I got back very late. I knew Whitman would give you a ride."

"And just where did you go last night, Mike?" I asked.

"Well, I drove down to Fort Collins to see if that town was where Debbie Does Donuts was located. It wasn't there."

"Damn it, Mike, there is no Debbie Does Donuts. These horny Air Force guys would absolutely know if there were a place like that within a thousand miles. Whether there is such a place is not important. What is important is that I am angry with the way you are conducting yourself. You have spent the last two days doing nothing but bothering everyone in the E Lab and tying up the phones. Last night you took the car and left me stranded. All because of a bare breasted donut shop. You are acting like a jerk and you are making GTE look bad. You will stop this immediately and start working. Do I make myself clear?"

Mike got red faced; he opened his mouth to say something, looked at me, and decided not to. He walked out the door and slammed it shut as hard as he could.

Bill came into the E Lab just after 10:00 AM. He came over to where the three of us were seated. "Well, the Wing Commander and I talked to NSA. They are sending in a team to investigate and if everything is as we said, they will make us do a code change and, for them, the incident was closed.

"I have also arranged for the identical piece of equipment that we tried to test to be brought over from storage. When it arrives, the Air Force will insert the dummy P plug and check out the equipment."

Ed Bannon cleared his throat and softly said, "Err, Mr. Whitman sir," lost his courage and stopped.

Bill bristled. "Damn it, don't ever call me sir." He looked at Ed who was almost shaking with fright.

"Sorry," Bill chuckled. "It's not your fault I don't like officers. What were you going to say, Ed?"

"Could you have the Air Force run a self test on the test set before we use it to check out the equipment?"

"Good idea, Ed. Let me talk to the NCOIC and get that started."

After Bill left, Ed looked at me and asked "NCOIC?"

"Non Commissioned Officer in Charge. These are the guys that really keep the wing working. By the way, Bill spent twenty years saying "Yes sir" to people he had little respect for. As you can tell, he is a little touchy."

The rest of the day went smoothly. During the two hour self test of test set, one of the voltages was found to be out of tolerance. When this was corrected, the test set passed and then the equipment passed.

While he and I were reading each other's notebooks he asked me "What in hell did you say to Mike Andrews?"

I was a little puzzled. "Just a little father to son talk. Why?"

"Because he followed me around all day asking questions and talking about the tech orders. I was glad he finally came to work."

"Me too," I said.

The four of us went out together that evening. Our plane left earlier than Whitman's so we said our goodbyes fairly early and I went to bed.

Before we drove to Denver the next morning, I left him a present at the front desk. It was a donut wrapped in saran wrap and placed in a small white bag. Along with the donut was a centerfold from Playboy on which I had our waitress inscribe "To Bill from his most ardent admirer—Debbie"

Secretly, I will admit that I always hoped Mike Andrews would have found "Debbie Does Donuts."

Don't Ever Lend Captain Peachy Any Money

As I think about it, I do not know why our division moved from Needham to Westboro. I would like to believe that the corporate officers wanted to isolate their most troublesome children from the rest of the staid firm. That wasn't the reason though. The cold hard fact was that the divisional vice president decided to move to a more prestigious looking building after GTE/Sylvania, along with all our big minuteman missile contracts, won a huge contract on the MX missile. Whatever the reason, the strategic system division moved into a brand new building eighteen miles west of the GTE complex in late fall of 1986. It was the first building finished in what was to be a huge industrial development; a four story glass and aluminum structure built right off of Route 9.

We moved desks, laboratories, equipment, and file cabinets in on weekends during the fall and winter, trying not to lose either our customers or our sanity. Overcoming inertia and transferring lethargy is always a painful process. But we persevered and by the beginning of spring we were back to our normal standard of organized chaos.

Just two weeks after the move was completed, I was in the

cafeteria line about 9:30 AM getting a cup of coffee when a Klaxon sounded over the public address system. It was so loud and insistent that everyone heard it; but having had no instructions, no one knew exactly what it meant.

When I got to the cashier, she took my money, gave me the change, and asked, "What does that siren mean?" I answered, "I guess it is the fire alarm system. But I don't know if it is just a test or the real thing."

As if in response to my quandary, a voice came over the wail of the siren on the public address system.

"This is L. Alexander DuPont, the head of security. The siren you hear is from our fire alarm system. Immediately secure all classified material and evacuate the building. I repeat, immediately secure your classified material and evacuate the building."

We did this gladly and quickly because it was a pleasant day and it was like being young and playing hooky from school again. We milled around in the fresh air, walking aimlessly and talking and laughing; we were relaxed. Soon, in the background, was the sound of fire engines; louder as they came towards us, quieter when they went away from us. They came near us many times and they went away from us many times; but at no time did they ever arrive at our building. We wondered why they didn't show up. It was a week before we found out. The reason was that the building was brand new and the builder forgot to give the fire department the address when the building was completed. At the same time the alarm sounded inside the building, it also rang at the fire station. Since no one had told the fire department the location of this new alarm, they were ready to fight the blaze; they just didn't know exactly where to go to do it. So they cruised around looking for a fire to put out. We also found out later that the alarm was triggered in error. The fire alarm system had been miswired; it finally shorted out and sounded the Klaxon. It was a false alarm.

In the meantime, our security chief heard the engines and he assumed the fire brigade was on its way to douse the inferno; so he waited, and he waited, and he waited. After three quarters of an hour, our security chief got angry and he decided to call the fire station to see if he needed to make an appointment. When his call got through, the fire chief was furious because his men and equipment had been out cruising without finding where they were supposed to be.

When both men finally stopped yelling and swearing at each other and calmed down, the fire chief got our address and drove over. He inspected every inch of the building and said that we could all return and go back to work.

In the meantime, not knowing any of this, we had a three hour sunbath, courtesy of GTE/Sylvania. After the initial excitement of leaving work, people gathered in small clusters and settled down. The group I was with had about 20 people. Five or six of us were engineers and managers who had worked together over fifteen years, the rest were younger people who worked for us. I sat with my eyes shut, not talking, enjoying the idleness and letting my mind drift. I began to pay attention when Ed Lambeau said, "We have been out here almost two hours now. No smoke, no fire trucks, no fire; must be a false alarm."

Len Fortes replied, "Ed you are assuming it was a fire that triggered the alarm. What if it were something else?"

Ed asked, "What would that something else be?"

Len replied, "Why not a bomb threat?"

And that is what started a discussion that began calmly and ended animated and lively. The idea of a bomb threat was bantered back and forth until it became the question, "what would you do if you received a bomb threat?" Some said to notify security immediately, others said to notify personnel immediately. On the issue of who to notify first, an argument began. Each side defended their choice and denounced the logic of the other side.

I listened but I did not enter into the conversation, as I didn't think it would make much difference whether security or personnel was notified first. I doubted that anything would be done except to evacuate the building, and this could be done by either department. I thought that they were arguing needlessly.

Len Fortes said to me, "Jay, I know you are not asleep. Who do you think should be notified first if a bomb threat is called in?"

I sat up and looked around. This was my chance to get the subject changed, and I was going to grab it.

I began, "You guys continually show me that none of you has the foggiest idea of what to do in an emergency."

That got the result I wanted, I had their attention.

Len was snippy as he replied, "Charming as always, you bastard, what would you do if you got a bomb threat?"

I said, "Let me see if I have this right. I am at my desk and the phone rings. I answer it and a heavily accented says "There is a bomb planted in your building set to explode in 35 minutes' is that what you define as a bomb threat?"

"Yes" Len said, "Now just how the hell would you handle this differently and better than we could?"

"Very simple", I replied. "As soon as he says '35 minutes', I look at my wrist watch and write the time down on a pad of paper. That's the start of the thirty five minute clock. I then take my pad of paper and go up to the fourth floor where all the brass is. I try to see each of those fat cats in his own office and I say to him that I just discovered I left my wallet home, and could he lend me some money. I would write his name and the amount I borrowed on my pad to make it look legitimate. I would move slowly but I would keep my eye on my wrist watch as time is important. If I could finish the fourth floor, I would continue to the third and borrow money. After about 25 minutes, I would quit asking for loans and I would leave the building. Just before I got in my car, I would face the building, wave my arm, and say 'Thanks suckers'"

When I finished I looked around. My friends were grinning realizing my story was just to kid them. Most of the younger people were also smiling, but a few were scowling deeply.

Just then the chief of security came out with a hand held bull horn and announced that the building was now safe to enter. Slowly and reluctantly we went inside.

As I returned, I noticed a few of the people who had scowled talking with one of my friends, Joe Daddante. The conversation seemed deep and intense.

The next morning, Joe and Len came into my office carrying coffee for themselves and one for me. Since they only bring coffee when they are going to rag me, my day immediately brightened.

After we greeted each other and sipped our coffee, Joe said to me, "Jay how many times have I asked you to be careful of what you say in front of new troops?"

"Over the course of a lot of years, I would say many, many, many times Joe," I replied. "Why are you asking?"

"You know why I am asking. Some of those new people came up to me and asked if you would really borrow money and then let your fellow workers get blown up."

"Joe" I said, "That only proves what I have told you, time and again. Anyone who takes me seriously deserves what he gets, and before you lecture me, let me ask you a question. Since I have known you exactly as long as you have known me, I know that you are not immune from pulling someone's leg. So tell me how you answered these naïve waifs."

Joe smiled a cherubic smile. "To tell the truth, Jay, I added a little to their confusion. I told them I was not sure what you would do, and that was one of the reasons you were called Captain Peachy. I also told them how to avoid getting caught in a situation like that."

"Oh, Oh," I said, "Thank you for coming to my rescue. And what sage advice did you give these beauties who are dumb enough to grow up and become managers?"

Joe said, "I told them that whatever the circumstances, never, never, never, lend Captain Peachy any money."

With that the three of us drank our coffee and decided that a bomb threat could ruin a perfectly good day.

Donating Blood Proves Injurious to My Health

In 1945 I turned eighteen and was drafted into the army. At that time the outcome of the war was obvious and neither side, for reasons of their own, was concerned about my availability. However, I was; I wanted to be a paratrooper, jump out of a plane, land, and go into battle. I had hoped to make the army my career. Twenty years of leaping and shooting appealed to me. This shows that simple minds weave simple plans.

However, as I was finishing basic training my plan was cut short. I contracted rheumatic fever and I was confined to total bed rest in an army hospital for six months. During this time I thought about it and I realized I would not make twenty years in the army because I could not take orders from anyone I didn't respect. I knew I would get into trouble, so I made new arrangements.

I decided to take advantage of the GI Bill and go to college. So, when I was discharged, I went back to Boston and applied to several schools. I was accepted at the University of Michigan and came west to Ann Arbor. When school started, I quickly found out that I would need more money than I was receiving from the government. I got a part time job, worked about twenty or twenty five hours a week, and just about made expenses. Once a month I would sell a pint of blood to the University Hospital; once a month I would sell a pint of blood to St. Joseph's Hospital. Every two weeks it was either the one or the other. That was my beer money.

One thing I did faithfully was to make sure that I wrote on the questionnaire, and told the nurse who took my history, that I had had rheumatic fever. I did not want anyone to go through what I had endured my first four weeks of being sick. During all the times I donated, no nurse ever turned me away, no nurse ever told me not to give blood. As far as I knew, my blood was used to help someone.

After I graduated and started working, I always gave blood whenever the Red Cross had a blood drive. I considered it payback time and I gave it freely for whomever could use it. I still made it a point to write on the questionnaire, and tell the nurse, that I had had rheumatic fever. My blood was still accepted with no comments.

In 1970, I had been working for Sylvania for about twelve years. Except for my time in Thule, I had given blood in all of the blood drives; and I still made it a point to tell the nurse, as well as write on the questionnaire, that I had had rheumatic fever.

One day in August, I returned to the house from work, kissed Virginia, tousled my daughters, patted the dog, and scratched the cat; I was home. I sat at the kitchen table and talked with Virginia while she fixed supper.

"You got a letter from your girlfriend today. It is on the top of the pile of mail by your plate," Virginia said.

I picked up the envelope and looked at it. It was a plain white envelope with my name and address typed in the middle. The return had three initials, EMA, and a Brockton address.

"What makes you think that his letter is from my girlfriend?"

"If that letter had been from a man, he would have written his full name," Virginia answered.

"I guess that you are right. But you know that I only pick girl-friends who are illiterate; that way I don't find myself in embarrassing positions like the one that I am in right now."

I could not think of anyone I knew, male or female, with the initials EMA. I was sure that Virginia was kidding me; otherwise she would have opened the letter to satisfy either her suspicions or her curiosity. I will have to admit that I was very curious myself. But before I had a chance to open the letter some huge domestic problem arose. I think it was a spat among all three girls, and Virginia and I forgot about EMA.

The next morning I left for work very early, but there beside my lunch, was my letter. I took it with me, and, in mid morning I finally had a chance to open it. The first line was enough to dispel Virginia's theory.

It read "I should like to talk with you in regard to your recent Red Cross blood donation." The letter continued with a phone number and a time to call. It was signed Ellen M. Anenburg, R.N. Massachusetts Department of Public Health.

I gathered that my blood had been rejected, so I called the number, got hold of Ellen M. Anenburg, and introduced myself. She said that it was imperative to speak to me and she asked me to come to her office today. When I asked her what it was she wanted to talk about, and why today, she answered that she could not discuss anything over the telephone. I made an appointment for later in the afternoon and I hung up, totally puzzled by the secrecy. I looked up my boss, Walt Collinsworth, and asked him to fill in for me, and when the time for my appointment came, I left.

Mrs. Anenburg ushered me into her tiny office buried in the basement of the Brockton Hospital. She shut the door, squeezed by me and sat at her desk. She motioned me to sit in the visitor's chair and when I did, my knees bumped her desk. Mrs. Anenburg did not smile. She appeared harried, and she looked as if she had not had any fun in a decade.

She stared directly at me and asked, "Have you told your wife yet?"

I stared back at her, not knowing which way to go, so I simply answered, "No".

She replied, "She certainly deserves to know. When had you planned on telling her?"

I got angry. I have a hot temper and I totally enjoy getting angry; but I also knew that speaking in anger would not help this situation.

So I inhaled deeply, exhaled slowly and finally replied, "Lady, you are correct, my wife does deserve to know. For that matter, I also deserve to know. If you will kindly tell me what the hell is going on, I will tell my wife."

She glared at me with disdain, "Mr. Carp, why are you pretending to be innocent?"

"Lady, I am not pretending anything. I am telling you, flat out, that I have no idea what you are talking about."

"Let me make this easy for you then, Mr. Carp. You have failed the Hinton test."

"Lady, I didn't even know that I had taken the Hinton test. Would you please tell me, in layman's terms, what it is you are trying to say?"

She answered from her high horse, "You are just going to have to come to grips with this, Mr. Carp. You have syphilis." Even though she continued to stare at me in disapproval, my anger faded. Whatever Mrs. Anenburg thought, I knew that I did not have syphilis. The situation was so stupid as to strike me as being funny; I started laughing. I must have laughed for two minutes before I stopped.

Mrs. Anenburg sat there watching me, not at all amused. "I fail to see what you are laughing about. There is nothing funny about having, and spreading, syphilis."

I began to get angry again. "Lady, if I had syphilis, and I were spreading it around, you would be correct, there would be nothing funny about it. I don't care a whit about your Hinton test, I do not have syphilis."

"Surely, Mr. Carp, you have had sex with some women other than your wife."

I was angry again. I did not like her attitude; I did not like her approach. And I certainly didn't like discussing my family life with anyone, let alone disapproving strangers. Yet, I did owe it to Virginia, to correct this woman's impression. Mrs. Anenburg, in her own way, was trying to help my wife. So, instead of a flip, very ribald answer, which I thought she deserved, I told her the truth.

"Lady, you are dead wrong. I have been married for over fifteen years and I have not strayed, not even once. If I caught syphilis, which I haven't, it would have had to have been from a toilet seat."

"Mr. Carp, that is not how this disease is transmitted" said Mrs. Anenburg. Her acid level seemed to be a bit lower. "If you are sure you have not been exposed to catching syphilis, I shall have to find out what caused a false reaction to the Hinton test."

She got the medical form that the donor filled out and we talked about each item as we came to it. When we got to rheumatic fever she spent a long time questioning me about the details of that disease which had occurred twenty five years earlier.

When we finished the entire form, Mrs. Anenburg said, "Mr. Carp, with your permission, I would like to set up an appointment to take another sample of your blood. I want to have some tests done including a repeat Hinton. If that fails, and it probably will, I would like to do a TPI. That is a test that will determine what is causing the Hinton to fail. The TPI is a sensitive, accurate test, not ordinarily performed, and the closest hospital that can do it is the Massachusetts General Hospital in Boston. Would you be willing to take the TPI? I really would like to get to the bottom of this."

She was acting more reasonable and less belligerent than she had been. I decided to respond in the same way, so we set up a time for me to give blood and then I left.

Virginia was waiting when I got home. She knew that I would

not answer any questions until I kissed, tousled, patted, and scratched, and felt at home, so she waited. When I finished, she asked, "Where have you been? You are late. I called work and Walt told me you left early. I was getting concerned."

She stopped, thought for a second, and then smiled. "It couldn't have been your girlfriend could it? You never did show me that letter."

I handed her the envelope with the letter inside, "As a matter of fact, it is because of this letter that I am late. I have had one hell of a day. My wife accuses me of having a girlfriend, my purported girlfriend accuses me of having syphilis, and the medical profession is going to examine my blood."

I certainly had Virginia's undivided attention, "What do you mean? What is going on?" She opened the letter and read it and then looked at me. "What in heaven's name is happening? Please, tell me."

During the next hour and a half, I told her the entire story in detail, and then totally repeated it. At first she was shocked, and then she was angry at Mrs. Anenberg's attitude. She finally regained her composure and she could see some humor in this bizarre episode.

A few days later I gave a sample of my blood for a repeat Hinton and whatever other tests EMA deemed necessary. I came home from work shortly after that and found a letter on top of the day's mail, sitting by my dinner plate. Although addressed to me, it had the initials EMA on the return, and it had been opened. Virginia certainly had as much right to read it as I had. The only subject of the letter was the details of an appointment for a TPI.

I took the TPI. To this day I do not know the results because I never heard from my girlfriend, EMA, again. I gather the TPI cured my syphilis.

Since then, I have not given blood. I am sure that there is a need for it, but I am afraid it would not be used and I would meet another person like EMA. Since I don't want another case of syphilis, I just don't donate blood.

Helen Hill's Writing Group

It is a fact that, like all the other members of this writing group, I also had a childhood. However, unlike the majority of you, I can not easily recall many of my experiences. I would listen to your stories of childhood and youth with rapt attention because I wondered how you could each remember so much. I had been born and I had passed through the same ages as you had; hadn't things happened to me?

After much thought I decided that things must have happened to me, I just have never given much thought to my childhood. Occasionally, isolated memories, like shards of broken glass glittering in a flashlight beam, would shine through my subconscious and catch my attention. For example, I remember that once, as a Cub Scout, I went on a hike through the woods in Norumbega Park. I remembered this adventure for two reasons. The first was that the hike was in winter and it was bitter cold; when we stopped to eat the sandwiches we had each packed, the bread was almost frozen. However, the major reason I remembered the hike was the tower that we unexpectedly came across. There, in the middle of those woods we found a round stone tower about thirty feet high. The tower was nothing more than a staircase leading to a small parapet on the top, from where the Charles River was visible. Embedded in the base was a metal plaque that said the tower had been erected to the memory of Leif Ericson. After I climbed to the top and came back down, I asked our troop leader how Eric the Red had gotten to this particular spot and how did anyone know that he had. He never really answered.

Aside from this, and a few other meager remembrances, I had managed to grow from childhood through my teens with an amazing amount of amnesia. As I listened to each of you give detailed descriptions of your individual pasts, I decided that I should revisit my own. What if I were an heir to a throne somewhere or what if I had won a baby pageant?

The question was how to begin? My mother and father were both dead and I had lost contact with my family years ago. Essentially, I had lost all connection with the past. So, I started by listing the house we had lived in when I was in high school and I then worked backwards trying to recall all the previous addresses. I came up with at least seven other homes; there might have been another one or two but I didn't think so. There was Hawthorne Road and Wyoming Avenue in Malden. Alton Place in Brookline, Chiswick and Sutherland Roads and Bostonia Avenue in Brighton, Stanwood and Brunswick Streets in Roxbury. It was at this point that I ran out of memory.

After I made my list, I started to study each address just trying to conjure up whatever memories I could gather. I am still in that process and I have made some progress; I have been able to go from an almost total blank to a very fuzzy recall. For example, I met Eric the Red while I was living on Chiswick Road, and using that as a basis, I have been able to think of other incidents that took place while I lived there.

At the present time, it is the home on Sutherland Road that is becoming the clearest to me. I was about nine or ten years old when we lived there. Sutherland Road is about a mile long and it runs between Commonwealth Avenue and Beacon Street. It joins Beacon Street at a rotary called Cleveland Circle, which is where Beacon Street and

Chestnut Hill Avenue intersect each other. My family lived close to the Commonwealth Avenue end of Sutherland Road and I didn't usually go down the street to Cleveland Circle.

I remembered that Cleveland Circle fascinated me whenever I got there because, in the middle of this grassy rotary, was a large, granite fountain sitting there with no water in it. The fountain was not used; it had been installed many years ago as a trough for horses and it had long since been dry. I used to sit there and pretend that there were a lot of horses for me to watch.

Cleveland Circle had one other fascination for me. The Boston Marathon ran from Hopkinton to Boston by way of Cleveland Circle. It was not as much of a media event back when I was young. There may have been two hundred runners and the sidewalks were not jammed with spectators. A child could see the race without being pushed and jostled. I would watch these runners as they ran by, four miles from the finish line, and just wonder at their stamina.

With two or three friends, and I don't remember their names, we would occasionally hike to Hammond Pond. It was probably only about a three-mile hike, but for us, it was a thrilling adventure. We would cross Cleveland Circle and walk through a huge playground and baseball field. At the far edge of the playground was a large building that always appeared deserted. As we approached, we could hear the noise of heavy machinery working, and as we got closer, the noise became louder. The building was the pumping station for the Chestnut Hill Reservoir. We would get right up against the windows and gaze through and be fascinated by those large pumps that always turned and never seemed to stop. We talked about slipping inside the building and looking around, but we never mustered the courage to try.

After that, we would leave the pumping station and walk directly behind it to a set of railroad tracks. We would walk down the railroad tracks until we reached Hammond Pond. These tracks were the main line between Boston and New York and there were trains constantly travelling between the two cities. We were frightened so we always watched and listened for trains moving in either direction. When we heard a train we would run off the tracks and get as far away as we could; most times we had about fifteen feet of space, sometimes as much as thirty feet. The trains would pass us, scaring us with their speed, their noise, and their vibrations, which we could feel through our sneakers. Occasionally, we had trains going in opposite directions that passed each other right where we were huddled by the side of the tracks. The extra noise and vibrations would leave us almost limp. Often, we thought about leaving a penny on the track and seeing how flattened it would be after the train ran over it. However, we decided that the vibrations would knock the penny off the track before the train would crunch it, so we never did.

Whenever we came to one of the three small trestles that were on our route, we would look up and down the tracks and then dash across the bridge as fast as we could. The trestles really weren't very long, maybe twenty feet, but we would act as if we were out of breath after we reached the other side. We would stand there panting for a few minutes before continuing our trip.

When we arrived at Hammond Pond we would walk around its edge, throw stones into the water, try to catch frogs, and look for signs of animal life. We would eventually sit down, eat candy bars, and talk about everything that ten-year-olds talk about. After we got tired of hanging around, we walked back along the same stretch of tracks and went home. As near as I can remember, we always went straight home; we never stopped to visit the pumping station on the way back.

As I listen to your stories, and as I recall my own past, I am struck by the diversity among us. We each have lived a full life before enrolling in this writing group and we each have come to this table by travelling separate and unique paths. Yet, when all of us talk about our younger years, we do have one thing in common. There is a patina of wonder, artlessness, and straightforwardness about our reminiscences that we don't carry forward to our later years. The trust and sweetness that accompanied our youth became tempered as we learn more about life. We may gain knowledge but we do lose our innocence; and from that point of view, experience is a hard teacher. Perhaps that is why we treasure our childhood so dearly.

Honk If You Love Jesus

In 1972 I was living by myself in Silver Spring Maryland when spring arrived. It was a welcome change to the cold, raw, damp days of winter. The dirty snows of winter begin to melt slowly as the warmer days shyly make their appearance. At first, the sun lingers a little longer each day. The cold changes to cool, and winter coats, as they become unnecessary, begin to feel hot and bulky. The air becomes moist and perfumed with the smell of vegetation coming alive after being dormant. The birds begin to put heart and gusto into their calls. The spring flowers, Jonquils, Iris, Lilies of the Valley, and Bluebells, stand up and proudly display their brilliant reds, yellows, blues, and whites. Spring in Maryland brings the promise of new life with every breath you take.

One of these rare and precious days occurred on a Saturday in early April. It was on a weekend that I was not driving to Massachusetts to see my wife and children, so I had almost nothing to do. I decided that I would enjoy the day and revel in being alive. I left my room very early in the morning and drove on back roads and country roads as slowly as I could. I stopped and watched brooks running, horses gamboling, and a farmer chopping down a tree. It felt good to breathe the hint of hope and happiness that early spring brought.

And I needed a hint of hope and happiness. Two years earlier, I had been laid off by GTE when a government contract had been cancelled. At the time, that was neither unique nor hard to do; thousands of engineers were out of work in the New England area. What was hard to do was to find a job. There were men with doctorate degrees driving cabs in downtown Boston; the electronic sector of the economy was in bad shape.

My layoff, after thirteen years with the company, took me totally by surprise, but there was absolutely nothing I could do about it. I needed money as I had three young daughters, a wife, a mortgage, two automobiles, and a lot of debts. Unemployment compensation did not begin to cover my expenses; I needed to work as many jobs as I could for the money. My motto became, "Anything for Income."

The first week of my layoff, I went to the Foxboro Town hall and filled out an application for the highway department. The highway department supervisor attended the same church my family went to, and I knew that he was always hiring. His crew included high school dropouts, marginal alcoholics, men with minor criminal records, and under achievers. He had a high rate of turnover. So, I was not surprised when I was hired; after all, compared to his other applicants, what could he lose? He knew that, for however long I worked for him, he would have someone who was dependable.

He made a dump truck available to me so I could learn to drive it, and I practiced for hours. When I had learned the necessary skills, I passed the Massachusetts driving test and was promoted to truck driver.

After about a year with the highway department, Vitro Laboratories in Silver Spring, Maryland, contacted me. They worked for the U.S. Navy testing submarine Inter Continental Ballistic Missiles (ICBM). Vitro offered me a job as a test engineer. I parked my dump truck, took a hot shower, and returned to the missile world.

Although I was thankful to get this job, it posed a terrible dilemma for my family and me. At the time I accepted their offer, Vitro offered to relocate my family to the Silver Spring area. After discussions with Virginia, we decided to delay moving the family. My oldest daughter was starting her senior year in high school and Virginia was very reluctant to leave her home and friends. So, I asked for, and Vitro agreed, to postpone my relocation package for a year.

When I arrived at Silver Spring that late spring, I rented a room in a house that was near Vitro Labs. For the first three months I would drive four hundred miles to Foxboro every Friday night, and four hundred miles back to Silver Spring every Sunday night. After that, for the next eight months, I drove home every second or third weekend. By then, I was tired, the car was tired, and the gas embargo made it Hell getting gasoline.

To make matters worse, the personnel office at Vitro wrote me a letter saying that, if I had not relocated my family and furniture within the year that we had agreed to, Vitro had no responsibility to pay any expenses. I couldn't argue, but it did mean that we were facing a real deadline. We knew that we would have to move, but Virginia really wanted to stay in Foxboro. We were as frozen as the winter weather, looking for a thaw, but fearful of what the thaw would bring. We were uneasy and unhappy.

And yet, in the midst of our slogging through our problems, changes were on the way. We did not sense them, but they would profoundly affect us. And the first of these was the loosening of the cold, raw winter weather and the sweet arrival of spring.

By mid morning I was lucky enough to be lost on a small, winding road that had no traffic and didn't seem to go anywhere. As I rounded a bend, I saw a car ahead of me, going in the same direction, but moving more slowly than my car. As I got closer I could see that the car was an old station wagon that had its rear window down. The bottom panels were rusted out and the entire car was caked with dirt and grime.

When I got about thirty feet from the car, a boy and girl suddenly appeared in the back compartment facing my direction. The boy was about six years old and the girl was about five. They were both tow heads; the girl had her hair braided, and the two braids hung in front of her. The boy had long hair clumped in spikes. Judging by their looks and coloring, they were probably brother and sister.

I could see them talking and, finally, the boy raised his hand and gave me a small wave. I smiled, put my hand out of the window, and waved back. Immediately, he grinned, and his second wave was much larger and more vigorous than his first. When I responded to that one, he really began to wave. His sister, who had been watching us without moving, joined in and began to wave. Within a minute or two, both of them were laughing, waving, and cheering.

When my car got about fifteen feet from their car, I noticed two legible bumper stickers in the back. One had a picture of the stars and bars, the Confederate flag. The other had the printed motto, "Honk if you love Jesus." Since I figured that was well within the spirit of the game that we three children were playing, I gave the horn three gentle, quick taps. The horn beeped no longer than a hemidemisemiquaver, a 64th note.

From behind, I could see the woman driver's blond head move to look out first her rear view mirror and then her side mirror. She slowed her car even more and lowered her driver's side window. She put her left arm straight out of the window, and then she bent her arm, at the elbow, straight up in the air. Slowly and distinctly, three separate times, she gave me the finger. After that, she stepped on the throttle with such force that the two children rolled on the floor, and she roared off.

I laughed so hard that I had to pull over to the side of the road so as not to lose control of my car. I thought her response was hilarious. From that day to this, I never use my automobile horn to express any religious views whatsoever.

Oddly enough, it was the Monday following this incident that I got a call from GTE asking what it would take for them to be able to rehire me.

I Can Hardly Hear You

With the advent of electronics, it appears that talking has now become our national past time. Cell phones are as common as earmuffs in a snowstorm. And, with the newest gadgets, text messaging has elevated the thumb, which used to be used for hitching a ride, into the queen of communications.

For anyone who can remember when there were phone booths on street corners and pay phones in small stores, today's wireless systems are frightening and mind boggling. The World Wide Web, cell phones, text messages, E-mail, and the Global Positioning System are recent examples of the tidal wave of instant communications. Personal privacy is being drowned in a sea of radio waves. Everywhere you go you hear the sounds of beepers, pagers, and cell phones buzzing, ringing and going off. Nowadays, you can get in touch with anyone, anywhere, any time, under any condition. However, this amazing capability begs two questions. Isn't everyone just talking? Is anybody really listening?

Almost every time I go shopping for groceries, I come across a young shopper who will suddenly pull a phone out of hiding, tap numbers into it, and breathlessly ask, "Honey, was it the big jar of sweet pickles or the small jar of dills you wanted me to get?"

That's fine; it solves the menu problem but it leaves me wondering if this couple, or any other couple, ever sit down and discuss anything before leaving for the store? And, more important, whatever happened to shopping lists and pens and pencils?

Before I moved to Milan a few years ago, I went over to my step daughter's house, in Ypsilanti, for Thanksgiving dinner. She always took great delight in having a crowd over Thanksgiving Day because she made it a point of personal pride to have all of her Christmas decorations up and her lights on the day before Thanksgiving. She invited her sisters, her husband's relatives, their friends, and the friends of her two teen age daughters over to see her display and eat dinner. That made me, whenever I went, the senior citizen at the feeding trough.

There was always a crowd and her small house was noisy and smoke filled because almost everyone smoked. On this particular holiday, I arrived after the Thanksgiving meal had been served. My step daughter and I hadn't seen each other in a long time and, to catch up with each other, I sat and ate in the kitchen and talked with her and her husband while they washed the dishes. As we chatted, her friends and relatives wandered through the kitchen and stopped and spoke with us, so we were there a long time. Just before I finished my dinner, my step daughter and her husband finished cleaning up, excused themselves, and joined their guests in the living room.

After I finished eating, I put my dishes in the sink and started to enter the living room to join everyone else. I stopped in the doorway in complete disbelief; it was a sight I had never seen before. The Christmas decorations were blinking all over the room, the Christmas tree was blazing with lights, Christmas carols were playing on the hi-fi sct, and the television was blaring away with a football game. But, more important than the noise or the lights, was what the people were doing. I counted fourteen people sitting or standing and not one of them was paying attention to any other person in the room. Everyone in that room was talking on their own cell phone. Since I didn't have a cell phone to call anyone, I left.

This summer, my wife and I took my daughter and her husband, who were visiting us from San Antonio, to Sault St. Marie. They had never been to Michigan but their son had been here last summer and he had raved about Sault St. Marie. After watching the traffic go through the locks we went to Antlers, a very popular restaurant, for dinner. It was completely filled with diners and we were seated at a table for four in the middle of the dining room. Suddenly, my daughter got a phone call on her cell phone. The ring tone was the distinct, loud sound of a yowling female cat in heat.

The result was instantaneous. From the very first wailing sound every person in the room started to look around to see where the cat was. The whole dining room suddenly became absolutely still as the diners craned their necks looking for the cat. My daughter at first didn't realize that her phone was causing the commotion and it yowled three or four times before she began grabbing for her pocketbook. She had trouble opening her purse and even more trouble trying to locate her cell phone.

The result was that the cat yowls were many and frequent and we were the center of attention. By the time Cynthia eventually answered the phone, the restaurant was the audience and our table was the stage. Everyone was silent watching and listening as our daughter carried on her conversation. The phone call itself was trivial and mundane, not worth interrupting dinner; her daughter called to tell her that she had gone shopping and had bought a new dress. After she hung up our audience slowly got back to the business of dining. I asked my daughter if the four of us shouldn't stand up and bow. Eventually, the restaurant returned to normal.

Why my daughter never turns her cell phone off is a mystery to me.

The point to all of this, if there is a point, is that there is a gap between those that use electronic devices and those that don't. It is more than an age or an attitude difference, it is a complete cultural gap.

Electronic users believe they absolutely have to be in contact with their peers constantly and instantly. They believe that they have the right to use their devices whenever and wherever they so choose. It might not be defined exactly that way in the Constitution, but they believe it is inferred.

Nonusers believe their privacy rights are being shredded by yakkers and hackers. Their movies, concerts, and gatherings are constantly being interrupted by not only the bells and whistles that announce messages but also and talkers who answer. A converser at a concert always seems to have a loud voice that interferes with what the audience is trying to hear. Nonusers also consider people who drive while using their cell phones as dangerous.

Both sides have elements of truth in their complaints, but both sides are missing an important point; there is no way to go back to the phone booth. Modern communications are not only here to stay but they are going to get smaller, faster and more intrusive. We are going to have to live with them and we must learn how to get along with each other.

That's going to take a lot more patience and respect than we have shown to each other in the past. We can all show our determination to do better by observing a moment of silence during which we will not use any electronic devices.

I'm absolutely ready.

Are you?

I Finally Catch Up With the Past

It certainly was not the fault of the teachers at Malden High School that I learned nothing about the Civil War. I took their classes, I read their assignments, I even remembered enough to pass their tests. But, long before I began studying it, I decide that I did not like the subject, and I quickly and gladly put the Civil War out of my mind.

My attitude, though not correct, was extremely simple. At the time I was going to Malden High in the early forties, the Civil War had been over for almost 80 year. For teenagers, that classifies as ancient history. The United States was then fighting in the biggest war ever, the Second World War. All that I really wanted to do was get out of school and join the paratroopers. So why should I care about a war that had taken place long before I was born but also before any of my family got to this continent? Besides that, I could not understand why these armies went back to the same battlefields every year to fight the same battles. Rather than think about the Civil War, I dismissed it as a dry subject, and really not important to me. Which shows that, even back then, I was not too awfully bright.

I remained in this state of total ignorance for almost 25 years.

During this period, I went into the army, although not in the para-troops, came to school in Michigan, got married, and went to work, all without ever giving the Civil War a second thought. I was too busy living in the present to pay any attention to what had happened in the past, especially towards something that was not relevant to me.

My perspective changed when my circumstances changed drasti-cally. First, the company where I had been employed lost its govern-ment contract and laid me off after twelve years. Second, the economic conditions in New England were so bad that I ended up driving a dump truck for a year before finding another job in my field. Third, the company that hired me was located in Silver Spring, Maryland. Because two of my daughters were starting high school, my wife and I thought it best for me to leave the entire family in Foxboro while I went to work in Maryland.

The distance between Foxboro, Massachusetts and Silver Spring, Maryland is just over 400 miles, and I drove that distance once a month to see my wife and daughters over a weekend. That gave me many weekends when I was on my own. At first, I visited all the gov-ernment buildings, museums, and monuments in Washington, D.C. Then still needing things to do on the weekends, I began to walk the battlefields around Washington.

Of course the growth of our cities has drastically altered almost all the battlefields. They are not at all what they were like when the war took place, but I could easily imagine the course of the battle when I visited Bull Run, or Mechanicsville, or Fredericksburg, or any of the other battlefields. Touring them brought them to life for me, they became more than just dusty names from the past. At all of these battlefields, men had been courageous and cowardly, had sweated and bled, had lived and died. Suddenly, the Civil War became alive and pulsating when I began to realize what both armies had gone through.

It was when I went to Antietam that the enormity of the conflict struck me. In a single day, still the bloodiest day in the entire history of our country, 14,000 union troops and 11,000 confederate troops were killed or wounded. That was more than the population of Foxboro. 25,000 men in one day? How could I have thought that our past was dry and academic? I smiled ruefully when I remembered that all of this carnage was done with what I had called "outdated weapons".

From about that point on, I did a great deal more reading about the Civil War than I did battlefield walking. Although I was interested in the soldiers as individuals, I was not too keen on battlefield maneuvers; I guess that attitude was a hangover from high school. I found myself drawn more to the people, and the problems of that time, than the mechanics of the battlefields.

As I read everything I could find about the politicians of both sides, I got two impressions. The first is that I found the majority of the politicions were no different than the mediocrity we presently have. There was absolutely no lack of hate mongers, rabble-rousers, and incompetents. There were so many of them that my second impression was hard to reconcile with the first. The political leaders were outstanding; by far they tower over what we suffer with today.

I say that because their leaders made up their minds based on their convictions and beliefs. I don't agree with some of what they did, but I do admire them for trying to make choices based on their conscience. Contrast that with today's leaders who won't take a stand on anything without having a poll taken.

Of the two leaders, everyone knows about Lincoln; but, hardly anyone pays attention to Davis. He was an outstanding man. I had been prepared to dislike Jefferson Davis because he was president of the confederacy, he was quite a cold person, and, I thought, he had dressed in his wife's clothes to escape capture. I have since come to admire him. He was a graduate of West Point who did not want to leave the Union. He did not want to be the Confederate President. It is true that he did have a problem dealing with people. However, he gave everything, including his health, for a cause he believed in. He had personal tragedies stalk him throughout the war. Like Lincoln, he lost a child while he was in office, but he absolutely persevered for what he thought was right.

The people that Davis and Lincoln dealt with, and relied on, are just as fascinating. Their wives, Verina and Mary, are remarkable women, rich in irony and contrast. The cabinets of each president had men as dedicated as their leaders; Benjamin and Mallory of the South were just as important for Davis as Stanton and Seward of the North were for Lincoln.

The generals of the period were also interesting larger than life characters. There was Lee, who did not believe in slavery but loved his native state of Virginia too much to leave it, and Grant, who was an excellent general but who suffered from the reputation of being a drunkard. And under them were Beauregard, Sherman, Sheridan, Jackson, Butler, Longstreet, Chamberlain, and a host of others. Each of them made for fascinating reading.

Outside of both governments, the civilians caught up in the war were charismatic; each side had their fierce loyalists, Harriette Beecher Stowe, Horace Greeley, Mary Chestnut, Frederik Douglass, are apt examples. The list of passionate patriots willing to sacrifice their lives, and fortunes, for their beliefs is almost endless. There was not much apathy during that time; people were either strongly for, or strongly against, state's rights and slavery.

I was visiting Appomattox Court House, that quiet and serene place where this bloody conflict ended, when the truth finally dawned on me. We are connected by the Civil War. If the south had won, the concept of state's rights would have prevailed, and instead of one country, composed of fifty individual states, we would be any number of smaller, independent nations. We would be like the Balkans or Ireland. There would be constant bickering, if not open warfare, because, even now, we have a hard time getting along. But the South did not win. And with the issues of slavery and the right of a state to secede finally settled, we try to work out our differences as free and equal people. After the war, the country grew, unevenly to be sure, but it did grow. The industrial revolution transformed our society, and today's electronic revolution is propelling us into an amazing future. I believe all these benefits began when a country that exhausted itself, stopped fighting and recognized that, despite all of our differences, we are really alike.

There is injustice and inequality in our system, but it does work. And it is better than what we had before the Civil War.

Is Being Old Fashioned the Same as Being Old?

O n Saturday, October 31 of last year, I turned off the lights and timers in my house, locked all the doors, and, as dusk approached, I went to a movie in Fox Village. It was the second consecutive year that I have turned my back on Halloween. That is because, for me the fun has gone out of this pagan celebration. It has become a ritual, done almost by rote, that does not bring nearly as much joy, as it once did, to either the giver or the receiver.

Now, I believe that everyone should beware of geezers who start off by saying, "Well, back in the good old days", because this type of geezer, whether it is a girl geezer or a guy geezer, is either not remembering things honestly or has Altzheimers. However, when it comes to Halloween, these geezers may have a point.

As a geezer myself, I have been trying to remember my own Halloween experiences. I have not had much luck picturing those past events. Now, please do not even bother to ask me, "Was Halloween even invented when you were a youngster?" The answer is, "Barely." But try as I might to recall what it was like when I was a child, the details remain fuzzy. I know we carved pumpkins and put candles inside. I remember a couple of community parties for youngsters, and I may be able to conjure up some small forays over to neighbor's houses for apples or goodies. But nowhere can I reconstruct these massive candy attacks that nowadays take place whenever one's front door is opened even a crack.

I have more luck, and gentle memories, when I think about Halloween during the time that my three daughters were growing up. They were born in 1956, 1958, and 1961, and, when they were young, they did their Halloween patrols in East Foxboro. We lived there in a small development for many years, until we moved to Grand Forks.

These were fun patrols. My wife always deferred from taking the girls; she preferred to stay at home and visit with the neighborhood children when they came around to trick or treat. So, by default, I was the shepherd. And it was delightful. We would start early, as the girls were young, and we stayed within our neighborhood. As they would knock, our friends and neighbors would pretend they didn't recognize these costumed and masked kids whom they saw almost every day of the year. They would chat with my daughters and me for a while, and then I would take my flock to the next house. We casually made our way around collecting apples and candy bars. I do not believe that the candy makers had gotten around to making the smaller candy sizes that have become popular today. I also remember some cars from other neighborhoods bringing their kids into our neighborhood to trick or treat, but not many. It was a leisurely pace and we got through in time for me to get home and help greet some of the older children.

We celebrated Halloween in Grand Forks in almost identical fashion as we did in East Foxboro, with one important addition. The first of the two years we were there, I made a big pot of chili that we ate before we went tricking or treating. Thereafter, chili was incorporated into any Halloween plans that we had, even after my daughters were too old to go tricking or treating.

It was not until we returned to Foxboro in the late 60's, that the flavor of Halloween began to slowly change for me. We bought a house much closer to the center of Foxboro on a quiet, residential street so that we were no longer in the New England boondocks. As Halloween approached, I was told, by all the neighbors, to expect at least three times the number of kids than lived in the neighborhood. They said to expect an influx, driven in from out of town, probably Sharon, which was the next town over, by their parents. I got five times the amount of candy I thought we would need and still we almost ran out. I was not at all upset by the large number of children who came to our door, but it made me wonder why parents would throw their kids into cars and drive for miles just to let them pick up a lot more cheap candy. I am sure that a lot of the stuff was pitched after a couple of weeks. It did not make much sense to me.

What really bothered me, though, and what really began to take the shine off of Halloween, was the era in which razor blades and poisons started to be put into the goodies handed out to children. I thought to myself, "How could anyone take advantage of a child's innocent trust?"

It is true that Halloween survives and we have developed countermeasures to insure that what is handed out is safe to consume. Nowadays the police, Macdonald's, and social organizations will screen a child's loot for safety. But doesn't that take away from the joy and the spontaneity and the innocence?

From that time on, Halloween started to lose its flavor. I will admit that it is a pleasure to give candy to a really young child, with his or her face painted, when they hold up their tiny palms and say "trick or treat." It is equally nice to hear a parent in the background say to their child, when they think the child will forget, "Thank the man for the candy, Dear."

Unfortunately, I do not see that nearly as much as I see older children rush up to the door, grab the candy, maybe say, or not say, "Thank you," and hurry to the next house. Or, I can't help but notice that the person who is tricking or treating is taller than I am, surly, and only intent on collecting as much candy as he can jam into the pillow case he is carrying. Sometimes it seems that parents cross all township, county, and state lines just to keep their kids gathering. Getting as much as possible seems to be the reason for Halloween.

I once had a dream in which these supercollectors, and their parents became like Santa Claus; they developed bottomless packs and they would travel to every single household in the entire world overnight. I certainly hope that never does happen.

At any rate, as the years went by, I did not enjoy Halloween nearly as much as I had in the past, and, after my wife died, I stopped doing it. So, while sitting in the movie theatre, at Fox Village waiting for the movie to start, the question popped into my mind, "Is being old fashioned the same as being old?" I am still mulling that question over because it may very well be that it is a trick question.

When you think about it, not everything that was old fashioned is good, and not everything that is new fangled is bad. And trying to compare one against the other is fraught with danger because it is difficult to balance the old against the new. For example, our child labor laws protect our children from the terrible conditions that existed when the industrial revolution began devouring them as a cheap labor source. That certainly is good for us, but look at the children in the third world countries today. Because of the insatiable appetites of modern society, there are far more children in bondage today then ever before. Even though they are further away, they should weigh heavily on our conscience.

Or take the practice of medicine, as another example. People live longer today and our modern day drugs can do wonderous things. But the medical profession, the insurance companies, the government, and religious groups are so tied up in knots and conflicts that every one who is a patient of any doctor is fearful of the medical system and terrified of the paperwork. Is that better than it used to be? I certainly don't know.

I am not inviting everyone into a round table discussion on these matters. You are all free to have your own opinions, just as I have my opinion on Halloween. I am only pointing out that it is hard to weigh the now against the then and come up with an impartial judgement that we can all agree upon.

And, the reason for that, I think, is that as we are all unique individuals, we have had different life experiences and they give us different values for the same set of circumstances. This is good, because your experiences probably prevent any of you from completely agreeing with me about Halloween. That is the way it should be, and, in this way we can each agree to disagree with one another and the world will not slowly stop spinning on its axis.

I think that there are a few things that we can agree upon. I am sure that each of you is keenly aware of the total lack of civility, respect, and friendliness, in our society today. Road rage, drive by shootings, violence in the workplace, all modern day, newly coined terms for the hate and distrust that is prevalent. It is no wonder that people think that the past may have been a better time. It is what we are lacking, not what we have, that causes geezers to harken back. I can wish along with them, but life is a onetime experience, and dwelling in the past too much will blight the future. It is best just to go on.

So, I do not know how to answer my own question. Halloween, which was once fun for me, will continue to thrive and become more commercialized as it continues. I will sadly, participate much less, and Halloween will not notice, and not much care.

So, I guess the answer for me, specifically regarding Halloween, is a sorrowful, "Yes, being old fashioned is the same as being old."

What would your answer be?

Joel Greenstein is a Non-Denominational Pain in the Ass

During the years that I was the GTE test supervisor, the first thing I did when I got to work each day was to read the logbooks of the test engineers who were running tests. Their last task, during each shift, was to place their logbook on my desk. These logbooks were not the official records of the test, nevertheless, they were invaluable to me as an indicator of how the test was going. The logbook was supposed to be a summary, by the engineer responsible for running the test, on how his test was proceeding and if any problems were encountered. All that I asked the engineers to do with their logs was to keep them brief and accurate. That way, I could generally scan the log and determine if a particular test was on track and if the test engineer was performing as he should. At times I would have to go to Quality Control and examine the official test data in more detail to determine specifically what was happening, but I always started with the engineering log.

Our test bed was an exact duplicate of the Minuteman missile system that was installed in North Dakota and Montana. As such, it was the only location anywhere where tests could be run without interfering with the actual missile system. The tests ran the gamut in complexity, from checking out a newly authorized electronic component, or installing a modified sub-system, to handling real time field problems that were being encountered in North Dakota or Montana. Small tests used only some of the equipment in the missile system, large tests used all of the equipment in the missile system; but it made no difference whether a test was big or small. Every test conducted on any portion of the Minuteman Missile System, followed exactly the same rules.

And the rules were stringent. The Air Force and their technical advisors, TRW, wanted hard copies of every aspect of each test. They wanted nothing left to memory; everything had to be documented, and an independent observer, in our case, GTE Quality Control, stamped each step of the test procedure as either accepted or rejected. Considering that the mission of Minuteman was to deliver a nuclear bomb anywhere in the world, everyone involved with Minuteman fought continuously for accuracy. Not paying attention to details could cause system degradation or system compromise or mask a system deficiency. So each test had to be done correctly and every discrepancy had to be explained and accounted for.

One of the facets of my job was to make sure that the intent of each test was followed. That meant I reviewed each test procedure, monitored the progress of the test, and helped edit the final test report. Any problem that occurred during testing automatically was laid at my doorstep; and it was part of my responsibility to work with a team and determine if the problem was either equipment failure or an actual system problem. To investigate, I had help, lots of help, lots and lots of help, often much more help than I really wanted. But I understood that everyone wanted to be part of the solution, so I tried to listen as patiently to nonsense as I did to good sense. Then we would all go and try to winnow the wheat from the chaff.

One day, my boss, Ben Hank, called me to his office, and when I arrived I found him and Jaques Mitterand sitting there. Jaques was manager of System Engineering and he and Ben were friends who had grown up together in New York City. Ben had gotten Jaques his job at GTE quite a few years ago. They lived near each other, carpooled together and, on and off the job, they were inseparable. I gathered that they had something they wanted to discuss with me so I greeted them and sat down.

"Jay," Ben began, "Jaques has a problem, so he asked me to help him. He is short of system engineers with full knowledge of Minuteman, two are on special assignment and two are in the field at Grand Forks. You know, of course, that he is shorthanded; and you also know that we have some difficult tests coming up. So, he is trying to juggle his man-power load and I am going to loan him two men from our group. Before assigning tests to individuals we wanted to know what you thought about System Test 109."

I paused a second; I had a hunch about what was on Jaque's mind and I wanted to try to change it before it became set in cement. Jacques was a very stubborn man. "That test is going to be a very difficult test to run," I replied.

"Why is that?" Jacques asked. "I have read it and it is nothing more than exercising all the system commands and interrogations the system uses to launch all its missiles, isn't that correct?"

"That's the first part of the test, Jaques. The second part is trickier. SAC wants to make sure that, in case of operator error, nothing can go wrong with the system. So they have instructed us to do things and send commands in combinations that are absolutely forbidden in the live system. The test goes out of the way to try to trick the system into doing something wrong. This test engineer will have to know what is happening if he is going to be able to interpret what the system does. The guy running this test will have to be damn good."

Jaques leaned forward and looked straight at me and said, "I am thinking of letting Joel Greenstein be the test engineer on this test. What do you think of that?"

My hunch proved correct and I was sure that Jaques had already made his mind up, but he had asked my opinion and he definitely was going to get it. I answered, " I think that would be a mistake."

Jaques turned to Ben and raised his voice, "See, didn't I tell you that he doesn't like Joel?"

Ben looked at Jaques and said, "Calm down, Jaques. You did not ask if he liked Joel, you asked if Joel could handle this test. I have worked with SAC to set this test up; it is a very difficult test and it will have very high visibility while it is going on. Jay, what are your objections to Joel running this test?"

"Ben," I replied, "Joel Greenstein does not know how the missile system works, he does not know how to get things done, and he does not get along with people. All his tests, since he got into System Engineering, have been small ones. That is not his fault, because that has been his job. But he has never come into the capsule to sit in the operator's chairs and monitor and exercise the system. Every other system engineer tries, when the system is available, to learn Minuteman. Joel makes no attempt, he believes he knows more than he does. I think that there are test engineers better qualified and with more experience than Joel.

"Also, he has a problem with paperwork. He won't write down changes to the test procedures when he decides to do things that are not on the test. He wants to decide what he has to write and he has, many times in the past, disregarded all of the rules of testing. Jaques, you yourself have spoken to Joel about not keeping track of what he has done. On this test especially that kind of an approach will be a disaster."

"I have spoken to him about this, Jay, and he has promised to cooperate with you and with Quality Control on this test," Jaques told me. "But, Joel's biggest fear is that you do not like him and that you won't help him."

In truth, there was not much to like about Joel Greenstein. Physically, he was short, maybe five feet five inches tall, and plump. To me, he seemed to offset his small stature by developing one of the most obnoxious personalities I had ever come across. He was arrogant, rude, opinionated, and smug. He rubbed almost everyone the wrong way.

For example, when he first came into the test group, he came over to me one day and said that he would like to supply our coffee club, which was run as a convenience for our test personnel, with fresh donuts daily. That sounded like a good idea, so after talking it over with Tom Kerby, who ran the coffee club with me, we allowed Joel to bring in fresh donuts daily, sell the donuts, and collect his money out of the daily cash. For the first two weeks it worked very well. Then, some of the people started to complain that the donuts were not fresh. Also, Tom mentioned to me that the money in the cash box seemed a little less than he thought it should have been.

One morning, one of the crew was in Dunkin Doughnuts just as Joel was picking up his daily order. He discovered that Joel was buying the day old doughnuts, at a discount price, but he was still collecting the price of fresh doughnuts. When we asked him about it, he was not fazed in the slightest. He said that he was certainly entitled to a profit for the services he was providing. Tom and I went out of the doughnut business immediately.

I had no intention of telling Jaques anything about Joel Greenstein, he wouldn't believe me anyhow. Joel's biggest fear was his problem, not mine, and that fear would change whenever it was convenient to develop another fear. What annoyed me was Jaques buying the idea that I would not help Joel.

"You listen to me, Jaques Mitterand. My feelings towards anyone is not an issue: it never has been and it never will be. That is because I dislike everyone exactly the same amount; and that definitely includes Joel. Whenever anyone runs a test they step into my ballpark and they will follow my rules. And, as long as they follow the rules they will not have any problems. When they do not follow the rules they will have problems. In all cases, they will get help from me if they want it. That is my job, and I will always do my job. And I do not appreciate any inference that my attitude towards Joel will color the way I do my job. All he has to do is follow the same rules that everyone else does and I guarantee that he will have no problems with me. Do you understand?"

Jaques seemed taken aback. "Jay, I didn't say I agreed with him. I am just telling you how he feels. He also thinks that you are anti-semitic."

I sat there for a few seconds deciding whether to laugh or get angry at him. Being called anti-semitic was the last thing in the world I thought that I would ever be accused of. Although both my father and my mother had been non-practicing Jews, I had gone through all of my younger years fighting the same fights and prejudices that all Jews did. I practiced no known religion and I allowed others the option to choose what worked for them. I never discussed this anywhere as I felt it was no one's business. So, I decided to treat Jacques to one hell of a display.

I slammed my fist on the desk to get his attention. "Goddamn it, this is ridiculous. You pick Joel as a test engineer and all of a sudden I am on trial for my attitude. Jaques, in all the times we have argued and fought, have you ever felt that my differences with you were based on the fact that you are Jewish?"

"Well, no Jay. I can't say that I ever felt that way."

Next, I turned to Ben and said, "In all the years you and I have worked together, have you ever thought I said anything to you that was anti-semitic?"

"No you have not, Jay," Ben replied.

I pointed my finger at Jaques. "This is plain bullshit. I had not planned on saying this, but, since you brought it up, I will tell you something about Joel. He is different than you and Ben. Neither of you feel apologetic for being Jewish, but Joel uses it as an alibi for everything that happens to him. He is a walking wailing wall. If someone disagrees with Joel, Joel says he is anti-semitic; if someone disputes Joel, Joel says he is anti-semitic. Judaism is his cloak that he uses to hide his short comings.

"I will say no more about Joel, I have said enough already. You will do as you please anyhow. Just remember that he will follow the same rules that everyone else follows or he will tangle with me.

"Ben, unless you have something else for me, I would like to get back to work." Ben winked at me, shook his head, and I left his office feeling dissatisfied with the whole conversation.

Ten days later, Jaques announced that the test engineer for System Test 109 would be Joel Greenstein. The normal procedures were followed and the test was given a start date and assigned a time to run on the second shift. A week before the test was scheduled to begin I was called to Malmstrom Air Force Base at Great Falls, Montana, and was out of touch with the test bed until I returned.

When I got to my office on Monday morning, my desk was littered with paperwork. As I worked my way through it, I got a total surprise, System Test 109 had been moved up and had been running the week that I was gone. I immediately looked for Joel's engineering logbook, found it, and began reading through it as quickly as I could. It was a mess. No where did he list the steps attempted, the steps accomplished, or the progress of the test. I went over to the quality control area and reviewed the test documentation of ST109; the data only confirmed my suspicions. A full week of testing had been wasted. The test was going nowhere.

Ben Hank had just arrived at work when I entered his office. He was getting ready for our daily review meeting, which we both attended.

"Good morning, Jay," he said. "Nice to see you back. I hope your Montana meeting went well."

"It went pretty well for G.T.E. Ben. You will see that when I hand in my trip report and my expense account. But, right now, I have other things on my mind. Why was ST109 started early?"

Ben smiled, and said, "I knew you would not like that. But Jaques told me that Joel was getting itchy to get started, and that Jaques could supervise Joel and make sure that the test was being conducted properly. So, with that assurance, the test was started five days early."

I asked, " And how is it going, Ben?"

"According to Jaques, who speaks to Joel every day when Joel comes in on the second shift, things are going quite well. He says that it appears as if your fears were well meant but entirely unfounded."

"Ben," I said, "Tell me something. Why does Jaques place so much faith in Joel?"

Ben replied, "I am not sure myself. I think that Jaques feels sorry for Joel. I think he believes that Joel is a nice, young Jewish boy who has been kicked around and never been given a chance to show what he can do. Maybe Jaques sees himself in Joel. I don't see Joel in the same light, but Jaques can be stubborn and pigheaded when he makes his mind up."

I wasn't sure exactly what I was going to do. The test was not going well, and neither Ben nor Jaques recognized that fact yet. I decided to wait and not say anything until I spoke to Joel, hoping that I might be wrong. So, I again went through all the data, listened to the ST109 voice tapes, and waited for Joel. The more I investigated the more uneasy I became. When Joel came into work, I asked him to come to my office with Jaques Mitterand.

He showed up alone. "Jaques says that I can handle this by myself. Since my test is going so well I told him that I can answer any question that you can think to ask me. So go right ahead and try to trick me, if you can."

"Joel," I said, "this is not a game and I am not trying to trick you.

I am just trying to figure out what the hell is going on. Tell me, what makes you think your test is going so well?"

He replied, "Of course it is going well. I have been running for five straight days without any interference from you and Jaques is completely satisfied with me. He says that he knew I could do it. I didn't realize how easy it is to be a test engineer."

I thought to myself, "Beautiful, he doesn't have the foggiest idea of what he is doing."

"Joel," I said to him, "where would I go if I wanted to look at the test data?"

"What do you mean? What about the test data? What are you talking about?"

I breathed deeply before I replied, "Joel, your test has been running five days now and not one section of the test has been completed and signed off. Worse, no two consecutive steps of the test have been approved by Quality Control. If TRW and the Air Force were to come in right now and ask you what the test is teaching the community about the Minuteman Missile System, what would you tell them?"

"What would I tell them? Why, the truth, of course. I have been ready for five days but I have been plagued with people who don't know their jobs, and the test procedure is not correct."

I began to feel my temperature leaving 98.6 degrees. "Joel," I said, "all test procedures are examined by people who know the system and, of course, errors will appear, it is unfortunate but inevitable. But it is the duty of the test engineer to correct the document and write up the corrections. Have you been correcting the test procedure?"

"Me? Write up corrections? That is Q.C.'s job. But they have been too busy nitpicking me and finding fault and rejecting steps to make corrections."

"Joel, let me tell you categorically that it is not the job of Q.C. to correct the errors in a procedure. Their job is to make sure you follow the procedure and write up all anomalies and discrepancies. You are the test engineer and are responsible for everything that goes on during the test. And that includes writing all the changes to the test documents."

"See, you are trying to put all the blame on me. None of those people are trying to help me, they don't know what they are doing, and you think I am responsible for their mistakes."

Joel still did not understand, so I tried again. "Joel, as test engineer it is your job to make these people do their jobs. You are responsible for everything that takes place during a test, every damn thing that happens. If you have problems document them and run the test; if you don't have problems just run the test. What could be simpler?"

"What could be simpler?" Joel got upset, "You obviously don't understand. These people don't like me. Probably they don't like being ordered around by a Jew. Not even the guys in your section are doing what I tell them to do. I can't help it if I am not getting their co-operation. I think I am doing a good job despite all the problems I am having."

My patience, what little I had, was beginning to wear thin. "Joel, if you are not gathering data after one week of starting a test than you are not doing your job. Those people you are working with, quality control, instrumentation, the test technicians, they are all snotty nosed and hard assed, but not one of them will sandbag either you or anyone else. It is your job to control them and run the test. I just don't think that you are ready to be the test engineer for this test."

Joel yelled at me, "See, I knew what I told Mitterand was absolutely right. You hate me and are an anti-Semitic. You just don't want to give me a chance to succeed. You want it so that you goys can run this missile system." It was as if a dam had broken, he kept on talking garbage and nonsense.

He angered me, and worse than that, he wasn't listening to what I had said. I decided to get through to him and Jacques. As he continued to rant I held up my hand like a cop stopping traffic. Joel stopped speaking and just stared at the palm of my hand. I stood up, put both hands on my desk, leaned forward so I was close to Joel and looking down at him, and very quietly said, "Joel Greenstein, until I met you I never realized that Adolph Hitler had stopped one short."

He gurgled, got beet red, and ran out of the office.

I did not have long to wait. Within five minutes Jaques Mitterand and Ben Hank came into my office. Jaques slammed my office door shut, pointed his finger at me, and shouted, "You son- of-a-bitch. You have upset Joel and you have made me furious. I knew you hated him and you have just proven it."

It was time to counter attack. I leaned back in my chair, put both my hands behind my head, and asked, "Jaques, you never even bothered to read Joel's log book did you?"

He blinked, frowned, and answered, "No, why should I? He told me everything that was going on. I am too busy to go through all of the stuff that you go through. I take him at his word."

"And," I continued, "You never looked at the data in Q.C., did you?"

"No. I tell you I am a busy man."

"Well now, Jaques Mitterand, let me tell you something. By being too busy to check on Joel you have put me, and Ben, and GTE, in one hell of a bad position."

That stopped Jaques in his tracks and brought Ben into the picture immediately. "What do you mean, Jay?"

"Sit down, both of you," I did not reply directly. When they were seated I handed Jaques Joel's logbook. "Read the entry for the first day of testing, please Jaques."

He took the book, found the entry, and read, "Monday, January 17. This is the first day of System Test 109 and I have had a lot to over come. The test procedure is not correct in many spots and QC does not want to take the time to make the necessary corrections. They are arguing that it is not their responsibility. I have considered trying to help them but I have spent most of the shift trying to get instrumentation straightened out. They are totally unprepared to start testing and want to spend too much time calibrating their equipment. I will not allow them to continually hold me up."

I handed Ben a sheaf of papers and said, "Ben, these are the QC summaries for ST109. Read the first day's entry."

Ben read, "Monday, Jan. 17. ST109 began second shift today. Seventeen of nineteen steps attempted in the test setup procedure have had to be rejected. Test engineer has not written explanations for rejections. None of instrumentation connectivity and setup has been accepted because the test engineer wants to change connectivity. Test supervisor not available so problems are unresolved"

"Oh Jesus, Jay, are all the entries like this?" Ben asked.

"They get worse, Ben. Jaques read Friday's entry."

Jaques shuffled through the log and read, "Friday, January 21. Because Q.C. won't make corrections I am trying to update test procedure. Their paperwork is sketchy and I don't remember what the exact steps were that we have done the last few days. Will have to start over again next week. I may have to ask for a new crew, this one seems incapable of performing this test."

Ben had gotten out the Q.C. report for the same evening. "Friday, Jan. 21. No testing and no progress to report this shift."

Ben turned to Jaques, "Jesus, Jaques, the Air Force and TRW have these QC summaries in their hands; luckily our engineering logbooks are proprietary and not available to anyone outside of GTE. We are in trouble; that test is just spinning around. Unless we get 109 straightened out fast, they will be calling us and demanding to know what we are doing. And, believe me, the Boeing Aerospace Company will be making a pitch that they ought to be running this test bed, instead of GTE. I never should have moved that test up while Jay was out of town."

Jaques thought a moment, and he finally said, "Maybe my judgement of Joel was not too good. OK, so I did make a mistake. How do we get out of this mess?"

Ben looked at me. "You are the test supervisor, you tell us what needs to be done."

"OK. Name a second test engineer to work with Joel. I will go on second shift, starting today, and straighten this mess out. My hunch is that, although Joel is responsible for this mess, that crew is not lifting a finger to be the least bit helpful in any way. And that is not right either. I will work through this second test engineer, get the test on the right path, and you can leave Joel where he is. Despite what you think, Jaques, I am not out to get him. He just can't handle the job you gave him. Let him stay on second, maybe, with the pressure off him, he might even learn something."

My surpise came when I found that Jaques Mitterand named himself as the second test engineer. He got off his high horse, I got over needling him, and we worked well together. The cockpit problems were corrected and the test was completed with dispatch.

Did Joel learn anything? Well, as test engineer, he started the post test meeting off by saying, "Although ST109 got off to a shaky start, by the middle of the second week I had everything under pretty tight control."

That was my cue to wink at Ben Hank and shake my head; he winked back.

Lambeau's Ups and Downs

During the thirty-five years I have known Edwin Lambeau, he has often left me shaking my head either in total wonder or in complete dismay. Yet, for the first two or three months after I met him, I paid little attention to him. At that time, Ed was working the counter in our stock room and he would supply me with whatever equipment I needed. We talked almost daily, but they were brief conversations and only dealt with specific details of our jobs. I was busy and he seemed busy, so our talks were usually short and impersonal; Ed seemed aloof.

When I returned to Massachusetts, after fifteen months in North Dakota, I was assigned to Sylvania's Minuteman Test Beds as Test Supervisor. It was at the main test bed where I met Ed Lambeau. Whenever test equipment was required, I would go to the stock room and make sure the equipment was available. The stockroom was thirty feet long by forty feet wide, and it contained row after row of twelve-foot high shelves containing thousands of items, each one catalogued and specifically located.

The person I dealt with was a red headed man who introduced himself as "Ed." After a couple of months Ed said to me, "I'm a little busy. From now on, reach inside, unlatch the door, and come in and get what you need. Just let me know what you are taking. You know what you want, so why should I wait on you?"

That is how I happened to be in the room, about two weeks later, when the phone rang and Ed answered it. I was close enough to hear a man's voice on the other end, but I couldn't hear what he was saying. The tone was short and angry. Ed listened for almost a minute and then he replied just as angrily, "No, Damn it. I said no and I damn well mean no."

My first thought was that this was a personal phone call and that I should not eavesdrop, so I started to leave the stockroom. Then I heard Ed very slowly say, "Screw the General." I stopped immediately. Now I was all ears; this was not a personal call.

He continued, "I said, 'Screw the General.' Until SAC tries what I suggested, I am not going out to look at this problem again. I have been out to that site twice; going out there once more won't change my mind. I don't have to go again because I know what the problem is."

Later, I found out that the phone call was from The Strategic Air Command (SAC) headquarters in Omaha, Nebraska. The Air Force was having a problem with our equipment in Montana. When they had asked Sylvania for help, Lambeau had been dispatched. He investigated the problem, and, based on his suggestion, Sylvania made a formal recommendation to fix it. The Air Force, disagreeing with the recommendation, had ignored the advice. Now, when the Air Force asked him to return and look at the problem again, Ed eloquently declined the invitation.

After I heard the story behind the phone conversation, I decided I had to find out more about this "stock clerk" who could give a general such clear, specific instructions. I enjoy people who like to tweak the system.

Ed Lambeau was not a stock clerk. He was an engineer from our Needham plant who had helped design the Minuteman system; he was hanging around the stockroom in Waltham because he was feuding with his boss and needed a place to stay. His office in Needham was so cluttered with junk that no one, including Ed, could get into it. It looked so disgraceful that his boss told him to either clean it up or keep the door shut. He just took his largest tank of goldfish out of his office and moved up to Waltham.

Ed was unique. When he was a senior in high school, he declined a total scholarship to the Massachusetts Institute of Technology to attend a smaller engineering school in Boston called Northeastern. He turned M.I.T. down because they stressed theory and they discouraged their students from touching equipment. Northeastern was different; it was a co-operative engineering school that encouraged its students to work on equipment.

Theory came so easily to him that he also wanted hands on experience. Ed loved hands on; he could not keep away from equipment whether it was electrical, electronic, or mechanical. He just had to assemble or disassemble everything he saw.

At lunchtime, he would be out in the parking lot, in coveralls, working on secretary's cars. He would time the engine, repair the radio, or fix the air conditioning. Many times I have seen someone from Sylvania pull him from under the hood of a car to explain a missile problem to a visiting Air Force officer or an engineer from an aerospace company. They would stare in puzzled amazement, as he would explain everything completely to their satisfaction and then go back to working on the car.

He had almost total recall when it came to blueprints or schematics. The division of Sylvania that made televisions and radios would call him when one of their dealers had a problem that they could not fix. He would ask the model number and the year of manufacture. He would then ask what the problem was and what they had done to troubleshoot. After listening, he would suggest from memory replacing a particular component, such as a transistor, a diode, a capacitor, a resistor, or a thermistor. He would give the component he was referring to the specific number it had on the schematic. Most of the time, that would solve the problem.

He became interested in photography and began taking still life pictures of scenery and flowers. He won so many prizes that the walls in the Needham corridors were covered with his prize wining pictures. About this time he earned a Master's Degree in programming by attending night school.

Ed Lambeau was a cornucopia of technical intelligence and ability. That was his positive side. His negative side could be equally impressive. For example, if he lost interest in something, he would walk away from it. That was part of the reason that his office looked like an abandoned junkyard. His office was stacked with toasters, televisions, blenders, radios, stereos; items that he had promised his fellow workers he would repair. If he didn't fix it in a few days, it could sit for a year.

He was the same way in his own home. A heavy television antenna sat on the dining room table and prevented his family from eating there for almost two years. He left a motorcycle he was repairing in the middle of the kitchen for almost six months. He finally moved it when his wife, Tanya, threatened to slash the tires.

Ed was thrifty and frugal to the point of being cheap. He was obsessed with saving money. Many times I would be driving with him in a car and he would ask me to stop. He would get out and return a few minutes later carrying some cans and bottles to recycle for five cents apiece. I didn't mind, but his bosses would feel a little uncomfortable when one of their lead engineers would show up late for a meeting carrying a bag full of clanking empty cans and bottles.

Ed was very sloppy about paper work. Even though he was a friend of mine I denied him access into any of out test sites unless I gave him permission. He was allowed in only after he had an engineer and a quality control person accompany him. Their job was to write down everything that he did while he was on site. Friendship or not, no one was allowed to deconfigure Air Force equipment. I slowed him down because that equipment had to be kept exactly in the same configuration as the real missile sites in North Dakota and Montana.

Ed's guilelessness drove his bosses crazy. He would do things on the spur of the moment without thinking of the consequences. For example, we were out at a meeting at Hill Air Force Base and we went into a fancy restaurant to eat dinner. Near the end of the meal, while he was still at the table, Ed took a citizen's band radio out of his pocket and started to talk to any trucker he could contact. His bosses squirmed and couldn't leave the restaurant fast enough. Socially, they avoided him as much as they could and referred to him as an idiot savant.

Luckily for him, his wife filled in some of his social gaps. Tanya Lambeau was also, in her own special way, an outstanding person. She had been in an automobile accident when she was young, and as a result, she had to have plastic surgery done on her face and she had a glass eye. That accident did not lessen her zest for life.

Her formal education had initially stopped when she graduated from high school. She started to work as a nurse's aide, and, by going to night school, she became a registered nurse. She completed her education while raising a family of seven children; eight if you count Ed.

My favorite story about Ed concerns his buying a station wagon that Sylvania traded in on a new one. It had been used, and abused, by everyone at the test bed for four years and it was in fairly bad condition. That did not bother Ed; he could fix it up. He wanted it for Tanya because it had a tailgate that opened either to one side or from the top down. Tanya could use it to haul groceries and it was cheap.

Ed followed the sale of the station wagon closely. He found out which automobile agency was supplying the new station wagon and how much trade in was allowed on the old one. The day the test bed got the new station wagon was the day that Ed bought the old one.

He paid fifty dollars above the trade in value and got it in an "as is" condition.

Tanya loved it. She could go shopping, buy a week's worth of groceries for her family, and load it, by opening the rear door either way, quickly and easily. She enjoyed shopping when she had that big station wagon.

One day, the rear window got stuck one third of the way down. With the window stuck partially closed, the tailgate would not open in either direction. Grocery shopping became a nightmare for Tanya. She would have to open the side doors, lift the grocery bags over the rear seat, and put them on the floor in the rear compartment. When she got home, she had to retrieve the groceries the same way.

The rear window was not down far enough for her to put her groceries through it, but it was down far enough to let in rain and snow. Sometimes, her grocery bags would get wet and split when she unloaded them. Then she would have to lean over the seat and individually retrieve the grocery items from the rear compartment.

Tanya complained about the window to Ed. As months went by, and he did nothing, her complaints got louder and more bitter. Ed did nothing to fix the window, but he always promised to get to it shortly. It was almost a year before Tanya got completely fed up and figured out a way to get his attention.

One morning Ed got out of bed to get ready to go to work. In the bathroom was a yellow postem stuck on the medicine cabinet mirror. Written on it was a very terse message.

"If that rear window does not go up and down, I do not go up and down."

Edwin Lambeau Jr. arrived late for work that day because he spent the morning making sure that the window went up and down. What I do not know is whether or not Tanya reciprocated.

Lost in the L.A. Airport

Vandenberg Air Force Base, in California, is an oasis of beauty. It has almost forty miles of coastline left in their pristine state. Every time I went there, I would drive along the almost deserted coastal roads and ocean gaze. Occasionally, I would see herds of white tailed deer and wild boars amidst the ground cover of beautiful native flowers.

The weather is delightful. Usually the morning fog burns off by 10 A.M., leaving the sun shining in a cloudless blue sky. The sunlight warms your skin, your bones, your heart, and your soul. The temperature rarely goes above 85 in the daytime and under 60 at night. Since I had spent 15 months in North Dakota and almost a year in Thule, Greenland, I always looked forward to visiting Vandenberg. I considered it my payback.

This trip was a little different than my other visits. I had been on the road for three weeks before I got there and I had a strong urge to go home. This had been a hard trip and I wanted it ended. Everything went smoothly that week, and, on Thursday, the meeting at Vandenberg, concluded.

Friday morning I went to the Santa Maria airport and boarded a two engine propeller airplane, a puddle jumper, to fly to Los Angeles.

I checked my luggage, except for a small leather briefcase, through to my final destination, Boston. When the puddle jumper landed at Los Angeles I started to walk from that terminal to the United Airlines terminal to board the plane that would fly me home. The schedule originally listed the departure of the Boston plane as one hour and fifteen minutes after the puddle jumper landed, but there had been a forty five minute delay in Santa Barbara, so I only had a half hour between flights. That would give me enough time to get to the United terminal, but it was tighter timing than I liked.

As I was walking down a long corridor I noticed the crowd ahead of me moving around something, or somebody, like a river flowing around an island. When I got closer, I could see that it was not a something; it was a someone, and the someone was moving very slowly. And, when I got directly behind this person I had to stare because I couldn't quite believe what I was seeing.

A big, black woman was inching her way along the corridor. She was tall, broad shouldered, and had heavy hips and thighs; more muscular than fat, but very chunky. She was wearing a blue sleeveless shirt that was soaked with perspiration. In her left hand she carried her purse and an overnight bag; in her right hand was a large valise and a draw string for a duffel bag which was lying on the floor. She would slowly take a step with her left foot, slowly take a step with her right foot, and then she would pull the duffel bag forward. Left foot, right foot, pull; left foot, right foot, pull. It was painful just to watch her. With every step she kept repeating, "Oh, sweet Jesus, please come and help me, Oh sweet Jesus, please come and help me. Oh, sweet Jesus, please come and help me."

I walked even faster as I started by her because I did not want to get involved. I might have made it, but I made a mistake. I glanced at her face. Tears were streaming from her eyes. I kept on going. Thirty feet in front of her I said, "Oh shit," and stopped. I must have spoken out loud because five or six people looked at me. I didn't care; I was furious.

I was not angry with this woman; who could be mad at anyone in such misery? I was not angry because I was going to miss my plane; I knew that would happen the moment I stopped. I was angry because I had tried to walk away from someone who needed help. Well, I was going to make amends.

Facing towards her, I waited until she came up to where I was standing. When she reached me, she stopped and said quietly, "I has got to go the bathroom."

"Beautiful," I thought. "What a great way to start a friendship." Looking up and down the corridor, I saw rest room signs just ahead of us. I pointed them out to her and she said, "Thank you, oh, thank you." She left her luggage at my feet and she went, very quickly, to the lady's room. While she was in there, I moved her luggage closer to the wall, out of the traffic flow, so we could talk.

When she returned, she asked, "Mister, would you please help me find my airplane? I wants to get out of here and back to my Momma in Louisiana." She was much younger than I had first thought; she was in her early twenties at most.

Her name was Cleona Courtney. Her Delta Airline ticket was from Los Angeles to Baton Rouge, Louisiana, and her plane was scheduled to depart in seven minutes. I didn't even bother to tell her that the plane would be departing without her.

I said, "Come on Cleona, I'll get you to the Delta ticket counter." I picked up her valise and duffel bag; she carried her purse and her overnight bag. We started walking, we had quite a way to go. Cleona thanked me, and as we walked, she told me how she came to be in Los Angeles.

She lived in a small town called Catahoula, and since her graduation from high school she had not been able to find a steady job. She wanted to be a bookkeeper or an accountant, not a counter clerk at McDonald's or Arbie's. So, her mother and father and six brothers and sisters saved their money and bought her a ticket to Los Angeles. She was going to live with her aunt while she looked for a job.

Leaving Catahoula was a mistake and coming to Los Angeles was a disaster. Cleona was homesick for her family and she did not like Los Angeles. She was going to go back to her mother and father and stay in Catahola and find a job even if she had to drive to New Iberia. She finished her narrative as we arrived at the Delta terminal.

We stood in line until it was her turn to show her ticket. The ticket agent was bald, pudgy, and he wore half glasses, which he peered over to look at Cleona. He glanced at the ticket and said, "Why this flight has departed. Do you want to wait and be booked on tomorrow's flight?"

He did not seem particularly concerned. I told him, "No, she can't wait. She needs to get to Baton Rouge as quickly as she can."

He looked over his glasses at me and then he began typing on his computer keyboard. "Oh here it is," he said after a while. "We can get her on a plane in three hours for Chicago. She will have a five hour delay at O'hare airport and then she can catch a plane for Baton Rouge."

"Wait a minute," I said. "She is going to fly to Chicago, wait for five hours, and then fly to Baton Rouge? A detour of half a continent? Isn't there any other way of getting her there?" I was specifically thinking that Delta might transfer her to another airline.

Now, he really stared at me. He asked, "Sir, may I ask what your interest in this passenger is?"

For the second time that day, I got angry. I did not like his tone or his suggestion. I leaned forward and said slowly, "I do not like that question, I do not like that insinuation, and I do not like your attitude. Please call your supervisor."

A tall thin man, who was standing behind the counter, heard our conversation and he came over to the ticket agent. "Paul, is there a problem here?" Paul peeked over his glasses and cocked his head at me.

"Are you the counter supervisor?" I asked.

He replied, "Yes, my name is John Wesley. What can I do to help you?"

Pointing to Cleona I said, "This young lady missed her plane to Baton Rouge. Your agent suggested a flight to Chicago, a five-hour layover, and then a flight to Baton Rouge. That's a long dogleg to travel. Isn't there a more direct route with less waiting either with Delta or another airline?"

John Wesley looked first at me and then at Cleona. It was a professional look without any malice. "That does seem like a long way for her to get home. Let me look."

He kept punching and punching at the keyboard. After a few minutes he said, "Paul was right. Unless she takes tomorrow's flight, Delta has no other way to connect her for the same fare except through Chicago. And that is ridiculous.

"Rather than rescheduling her on another airline, I will upgrade her ticket, at no cost to her, to first class through Dallas-Ft. Worth. She will have a two-hour delay and then she will fly directly to Baton Rouge. Will that be satisfactory?"

I said, "Mr. Wesley that is more than satisfactory. That is a very decent gesture. She has not done much flying and I don't believe she will understand what you are doing, but I do and I appreciate it. I thank you."

He took her old ticket, issued her a new one, and tagged her luggage. Cleona was ready to return to Catahoula.

I walked her to the gate; I was taking no chances on her getting lost again. "Cleona," I said, "You have to call your family, tell them that you missed your plane, and give them the information on your new flights."

She said, "Mister Jay, I am going to call them and tell them how you and the Lord Jesus helped me."

We found a pay phone and she placed a long distance, reverse charges, call to her family. She explained her misadventures to her mother and, after much repetition, gave her the new flight numbers and arrival times.

Before I left her to straighten out my own travel plans, I happened to think of something else. I asked, "Cleona, when is the last time you ate?"

"Why I had breakfast at six o'clock this morning, Mr. Jay." It was now four in the afternoon and her plane did not leave for another three hours.

I handed her a ten dollar bill and I said, "Listen Cleona, I am going to leave now because I want to go home too. You will be all right. You must be hungry, get yourself something to eat."

"Oh Lordy, I surely am, Mr. Jay. If you ever get to Catahoula you look us up. My family will be wanting to thank you."

I replied, "If I ever get to Catahoula I will Cleona. In the meantime be careful and ask directions only from people wearing Delta Airlines uniforms." We shook hands and I left.

When I got to the United Airlines terminal, I found that the only plane to Boston was a "red eye", which reached Logan Airport at six A.M. on Saturday morning. Even though I had a seven-hour layover, I was feeling good; I had helped someone who had needed help.

However, I did think it was ironic that the person who was responsible for me missing my plane was flying first class while I was stuck on an all night flight in cattle class. Who says there is such a thing as justice?

Matinee Musical

About a month ago, Hazel gave me a yellow flyer to read. It was an announcement for a concert to be held at the Jewish Community Center on the afternoon of Wednesday, November first. The program was a piano trio of Mozart and a piano trio of Beethoven. The pianist was a professor from the University of Michigan Music School, the cellist was the conductor of the Ann Arbor Symphony, and the violinist was the symphony concertmaster.

A few days later, Hazel said that she was interested in going to the concert and asked me my opinion. This presented me with a problem because I have just recently diagnosed myself as having CDD, the senior citizen version of ADD, Attention Deficit Disorder. CDD, Cultural Deficit Disorder, is the result of too many high-class events taking place in too short a time. When I am overloaded with culture, my brain goes numb and I easily tire and fall asleep.

My calendar listed a book signing for one of the authors whose book Hazel and I published on Thursday, November second. Also, there was a concert by the Ann Arbor Symphony on Saturday, November fourth.

So this concert was the first of three events in rapid succession. I didn't want to overdo and have a CDD attack but the afternoon concert did appeal to me. I decided that I would be all right if I took my non-prescription medicines, geritol and gin.

That Wednesday, Hazel and I arrived at the Jewish Community Center early, as Hazel wanted to nibble on the dessert that the flyer invited everyone to try before the concert. We squeezed into the last parking space in their parking lot. As we approached the front door, a white minibus from one of the retirement homes pulled up to the door and the driver helped the passengers get off. It was a very slow process. The people who needed walkers, canes, crutches, and wheel chairs outnumbered the people who could dismount without help. I wondered if they would be able to make it inside the building before the concert began.

We went into the large room where the concert was to be held. There were twenty-five or thirty round tables that had room for eight people at each table. Every table was covered with a blue plastic tablecloth and each had a pitcher of lemonade and a plate of cookies on it. We chose a table that was right in front of two music stands and a beautiful, black, baby grand piano and we chatted with the other people at our table as we nibbled on our dessert. Very slowly the auditorium filled to capacity and then to overflow. Concerts and cookies seem to nicely compliment each other.

Fifteen minutes after the concert was scheduled to start, a woman walked through the crowded tables to the music stands and the piano. She stood there, with a cordless microphone, until the talking subsided. Then, she greeted everyone on behalf of the Jewish Community Center, apologized for being late, thanked them for coming, and proceeded to give the musicians' background.

When she finished, the three musicians made their way to where she was standing. The three of them, although clad in different styles, were dressed in all black, black shirts, black pants, black shoes and socks. If the violinist and the cellist had not been carrying their instruments, I would have guessed that the three of them were a posse from a funeral home.

After they joined her, they introduced themselves to the audience and began preparing for the concert. The violinist and the cellist sat down and started to tune their instruments. The pianist raised the music stand on the piano and then lifted the cover. He lightly stroked the keyboard, jumped back, and then struck the keyboard with both hands.

He said in a very firm voice, "Men, we have a bad problem on our hands."

The other two musicians looked at him and, almost in unison, said, "What's the problem?"

"The piano is broken."

"Broken?"

"Yuh, listen," he sat down, played a loud chord, got up and walked away. The piano kept resonating with the sound of the chord. "See, the notes are not being damped. I can't play it. There is no way this piano can be used for this concert until it is fixed. Beethoven wouldn't appreciate it and neither would I."

The other musicians went to the piano and did exactly what the pianist had done, bang on the keys. The result was the same the piano was broken no matter who played it. The audience started to murmur, buzz, and soon, people were giving their advice, gratuitously.

"How about playing 'The Lost Chord?'"

"Let's change the concert to 'Two Strings and A Dancer.'"

"I have a harmonica I could lend you."

The woman who had introduced the trio came to talk to them. After a conference, she and the pianist left together and one of the other musicians picked up her microphone. "They have gone to look at an electronic piano that the Jewish Community Center uses. If it is acceptable, we will use it for our concert. In the meantime, we have called the piano company and asked them to send over a technician to see if he can fix the piano. So, please be patient, we are working on the problem."

In ten minutes, a spinet piano was pushed into the room and moved to where the music stands were. The baby grand piano was moved out of the way. The power chord of the spinet was plugged in, the musicians seated themselves, tuned their instruments and the concert finally began.

It was a marvelous performance. Not only was Mozart's music beautiful but, because I was sitting less than six feet away, I could watch the hands of the cellist and the violinist as they moved their strong fingers along the strings to get the sound they wanted. I could also see the interplay of the musicians, eyeing each other and nodding as they individually entered and left a musical passage.

During the third movement I caught sight of a man slithering on his belly under the baby grand piano. He was wearing a blue shirt so I could tell that he wasn't a musician. He would alternate between lying on his stomach and shaking the foot pedals and turning on his back and tightening something on the underside of the piano. He was quiet and caused no disturbance.

He emerged just as the musicians finished and were bowing to the audience. He walked over to the pianist, spoke to him, and they both went to the piano. After playing a few chords, the pianist jumped up and enthusiastically pounded the man in the blue shirt on the back. The spinet was unplugged, moved aside, and the Beethoven trio was performed using the grand piano.

As the concert ended, the audience gave the musicians a huge ovation not only because of their performance but also for their good humor and their willingness to overcome obstacles. It was a long round of applause and, afterwards, the musicians circulated into the audience, talking and signing autographs.

As Hazel and I stood up to leave, I became aware of something I had not noticed when we arrived. We had gotten there early and we were so busy talking to the people at our table that I had not paid any attention to the rest of the audience. When I was on my feet I could see almost everyone else. I thought, "Holy Nelly, I may be one of the youngest people in the room."

And, unfortunately, that probably was true. These were senior senior citizens. It took us more than twenty minutes to move less that one hundred feet, from our seats to the front door. As we were making our way around the tables, one elderly man asked Hazel to help him get his stroller as it had been pushed just beyond his reach by the thundering herd making its way out.

When we finally got to the car, we had to wait as six or seven minibuses were double-parked in the parking lot. They were loading their passengers to return to the various retirement homes that they had come from.

As we waited, we discussed the concert, the audience, the musicians, and whether any of these topics affected my Cultural Deficit Disorder. We decided that, as long as we got there early enough for the cookies, I could keep my CDD in check.

Despite my CDD, I am looking forward to the next MUSICAL MATINEE.

The Mileage to Milan

The driving distance from the intersection of Platt and Packard roads in Ann Arbor to the driveway of my condo in Milan is twelve miles. There is no mileage sign to that effect - I measured the distance myself. The reason I took this measurement is that I had no reason to take it, I was just curious. As it turns out, I have been curious about mileage signs for a very long time because, for me, they raise questions.

My first question concerns the accuracy of the mileage listed on the individual sign. I don't mean to the inch or to the foot, but did the guy doing the measurement start at Point A, drive the miles listed on the sign, get out of his truck, and then pound the sign into the ground? How else would he know the mileage between point A and point B? Or do they just put signs up without making measurements?

Which leads to other questions. Where is point A located anyhow? For example, when I was growing up in Boston the distance between Boston and New York was posted as 200 miles. Both metropolitan areas are huge, so is that the distance from the Boston Common to the elevators in the Empire State Building? I doubt it, but I would like to know from where to where that 200 miles is?

Many times, when I have seen a mileage sign, I have tracked the distance on my odometer and I have found that both measurements hardly ever agree. My odometer is usually at least two or three miles less than the posted mileage. This led me to wonder if point A of a given mileage isn't located somewhere in the downtown area of the city. I have no idea how those mileage figures are determined.

When I first got to Michigan I noticed a distinct difference in how people discussed distances and directions. Michiganders, and the rest of the country, talked in terms of mileage from point A to point B and they gave directions in compass terms, North, South, East and West.

Not so, Bostonians. Their roads are a tribute to antiquity and they intertwine with each other like a serving of spaghetti. A rider on a carousel has more use for a compass than a driver in Boston. The result is that Bostonians give directions in terms of driving times and left turns and right turns. When driving from say, Malden to Brockton, a Bostonian will say, "it's a 40 minute drive" not "it's 20 miles away". Couching directions in those terms masks the fact that it is almost impossible to go from point A to point B in Greater Boston.

I mention all of this trivia because I now commute between Milan and Ann Arbor. The several roads I can take depend upon where in the Ann Arbor/Ypsilanti area I need to go. I frequently use Moon Road to State Street and the Milan Saline Road to Main Street. Platt Road is the only road I have measured and that was strictly out of curiosity.

However, in commuting this last year, two things have happened. My questions concerning mileage were stirred and I learned that commuting to Ann Arbor is a much different experience than driving in Ann Arbor.

When I lived in Ann Arbor, I would strap myself into the car and take off for my destination hoping that traffic would not be too bad and that I would not meet any crazy drivers. My only goal was to reach my destination safely. There was no joy associated with driving around Ann Arbor. The thought that I might enjoy my drive or that I would see something beautiful was as alien as an anteater in Antarctica.

Commuting to Ann Arbor is different. Although I still have to watch out for traffic, especially in inclement weather, the serenity of the trip is something I look forward to. Almost every morning I drive up Platt road to the Washtenaw Recreation Center. I am usually on the road by 7:30 in the morning. All during the summer and fall it was pleasant to drive alongside the huge cornfields and soybean fields near Milan. The vast expanses of these crops made me wonder where all of the corn and soybeans were going?

Early this winter, when the weather was warm and the fields only had stubble, the morning mist would cling close to the ground and the sunlight, coming over my right shoulder, would ripple on the mist. Occasionally, a flock of Canada Geese would be pecking for food and their heads would appear above the mist as they made their way across the field.

Later, when the ice storms came and coated the limbs and branches of the bushes and trees, the sun would reflect off their icy coating and the trees looked as if they were made of polished silver. I had to shield my eyes against their glare.

However attractive the fields had been before, it was the snowstorms we have had that made for the most beautiful scenes. The sun shining on the snow made each day a magical light show. When there were no clouds, the sun made the snow look pure white. When there were a few clouds, the snow was the color of cream. All clouds made the snow appear gray.

I was reminded of a painting that I had seen in Chicago. Claude Monet had painted a winter scene and called it "The Magpie". I stood transfixed by the beauty he had created in that painting until I was almost pushed out of the way by other visitors. I couldn't get over how he had captured the cold essence of winter. As I drove I felt that his scene had come alive and I wondered what Monet would say if he saw the fields that I saw.

And each road has its own beauty. Moon Road has large, old

trees that seem to nestle the driver in their branches. The Saline-Milan road has huge corn and soy fields along the entire distance between the two cities. One stretch had corn planted so near the road that the stalks crowded both sides and made the lanes seem narrower. The green stalks loomed straight up and were taller than the automobiles that drove through. I called it "Corn Canyon" and, until they were cut down in late fall, I enjoyed driving through the maze.

However, there are signs that the enjoyment I get during my commute is in danger. Urban sprawl is encroaching on some of the fields now lying fallow and frozen. Just before winter, several of the fields on Platt Road had paved access ways constructed from the road to their entrances. These fields are going to be converted into apartments and a shopping mall. On Moon Road, several other fields are awaiting the same fate. One small victory was won when the neighbors around one Moon Road development convinced the developer not to destroy a beautiful old oak tree that is close to Moon road but is in the entry-way to his development.

I am glad that neighborhood action saved the tree, but it seems only like a stay of execution for what is happening all around, the irreversible march of urban progress. The way we continually take land away from nature and build on it makes me wonder what the future is going to be. If we do not change, America will eventually become one long strip mall, from sea to shiny sea. And that would be sad.

I hope we develop a more sensible approach to saving our land with its inherent beauty. In the meantime, I will continue to take pleasure in my commute and advocate a more sensible approach in expanding our urban frontiers.

Musing on Missiles

In North Dakota, Wyoming, Colorado, Nebraska, Montana, South Dakota, and Missouri, the Strategic Air Command, (SAC), has six Air Force bases that control the entire arsenal of Minuteman Inter Continental Ballistic Missiles, (ICBM's). There are 1,000 of these missiles, each one capable of flying halfway around the earth to deliver three individual nuclear bombs to selected targets. The multiplication is simple, 3 x 1,000; Minuteman has 3,000 nuclear bombs available. The mathematics continue, Minuteman forms only one third of a triad; thousands more bombs can be delivered by SAC bombers and by the submarine fleet of Navy ICBM's. These are tactical weapons, posed strictly as a deterrent; our battlefield nuclear capability is equally staggering. It appears that our military and political leaders are genuinely democratic in their desire to allot, to each man, woman, and child labeled as our enemy, one nuclear bomb apiece.

When you drive through a Minuteman missile field, you would be hard pressed to realize it. Every one of the six fleets is spread over thousands of square miles. The missile silos and the launch control centers are all buried underground, and any distinguishing features are very far apart. If you did not notice the above ground communication antennas or the silo lids, you would not know you were in a missile field. Even the local people are hardly aware of what is around them. Once, I had a flat tire on a rental car on a back road near the town of Knob Noster, Missouri. A middle aged farmer stopped his truck to help me and, when he asked, I told him that I was working out of Whiteman Air Force Base, which was about thirty miles away. He then asked if I could tell him anything about the deserted missile silo that was near his house. I didn't have the heart to explain to him that it was not really deserted, it was just not manned, and that a missile could come roaring out of that silo at any time of the day or night.

In the early 60's work was started on the sixth, and last, missile fleet at Grand Forks, North Dakota. The equipment of Wing VI, (The Air Force always uses Roman numerals for their wing numbers similar to super bowl games), was much different than the equipment of the other five wings of Minuteman. Our leaders in Washington, both the Pentagon and the politicians, knew that there would be installation problems and delays because of the new equipment and because the schedules that they had imposed were unrealistic. Claiming that Russia was much stronger than we were, they insisted that their schedules be maintained. This attitude resulted in millions of dollars being wasted and relentless pressure put on the Air Force personnel at Grand Forks.

As the physical construction neared completion, and SAC was getting ready to install their missiles, I started my missile career. My company, Sylvania, had won the contract to supply the command, control, and communications equipment for Wing VI. After some minimal training, I was sent to Grand Forks as head of a team of five engineers. We were to work directly with SAC, as they brought their missiles on line. The job of my group was to supply technical answers and information to all SAC personnel. They had been to school on our equipment; in fact, they had a lot more schooling than we had, but the system is very complex and they had a lot of questions, and they needed help. Because our company had designed and built the equipment, they would turn to us for answers. We were supposed to be walking, talking, textbooks.

We dispatched to the sites with the Air Force, we worked in the electronic labs with the Air Force, and we helped update and correct Air Force technical manuals and procedures. The first six months on the job the men in my crew worked long hours and I worked even longer hours. We were not paid overtime; I just couldn't walk away at the end of an eight-hour day and leave the Air Force overwhelmed with their problems. It was a very difficult time.

This rugged assignment taught me two things. The first was that I learned this missile system thoroughly. I worked on almost every aspect of it, from the 440 volt power lines coming into the sites, all the way through the electronic equipment to the computers that launched the missile. I did become a walking, talking, textbook.

The second thing I learned was to have a deep, abiding respect for the Air Force men and women tasked to keep these missiles up and running. They labored long and hard to keep impossible schedules and meet arbitrary deadlines. They bitched every step of the way, but they did what they had to do. Despite bad equipment, terrible weather, heavy floods, and desperate fatigue, they kept on working. A lot of good people got worn down, but, eventually, all the missiles were started and brought to the ready. (A status the Air Force calls Strategic Alert.)

After almost 15 months at Grand Forks my work was finished. I was called home to Massachusetts. From then on, until I retired in 1992, I worked on Minuteman, MX, which I called Son of Minuteman, and Rail Garrison, which I called bastard Son of Minuteman. My insight into Air Force procedures along with my system knowledge proved invaluable to Sylvania. I shuttled between System Engineering, Management, Specification Writing, and Field Engineering. I would be sent out to troubleshoot problems and/or attend technical interchange meetings. I was given free rein and I thoroughly enjoyed my work.

Grand Forks was buried deep in my past and I probably would not have thought about it except for a curious incident that happened to me in 1989. I went to Great Falls, Montana, for a three day Technical Interchange meeting being held at Malmstrom Air Force Base. It was dusk, almost dark, by the time we left the airport and headed for our motel. As we neared our destination, a vehicle crossed in front of us about three hundred yards away. What caught my attention was that it looked like an olive drab armored car. I asked my colleagues if they had noticed the vehicle and they said that they had, but they couldn't be sure what they saw; the light was really fading rapidly. I wondered why the military would need an armored car? I didn't think they did, so I let the thought go.

The next morning, after we got on base, we passed a parking lot where ten or twelve olive drab armored cars were parked. I was curious, so I asked the Deputy Commander of Maintenance about them.

"Oh, we have to use them, as escorts, whenever we change out an R/V," he casually answered.

I almost fell off my chair. R/V stands for Re-entry Vehicle. That is the euphemism used for the nose of the missile that contains the three warheads and the equipment that nudge each warhead to its selected target. When I was at Grand Forks, the only escort necessary for the R/V's was a jeep that had two Air Police. They carried loaded weapons and a radio for communications. I was even more curious now. Why were such elaborate precautions being taken?

The last day of the meeting, I went out for a beer with an old friend of mine, a Chief Master Sergeant. Senior NCO's are the backbone of the military; they know what is going on and they know how to get things done. When I needed information, I would always check with the senior NCO's. And that is what I was doing. We had a couple of beers and he told me about the armored cars.

Sometime after the mistrust and the bad feelings that Watergate and the Viet Nam War stirred up against the government, the military began to worry that some disgruntled fanatic might try to steal a nuclear warhead for his own purpose. To prevent any possibility of this occurring, they instituted new rules about delivering the R/V's from the guarded armory to the missile sites. There would be an armored car directly in front of, and directly behind, the truck carrying the R/V. Each armored car would have four Air Police with loaded weapons and two-way radios on a dedicated frequency. The front armored car would also carry a United States Marshal. This was because the Air Police would have no jurisdiction over a civilian crowd, and the Marshal would first have to tell the crowd to disperse before he could call on the Air Police for assistance. As this convoy left the Air Force Base and headed for the missile, a helicopter would begin to circle it until it reached its destination and the R/V was stacked on the missile. Back at the Base, another helicopter and its crew were kept on alert; if anything happened to the first helicopter, the second would be airborne immediately.

I could not believe what I was hearing. The amount of extra effort required to perform a relative simple mechanical task was staggering. It made a routine job that happens quite often, into a circus spectacular.

That evening, when I was alone in my room, my mind wandered over my past experiences. Over three decades ago, when I first became involved in Minuteman, the enemy was overseas and it was Communism. Now, our original enemy has disappeared, unfortuneately, our warheads have not. We have a new enemy to take the place of the old one. Our new enemy is the rag tag, lunatic fringes of our own society.

Where should we be aiming our missiles, our bombers, and our submarines?

My Older Brother

In the summer of 2004 my older brother Buddy, and his wife, Esther, came to visit me in Ann Arbor, Michigan. Until that summer, we had not communicated with each other in over thirty years. What made this stark fact completely senseless was that there was no logical explanation for the separation. There had been no quarrel, no argument, not even any angry words, between us. For all of these years we had just traveled our own separate paths.

Buddy was the oldest of the five of us. We were all born and raised in Boston as a family and yet, we all went our different ways. There was Buddy, our sister Marcia, myself, our younger sister Edna May, and our younger brother Richard. Edna May has passed away and Buddy has not heard from either Marcia or Richard in years. It seems that as we each walked out of the house, we closed the front door and never looked back. After Buddy's visit, I tried to trace Marcia and Richard on the Internet but I had no luck.

During our weekend visit, we discussed our separation and not one of the three us could come up with any valid reason why Buddy and I had lost track of each other. However, there was no denying that contact between us had been broken. Just before they left to continue on their trip, Esther summed it up by saying, "Both of you are horse's asses. Just look at all the time you have lost."

I couldn't agree with her more. For myself, I will plead guilty to stubbornness in the first degree and guilty to stupidity in the second degree. On the charge of not caring, I enter a plea of not guilty and I'll let the jury decide.

Since that first meeting, I have been in constant contact with Buddy and Esther. I went to Massachusetts in the fall of 2004 and stayed with them in their home in Worcester and we talk on the phone once or twice a week. While I was there, we drove to Connecticut to meet with their daughter, an only child named Wendy. I had not seen Wendy since she was a little girl and now she has a family of three of her own children. Before I left, Buddy and Esther invited me to visit them in their Florida condo sometime during the winter.

Around the First of March of 2005, I flew to Ft. Lauderdale to spend a week with Esther and Buddy. We did not do much sight seeing even though this was my first visit to the Ft. Lauderdale area. We were much too busy talking, recollecting, and asking questions of each other. There was little time to do much of anything else. We did manage a few diversions but, for the most part, we just enjoyed each other's company. It will take more than the few days we have spent together to fill in the emptiness of those missing years, but I am beginning to see the outlines of both Buddy's and Esther's individual personalities and character. And I am delighted with what I have discovered.

Buddy is my brother's nickname. Although the name on his birth certificate is Sheldon Carp, he was called Buddy as a child and he introduces himself as "Buddy". He has no idea how that nickname happened to be given to him. I don't think he has any preference and I know that he will respond to either name, especially if he is being called to the dinner table.

Buddy is older than I am by five years, which makes him eighty-four. He takes good care of himself and he and Esther go to the gym and workout almost every day. He follows a fairly rigorous exercise routine. In Massachusetts, their gym is a few miles away so they both drive to the gym together. In Florida, the gym is a mile away and Buddy walks over and back and leaves the car for Esther, so that she can come later. They had told me to bring gym clothes with me before I visited them in both Worcester and Ft. Lauderdale. I did because I also enjoy working out.

Buddy is of average height and weight and we look nothing like each other. We both claim to be the handsome one, but, truthfully, neither of us quite live up to that billing. However, I do believe that I come closer to that description than he does.

One thing I noticed immediately, from the first time I visited them, was their flag. Early every morning Buddy unfurls the American flag and puts it out in front of their home whether they are in Worcester or Ft. Lauderdale. At sunset Buddy retrieves the flag, refurls it, and puts it in the closet. He usually wears a battered, black baseball cap with the number and the initials of the outfit he served with during the Second World War. He landed in Normandy shortly after D-day as part of an anti-aircraft unit. After the skies were cleared of German airplanes he was assigned to drive a truck on the "Red Ball Express" and, later, he guarded German prisoners. He is proud that he served his country in World War II and he attends his army unit's reunions every year.

After I arrived in Ft. Lauderdale, as we drove into their condominium parking lot, Buddy said that he and I had a job to do. When I asked what the job was he pointed to a red car that had its covering tarpaulin half off and half on. The wind had ripped open a few of the seams and the sun was shining on the part of the red paint that was exposed. He told me that the car belonged to a lady who had not come to Florida this year because she had been very sick. The wind had recently torn the tarpaulin and Buddy wanted to repair it before the car finish faded from the sun.

We had to cut the steel wires that held the tarpaulin in place on the underside of the car, and we had to patch the holes in the tarpaulin. We finally got it repaired and we put it securely back on the car. After we finished, I asked Buddy if this lady was a good friend of Esther and his and he said no, not really. However, since no one else seemed to care that the finish on her vehicle would be damaged unless something was done, he felt that he should try to help her.

That was typical of Buddy. He is a caring person. For example, one of the few excursions we took in Ft. Lauderdale was to a butterfly farm. We entered into a large cage with hundreds of beautiful butterflies fluttering around us. There were signs all over asking patrons to move slowly and not to touch the butterflies. Shortly after we were inside the cage and were watching these lovely creatures, a woman with two youngsters, a boy of about eight and a girl of about six, came in. Her children were obese, as was she, and both children began running around yelling and trying to grab the butterflies. Finally, the boy caught one of them and started to shake it. Buddy went over to the mother and said, "Lady, perhaps you and your children have not seen the posted signs."

The woman became very indignant. She replied, "I paid good money to come in here. My children are not bothering anything and I'll thank you to mind your own damn business." Buddy walked back towards Esther and me shaking his head. I began to look around for one of the guides who were constantly circulating inside the cage, but, before I could find one, the woman, along with her two chubby monsters, left.

Esther and Buddy have been married for almost fifty-seven years. As I sat in their homes and listened to their private conversations I could easily understand how their marriage has lasted so long. They may disagree, or even argue, but they are never mean or disrespectful to each other. At best, they can come to an agreement, at worst, they can agree to disagree. And both reserve the right to shake their heads at their partners' foibles, which they do constantly. They also reserve the right to make comments about each other's foibles.

During their marriage they have lived through good financial times and bad financial times. They have both worked long, and hard, for whatever they now possess in their retirement. They have truly shared the vows they made on their wedding day. They enjoy each other and they celebrate each day with one another. As a couple, they have their rituals, routines, and conversations that they have perfected together over the years. Buddy looks to Esther for help in deciding what to wear. Esther looks to Buddy for help in deciding how to accomplish their daily tasks. It is a good marriage founded on their love and respect for each other.

I don't believe that Buddy is religious in the conventional sense. Esther may be more aware of her heritage than Buddy. When he and I were growing up in Boston, our family was more Jewish by birth than Jewish by piety. On the other hand, Esther was born and raised in Worcester and Worcester has a fairly large Jewish population. She and her family followed Jewish traditions more closely than we did. When Buddy and Esther were younger, I think they participated in the rituals of the Jewish religion more closely than they do today. I don't know that for an absolute fact, though. However, Buddy certainly knows a lot more about the Jewish religion than I, but I think he has backslid from the practice. Their daughter Wendy is much more devout than Buddy and Esther and she keeps a kosher home.

Because of my disbeliefs, I didn't ask Buddy about his beliefs. Outside of curiosity, I am not really interested because I am sure that he is religious in the sense that he cares about people, all kinds and all types of people. And, for me, that certainly is good enough.

During my Florida visit there were conversations that made me feel sad. My mother died in 1984 and my father died in 1987. We visited their graves in Margate, Florida, and Buddy told me that in our father's final years, he was blind. Buddy drove him whenever our father needed transportation. Because of dealing with Dad's helplessness, when Buddy is in Worcester, he makes himself available to drive any person who is blind and in need of transportation. It bothers me that I did not even know that my father was blind.

Buddy also told me about my younger sister Edna May. She had been engaged to be married twice and, both times, her fiancée was killed in a traffic accident. Edna May never married and she lived with Esther and Buddy before dying of cancer. That is a tragic story that haunts at me.

The night before I left Ft. Lauderdale, either Esther or Buddy, I can't remember which, told me the following story. After Esther's father died, her mother moved into a senior citizen apartment complex run by the City of Worcester. Every Wednesday she would call Esther and Buddy and give them her grocery list. Since Buddy worked in the fruit and vegetable business, shopping for his mother in law was no problem. He would buy whatever was on her small list, save the receipt, and then deliver her groceries after he finished work. His mother in law would examine each item and then she would look at the receipt. After that, she would get her pocketbook, pull out a handful of dollar bills and loose coins, and pay the exact amount, to the penny.

One bitterly cold winter she told Buddy that she would really enjoy having some fresh lettuce. When Buddy asked her why she didn't order a head she told him that lettuce was much too expensive and she couldn't afford it. The next two weeks Esther's mother repeated her lament that she would enjoy the taste of fresh lettuce but that the cost was too expensive.

When Buddy went shopping for her the following week, he picked up a head of iceberg lettuce, put it in the grocery cart, and, when he got to the cashier, Buddy told him to ring it up by itself. It was $2.75. He ripped up the slip and put the lettuce aside, in a separate bag. After Esther's mother had examined her groceries and paid her bill, Buddy said to her, "Oh Ma, I forgot to tell you. I was leaving the store when they announced a two-day sale on lettuce. Today and tomorrow only, iceberg lettuce is nineteen cents a head. So I picked you up a head and, since it was so cheap, it is my present to you."

She protested a little but she finally accepted the lettuce as a present and Buddy left feeling good about giving her something she had wanted.

When he got home Esther told him that her mother had called and wanted Buddy to get in touch with her right away. Buddy called her back immediately and asked, "Is there something wrong, Ma?"

"Oh no, Buddy, there is nothing wrong. But, when I told all my friends about the marvelous sale you found, they all wanted a head of that nineteen-cent lettuce. So, I need you to go back to the store and get seventeen more heads. Can you do that?"

Buddy bought the lettuce and never told his mother in law what the real price was. And this was at a time when money was scarce for Buddy and Esther. To me, this seems to personify Buddy and makes me regret the fact that we missed so many years.

All I can do is shake my head and repeat what I have known for so many years, "What fools we mortals be."

No "Geronimo"

I was 13 years old when the Japanese attacked Pearl Harbor. From the moment that hostilities began, I was gripped by the same feeling of patriotism that swept through our country. All through junior high and high school, I read about the war in newspapers, I heard about it over the radio, and I saw it in movie theater newsreels. Even though I was too young to enlist, I was already fighting our enemies. When Cary Grant, as a submarine skipper, sank a Japanese aircraft carrier, I was his navigator; when Clark Gable, as a squadron pilot, bombed German munitions factories, I was his bombardier. When Robert Taylor, as a paratrooper, parachuted into enemy territory, I jumped right behind him yelling the paratrooper battle cry, "GERONIMO."

It was not to be. When I graduated from high school in 1945, Germany had surrendered and Japan was on the verge of being the target of an atomic bomb. I was probably the only person who sulked when the war started to wind down; I was not at all pleased that our enemies would not wait for me. However, by this time, I had decided that I wanted to make the army my career. My only ambition was to be a paratrooper. I had no other plans. Since no one else in my family had even graduated from high school, let alone go to college, getting an education never occurred to me.

After I turned eighteen and was drafted, I was happy because I thought that I was starting my career. I was sent to Fort Belvoir, right outside of Washington, DC. Basic training was a piece of cake. I enjoyed the physical challenges and I reveled in the idea that I did not have any choices. Everything was decided for me; I was not responsible for anything. All I had to do was what I was ordered to do. For a while that was fine with me. I went about learning to be a soldier, and, after about a month, I put in my application for airborne training.

Even though I actually tried to do just what I was told, no more or no less, my experiences eventually began to cause me to get off autopilot and think for myself. Despite my reluctance to make comparisons, thoughts, ideas and impressions of what army living was really like began to filter through to me. I did enjoy the training and the physical rigors; I did not like regimentation and I bridled when I was ordered to do something I did not want to do. I began to wonder if an army career was such a wise choice. But I was already in so my only options were to watch and evaluate.

After the third week of basic training, I was in the PX with a couple of members of our platoon having a beer. We went almost every night to have a few just before bed check. We were sitting around and talking when "Muscles" Malone came into the PX. We called him "Muscles" because he was the strongest and quickest man in our company. He was twenty-four years old, almost six years older than the rest of us. He had lifted weights for years and was very proud of his physique. However, Malone did have a problem; his mind had developed inversely as his muscles. He answered every discussion he got into with an offer to have a fistfight. As a result, everyone avoided riling "Muscles" Malone. No one agreed with him, but no one argued with him.

Malone came in and, as he was walking over to where we were seated, he spotted the guy we had nicknamed "Pops". We knew nothing about "Pops" except that he was usually sitting at a small table by himself when we arrived. He was just below average height, thin, and much older that we were; his sparse hair had streaks of gray running through it. He always dressed in clean plain fatigues with no rank, no nametag, and no army patches stitched on them. He would quietly drink his beer, get up, and leave without saying a word. I was curious about him whenever I saw him; I wondered how long he had been in the army but he never talked to anyone, so I never learned anything about him.

A few nights ago, Malone had started to pick on "Pops" for some reason known only to Malone. He had gone up to his table and, in a loud voice, had said, "Old man, you should be in bed, not out with us young people. You had better get out of here before I have to throw you out." I do not know what "Pops" replied, but that was the extent of the trouble that night.

But Malone kept getting more aggressive each time he saw "Pops". He would say something nasty and stupid and "Pops" would leave quietly. Tonight was different. Malone went to "Pops" and said, "Old man, you are sitting at the table I want. Get up and give it to me."

"Pops" looked up at Malone and said softly, "I am almost through. If you can wait a few minutes you can have this table."

Malone became angry, "Old man, I don't want to wait a few minutes. I want that table and I want it now. Get up now or I'll beat the living crap out of you."

"Pops" just sat there not saying a word and not looking at Malone. After a minute of silence, Malone reached over the table and swept both the bottle of beer, and the beer glass, off the table onto the floor. They shattered on the floor and everyone stopped to watch.

"You should not have done that," "Pops" said quietly.

"Old bastard, don't tell me what I should not do. You come on outside and I'll show you what I should not do." Much to everyone's surprise, "Pops" stood up and followed Malone outside. There was a huge crowd and Malone, seeing such a large audience, played to the gallery. "Old man, I am going to show you that you are too old to wear an army uniform. It is a disgrace to have an old man like you pretending to be a soldier. I am going to beat you to a pulp."

He threw a punch at "Pops" but it never landed. I looked at "Pops" and saw that he had put his weight on the balls of his feet and he was fast enough to avoid Malone's punch. That made Malone even angrier and he swung three more times with the same result, he never landed a punch. "Pops" was good at avoiding Malone's fist. Malone decided to crowd the older man so that he could not slip away. When Malone did get close, "Pops" no longer tried to avoid him. "Pops" stepped towards Malone and threw two or three rapid chops of his arms. Malone fell to the ground and didn't move. "Pops" walked away without looking back. We all did the same thing.

It was a few days later when I took my application to an office in battalion headquarters that I saw "Pops" in his dress uniform. He was a chief master sergeant with a paratrooper badge, a combat infantry badge, row upon row of decorations on his chest, and five years worth of overseas chevrons on his arm. I asked the corporal who was helping me about "Pops". He told me that "Pops" was awaiting a discharge and that he had been one of the original volunteers for paratroopers. "Pops" had at least fifteen combat jumps and he had taught Karate for years. I never told Malone what I had found out about his "old man", I only wished that the army had such a thing as a molesting Malone medal.

After I finished basic training, I was put into a holding company temporarily until the next airborne training class started. That was supposed to begin in two weeks. There was little to do during the days and my evenings were free, so, on Wednesday night I went into Washington, D.C. I ended up at a USO dance, where I saw a very attractive girl. After watching her for a while I approached her and asked if she would like to dance. We danced; she talked and I listened.

We danced some more; I talked and she listened. We were very comfortable together. She was the first girl that I had spoken to in almost four months and I was delighted to be able to break my silence. Her name was Kathie and she had a delightful sense of humor.

After the dance she invited me to walk her to the bus stop and we stopped for coffee. We talked and talked, and, finally, Kathie told me that she had to go because her Mother and Father would be concerned if she didn't arrive home shortly. I asked her if I could see her again and she gave me her phone number and her address and invited me over to her house the following Friday. I went back to the barracks with the urge to wake every one up and tell them I had a date with a pretty girl on Friday night.

Luckily for me payday was Thursday; privates did not get much money back then and I was absolutely broke. Friday I went over to her house and met her father, her mother, and her older brother. They asked a lot of questions about my family, my upbringing, and me; until they were satisfied that Kathie would be safe in my company. We left her house and we took a bus downtown, went to a movie and then went to a restaurant and got something to eat. I was having such a good time that, despite Kathie's protests, I insisted that we take a cab back to her house. I don't know why I did, I just wanted to splurge. As we stood on her darkened front porch, holding hands and awkwardly trying to be graceful as we said, "Goodnight", I asked her if I could take her out again tomorrow night. She said that she had enjoyed herself and that she would be happy to see me tomorrow. We set a time, she gave me an innocent kiss, and then she went into the house. On my way back to Fort Belvoir, I started to feel a little chilly and, by the time I got to bed, I had a splitting headache.

When I awoke in the morning, my headache was gone but I felt a little tired. I ate a small breakfast and then I counted what money I had left. I had all of one dollar and eighteen cents to take Kathie out on a date.

"Damn," I muttered to myself, "What the Hell am I going to do?" There was no way that I was not going to see her this evening, but where could I get hold of some money? I thought about it for a while, and then decided on what to do. It was a little risky, but Kathie was worth it.

In mid afternoon, about three hours before our date, I got dressed in a clean, freshly pressed uniform and went back to downtown Washington. I went to the largest department store in the DC district and stopped at the entrance that was in the middle of the block. I picked this location so I could see, in both directions, and watch for any approaching Military Police. I then took an empty quart bottle of milk out of a paper bag and stood there, holding the bottle. People would walk by, notice me in uniform, and fumble for coins, and occasionally folding money, and put them in the bottle without saying a word. Every once in a while, someone would ask what I was collecting for, and I would answer, "For the cause." There never was the follow up question, "For what cause?" I was glad of that because I would have told them it was so that I could take Kathie out that evening.

After playing Robin Hood for almost two hours, my milk bottle was getting full. When I saw two M.P.'s wearing helmet liners slowly strolling down the street, I decided that my panhandling career was over, and I ducked into the department store. I rode several escalators, going up and down a few times to make sure that the M.P.'s were not tracking me, and I finally ended up in a small coffee shop where I got a cup of coffee and counted out my ill-gotten gains. I wasn't proud of scamming a lot of innocent people but I had tucked my conscience into my back pocket because I did want to see Kathie. And now, I had enough money to take her out in style.

Although I was glad to have the money, I was just not feeling up to par. I felt a little tired, my head was buzzing, and, occasionally, I would have hot and cold spells. When I got to Kathie's house, she asked if I wanted a tour of Washington, D.C. I had not seen our Capitol and that sounded interesting, especially since I soon would be leaving the area. So, Kathie walked me all over Washington, showing me our government buildings and monuments and giving me a fascinating history lesson. We went to an expensive restaurant and, afterwards, we took a cab back to her house. This time, I knew why I took it, I felt tired. We sat on her porch steps and talked. Kathie touched my forehead with her hand and told me she thought I had a fever. She thought that I might be catching cold and she wanted me to go back to camp and get some rest. I promised her that I would call her before I was shipped out of Fort Belvoir. I left Kathie not feeling well.

When I got back to the barracks, just after midnight, I fell into bed and started having attacks of chills and fever. I stayed in bed all day Sunday, every joint in my body ached. Monday morning, I did not make reveille and my platoon sergeant came into the barracks looking for me. He called for an ambulance and I was taken to the base hospital. Several doctors examined me and I was diagnosed as having rheumatic fever. I was confined to total bed rest for almost seven months.

After the first three months, my body started to recover. The swelling in my joints subsided, my heartbeat became regular, and I began to feel good. I asked a nurse to call Kathie and give her a message from me. The nurse reported that the number was no longer in service; evidently Kathie's family had moved. I never heard from Kathie again.

Lying in bed for so long gave me an opportunity to sort out what I was going to do. It was clear that I was never going to be a paratrooper; there would be no "GERONIMO" for me. That was just as well because I would have both gotten into, and caused, trouble if I stayed in the army.

The bright side though, was that I realized that I was eligible for the GI bill and that the government would pay for my education if I went to college. And that is what I did. After I was discharged, I went to Boston and applied for admission to several schools. I was accepted at the University of Michigan and I came to Ann Arbor.

Our Lady of the Water Hose

In 1970 the Air Force cancelled its contract with GTE and my flip and disdainful attitude finally caught up with me. I was laid off. That was a bad year around the Boston area. The electronics industry was laying off thousands of engineers, technicians, and managers. Graduates with PHD's were driving cabs and were thankful for the job.

I honestly had no idea what to do. At first I started going to a huge unemployment office opened by Massachusetts to help people in the electronics industry find jobs or get retrained. I soon learned that the job listings were non-existent or filled months ago. The job counselor, as he called himself, suggested that I get retrained as a salesman. I had no objections because I needed a job but when I asked what was available the job counselor replied "nothing." I left and never went back to that unemployment center. Somehow, the prospect of being out of work in two fields rather than just one was depressing to me.

However, I did need to work desperately; I had a family, a mortgage, and bills to pay. I finally ended up with two full time jobs; from

10:30 PM to 6:30 AM I worked on a production line making dynamite cans. From 7:00 AM to 4:00 PM I drove a dump truck for the Foxboro Highway Department.

I got the job with the highway department because I had lived in the town of Foxboro for twelve years and I knew the highway department supervisor. He always needed workers and to have someone who had no criminal record, was not a chronic drunk or was not a high school dropout, was almost a luxury for him. So he hired me and I drove trucks around the garage yard until I got my trucking license.

The following summer, the highway department's main job was to rebuild Beach Street, a street near the center of Foxboro. My job was to drive to the next town, Wrentham, to a Macadam Plant, load up six or seven tons of "hot patch" and bring it to Beach Street. I would back the truck to the spreader, unload the "hot patch" and go get another load. As the project got started, the weather became extremely hot and humid. The weather, along with the smell of diesel fuel, the heat and the stink of the "hot patch" made it a physically hard job. After two days, the entire crew of about thirty men was angry and short tempered with each other. The third day someone on the crew noticed something that helped make the work bearable. A woman came out of her house connected a water hose to her outside faucet, ran it to the edge of the street, and let everyone drink and spray themselves with her water. That simple kindness allowed the work to continue. Wednesday, Thursday, and Friday she just left the hose out so we could help ourselves. Starting on Monday of the second week, the woman sat at the edge of the road in a lawn chair reading and talking to the crew.

Our Lady of the Water Hose, as I thought of her, was thin, almost scrawny, but she had a pleasant face. She wore a bikini when she was out in that hot sun. Every time I delivered a load of "hot patch", I would drive my truck over to her hose, take a drink of water, splash my face, thank her and then drive off. There was always a group of at least three or four men with her so she and I never exchanged pleasantries or personal conversations. She certainly had enough male companionship to keep her occupied.

After three weeks of working on Beach Street, my luck suddenly changed for the better. I was hired by Vitro Lab in Silver Springs, Maryland. My job was as a technical writer to write tests to check out the Polaris and Poseidon missiles. These were the inter-continental ballistic missiles that were carried aboard the US Navy submarines.

I moved to Maryland, leaving my family in Foxboro. For almost a full year I commuted every other weekend from Baltimore to Foxboro. Just as I began to look for housing in Maryland, Tom Kerby, a personal friend and coworker at GTE, called and told me that GTE was in the process of getting in touch with me and wanted to rehire me.

I thought about not going back, but finally I decided to return to GTE. Twelve years of seniority weighed heavily along with the fact that I would not have to uproot my family from Foxboro. So I returned to GTE; not to the Waltham facility, which had been closed, but to the Needham complex.

After processing in on a Monday, I was temporarily assigned to an office that had two desks. The other desk was being used by a man named Bobby King. I had first met Bobby years ago in Grand Forks, North Dakota. We were never close friends because when he drank, which was often, he would become mean and belligerent. He was dark skinned and somber. He was proud of being part American Indian and he said that was why he was mean when he drank.

That Tuesday morning I came to work and started to read a backlog of technical papers to try to catch up with the changes that had occurred during my two year absence. As I was reading a women walked into the office carrying two styrofoam cups of coffee from the cafeteria. She said, "You are early whoever you are."

I looked up and I could not believe my eyes. There, standing in front of me, dressed for work, was my Lady of the Water Hose. I replied, "I always get to work early as it is the only sane part of the day."

She looked hard at me and frowned, "I have seen you somewhere before. My name is Carol. I am looking for Bobby King; he told me he would be early today. This week he is staying with his bitch wife in New Hampshire."

Too much information for me, I thought. "I haven't seen him since I moved into this office yesterday. My name is Jay," I said.

"Well, I will just sit with you and drink my coffee, if you don't mind." She sat down and started drinking her coffee before I could reply. "I swear I have seen you before but I can't remember where. Do you know where?"

I did not even get a chance to fib and tell her I didn't remember where we met when she told me, in detail, about her relationship to Bobby. According to Carol, Bobby's bitch wife was preventing the two of them from living happily ever after. When she finally finished with that subject, she went on to tell me some juicy tidbits of what went on after work stopped. Too, too much information, I groaned inside. An hour after starting time, Bobby finally arrived and Carol transferred to the chair beside his desk, not missing a beat in her gossip column.

One thing I did learn from her that totally surprised me was that she had worked for GTE for fifteen years. That meant we both had worked for the same company, and we both had lived less than two miles from each other in a very small town for over ten years without ever meeting. Wednesday morning was a repeat of Tuesday except that Carol stared at me more and she tried to remember where she had seen me. Her gossip started from where she had left off on Tuesday. Carol was a gushing fountain of sex scandals, and scoundrels. I began to regret that I hadn't transferred to this complex years earlier.

Late Wednesday afternoon I was given my own office and my first reaction was "Thank God."

I was premature. Thursday morning, bright and early, Carol bounced into my office with two cups of coffee. She sat down and said, "This is the way you drink it, black with no sugar, I bought it for you. Bobby won't be in until Monday because he has to do something with his bitch wife."

Luckily, I was busy with phone calls and meetings a large part of the day. This interfered with Carol's gossip but she was gracious about my interrupting her. I began to wonder if she had her own desk any where. She told me she had been a secretary who had been promoted to a data analyst. The only data I had heard from her concerned the personal lives of our co-workers.

Driving home Thursday evening I had to do something about Carol. It was not that I didn't enjoy a little gossip and dirt; it was that I was caught in a landslide. I wanted Carol out of my office.

Friday morning, as she sat down with two cups of coffee, and even before she could speak, I asked, "Carol can you keep a secret?"

"Why of course I can, Jay. I am the soul of discretion. Why are you even asking me such a silly question?"

I replied, "Carol it isn't silly. I finally remembered where I have seen you but I am not going to tell you until you swear that you won't tell anyone."

"Jay, I swear it on a stack of bibles. But why is it so important to keep what you are going to tell me as a secret?"

"Because, Carol, I could lose my job if you say a word to any-one." I was straight faced and somber.

"Jay, I wouldn't want anyone to lose his job. I swear before God that I will never tell anyone. Tell me, Oh, tell me." She implored; she was almost salivating.

"Well, OK." I said reluctantly, "Beach Street." It did not register for a few seconds and then her face lit up in a smile. "Beach Street, Beach Street," she started jabbing her finger at me as she screeched, "You were driving a dump truck on Beach Street."

"Hush, Carol," I said very sharply. "You have sworn you would keep a secret. If my boss finds out, I will be fired."

"My lips are sealed Jay. But how did you get from a dump truck to this office? I don't understand."

"I am not sure Carol. I will tell you, but please remember that I have a wife and family to support." I threw that in to lay it on heavily.

"You saw me bringing in 'hot patch' to Beach Street. Well, the Foxboro Highway Department laid me off. After that for almost a year, I couldn't find steady work. Finally, I saw and ad in the Boston Globe that GTE was looking for truck drivers, so I sent in my resume. About a month later I got a call to come in for an interview. I told the guy I interviewed with that I had a class two driver's license as well as a hydraulic license for backhoe, bulldozer and cherry picker.

"Nothing happened until two weeks ago. I got a registered letter stating that I was hired and to report to Needham. This last Monday, I came in dressed to drive a truck. I signed a few forms and then they put be in Bobby's office. At lunch time, I sneaked home and changed to a suit and tie. I can't exactly figure it out. But I think they switched papers somewhere. Now remember your promise to me."

"You have my word Jay; I swear your secret is safe with me." She smiled and almost vibrated as she quickly left my office.

Monday morning, it was Bobby, not Carol who walked into my office. He looked at me and growled, "You lying son of a bitch."

"Bobby, she swore up and down that she wouldn't tell anyone."

"Well she told everyone at work that cockamamie story. She told me Sunday night when I got to her house. After I told her the true story about you she got mad because you have embarrassed her with that fake story she spread around. She is not going to talk to you ever again."

Bobbie walked out.

You win some, you lose some, I thought. If she doesn't speak to me, I can always retain her image as Our Lady of the Water Hose.

The Shelbyville Cheer

When I graduated from Malden High School, in 1945, the federal government invited me to join the United States Army. At that time, the war in Europe was coming to a close but the fighting was still heavy in the Pacific. I had no other plans, and I was young and patriotic, so I was eager to leave this small, blue collar town which was just north of Boston. I wanted to be a paratrooper. The thought of jumping out of an airplane, landing, and shooting up the enemy, whomever the enemy was, appealed to me. As a matter of fact, I was planning on staying in the army for twenty years. I guess all young people have simple goals.

However, I never achieved my goal. As soon as I finished basic training, I got sick with rheumatic fever, and that automatically disqualified me from jumping out of airplanes.

After all the symptoms subsided, in about a month, I was left with a slight heart murmur. I was offered a choice, I could either get a disability discharge or I could stay in the army and be part of a study group to determine how to treat rheumatic fever patients. One of the few smart decisions of my life was to become part of that study. They confined me to complete bed rest for seven months and I was stuffed each day with aspirins. That was the only medicine they had, in those days, for treating rheumatic fever.

Two things happened to me during those seven months. The first was that, by laying immobile, my heart completely recovered. The second was that, by being confined, I had a chance to read and think. I read anything and everything I could get my hands on in the hospital and the base libraries. After all, what else was there to do lying in bed in a hospital ward?

Slowly, it began to dawn on me, that the government would pay to send me to college. That was something I had not ever thought of before. Even though I was the first in my family to graduate from high school, my older brother and sister had dropped out of school before I got to high school, I had never entertained the idea of going to college; I hardly entertained any ideas back then. When I finally was allowed out of bed, getting myself an education became almost an obsession for me.

I applied, and was excepted, at The University of Michigan, as an out of state veteran. For the first few semesters, I was housed at Willow Run Village, in Ypsilanti, and bussed to campus. At that time, there were miles of totally undeveloped farmland between Ann Arbor and Ypsilanti. Being transported to, and from, campus was like a day trip through the countryside and it was a pleasant experience.

Willow Run Village had been a housing project for the workers at the Willow Run bomber factory before the university used it for their veteran students. I lived there for a semester or two, before I moved into East Quadrangle.

Early one Friday afternoon, a group of us were sitting outside in Willow Run Village and just talking. It was a crisp, beautiful fall day and all of us had just cashed our monthly allotment checks; this made life just great. We were rich and young.

Someone, out of the blue, suggested that all of go down to Columbus, Ohio; it was their Homecoming Weekend and we were playing their football team on Saturday. Even though no one had tickets, or a place to stay, the idea spread like wildfire. We were all to drive the 200 miles as best we could, look up an Ohio State veteran's group on campus, and meet there. We would find out about tickets once we arrived. Those that decided to make the trip immediately started packing and leaving.

I ended up in an old jalopy with three older veterans of about twenty four or twenty five. Naturally, because of such orderly planning, everything seemed to go wrong. The car ran out of gas, we had a flat tire, and we got totally lost. By about seven o'clock that evening, we figured we were about twenty miles away from Columbus, but we did not know how to get there. We finally decided to stop, get something to eat, and ask the natives how they would get from where we were lost to Columbus.

We pulled into a small town, whose name I have forgotten. It consisted of a few houses, one gas station, one grocery store, one drug store, and a tavern. There was no problem finding a down town parking spot. As we entered the tavern we found that it was divided into two sections, the bar and the family eating area; we entered the bar area. There, everybody knew everybody else, except that no one knew us. So, as we walked in, the conversations tailed off for a few seconds. We ordered bottled beer and sat at a table.

Shortly after we were seated, two men in bib overalls came in and sat at the table next to us. They were middle aged, thin and sun burned; and, of course, we thought they looked ancient. One man wore a black fedora hat, the other was bald. Our tables were so close that they could hear our conversation and we could hear theirs. Soon, we merged in friendly banter and our conversations became common to both tables.

After a while the man in the black fedora asked, "Is your car the one with the Michigan plates on it, boys?" His accent was not a flat mid western twang; it was more like a southern drawl.

We told him it was our car.

"Well, would you boys be on your way to Columbus for the football game?" He smiled and pointed to his friend, and said, "His son and my son go to Ohio State. So you can see that we can't wish you the best of luck, tomorrow. We will be rooting for the Buckeyes."

We told him we could understand misplaced loyalty and that we respected their right to root for the underdog. We joshed each other for a good long time and finally the man in the back fedora said to me, "your accent is much different than your friends. Where do you come from?"

"Boston, Massachusetts is where I was born and raised. Are you from around here?" I asked him.

He replied, "I was born and raised in a town named Shelbyville, in Missouri, but I have lived here a good many years." He pronounced the state "Mizzura". He continued, "Now tell me, what is Boston famous for?"

"For many things," I replied. "Bunker Hill, The Boston Marathon, The Boston Tea Party, colleges, universities, hospitals, the list is almost endless."

He replied, "Those are things from the past. I mean what is Boston famous for recently? Even little Shelbyville is more famous if you talk about recent events."

"Wait a minute, I have never heard of Shelbyville. What is it supposed to be famous for?" I asked him.

"They certainly don't teach you everything at school. Have you never heard of the famous Shelbyville Cheer?"

"What the heck is it?" I asked my companions if they had heard of it and they shook their heads, "No." I continued, " None of us ever heard it, so how can it be famous?" By this time, a lot of the people in the bar were listening to us.

He looked around at his friends, shrugged his shoulders, and said, "They have never heard of the Shelbyville Cheer. Can you believe that?" As if on cue, they looked at the four of us, shook their heads, and one or two said, "They have never heard of the Shelbyville Cheer."

I said to the man in the black fedora, "OK, put us out of our misery. Tell us the Shelbyville Cheer."

"Well now," he replied, " It won't do you any good to give you this valuable cheer for nothing. You won't appreciate its value getting it free of charge. I'll tell you what I will do, though. You buy my friend here and me a couple of bottles of beer, and I will give you the Shelbyville cheer."

We waited for a while; we figured that that was an offer we could afford to refuse. After getting directions to Columbus, just before we left, our curiosity overcame whatever sense we had. We bought him, and his friend at the table, a couple of bottles of beer. The crowd of locals watched him as he took a bottle of beer, stood up, and, in a loud voice, rendered the Shelbyville Cheer:

SHELBYVILLE . . . . . SHELBYVILLE . . . . .
SHELBYVILLE . . . . IS . . . . . IT
S . . . . H . . . . FOR SHELBYVILLE
I . . . . T . . . . FOR IT
S . . H . . I . . T

SHELBYVILLE

The four of us laughed, said good evening all around, and left on the last leg of our trip to Columbus. My companions felt that we were taken by the locals and, for a while, I thought I agreed with them. I have since changed my mind. I get so much pleasure out of telling this story that I think the Shelbyville Cheer was worth the few bottles of beer it cost.

My only regret is that I do not remember who won the football game on Saturday.

The Aftermath of Christmas

To be perfectly honest, I had not planned on writing anything else about Christmas or the Christmas spirit. As a matter of fact, I had already aimed my pen at my next subject which, for absolutely no reason at all, was to be about my being laid off way back in 1970.

However, on December 26th, I came across three newspaper items with small personal stories about Christmas. Had I read just one story I would have shrugged my shoulders and not changed subjects. Had I read just two stories, I would have paused awhile, thought awhile, and still not have changed subjects. But after I read the third story my thoughts kept spinning around and bumping each other as if they were in a clothes dryer. I could not begin to tell you about being laid off until I cleared my mind of these vignettes. So, bear with me as I straighten up.

The first story was about a seventy year old man who had been working as Santa Claus for thirteen years. He was fired two days before Christmas because he refused to promise a youngster a gun for Christmas.

"Not so," said the ex-Santa. He said that his policy for thirteen years was that when kids ask for guns, knives or live pets, he would tell them that that is up to their moms and dads.

The child told his father that Santa wouldn't bring him a gun. The irate father confronted Santa while he was on a break eating a meal. Santa told the father that his policy was not to bring guns to kids.

The father complained to the Mall management and in turn they insisted that Santa apologize to the father. Santa refused. So, two days before Christmas they replaced him.

The second story was about a family that went shopping for a Christmas tree. Twelves years ago the Coyles—Mary, her husband Larry and their daughters, went to a tree lot. As they were leaving, the car ahead of them lost the tree that was on the roof. They chased the car, flagged it down, and told the woman driver of her loss. Both cars went back to where the tree had fallen off, but by the time they returned, someone else had picked up the tree.

The women started to cry as she explained that she had spent the last of her money for that tree and that her thirteen year old son would be heartbroken. The Coyles told the woman to stop crying as they wanted to help.

They went back to the lot, purchased a tree she selected and securely tied it to the top of her car. The women took down their names and phone number, and promised to repay them. She thanked them, wished them a Merry Christmas and drove off. The Coyles thought of that woman every Christmas since but she never contacted them.

This last Christmas, the woman called Mary Coyle. she told Mary that she had not forgotten the kindness shown her twelve years before. She had just come into some money and wanted to give the Coyle family a gift certificate for making her Christmas of 1985 such a memorable one.

The third story was about a letter that a young boy wrote to the company that had fired his mother. In July his mother was hired by Russer Foods. In August she was raped and as a result she missed fifteen to twenty days of work over the following three months. Russser Foods fired her a few weeks ago.

The boy was deeply worried and concerned about his mother. So, without either her knowledge or approval, he wrote to the Russer Foods. He explained that the missing work days was because of her being raped. He told them that she was presently out of work and he begged them to rehire her so that she could support her family. He closed by telling them that his "mother knows nothing of this letter. This is my Christmas gift to her."

Her fortune changed after the letter. She was rehired the Monday before Christmas and she and her family did indeed celebrate Christmas Day.

My reactions to the first Santa story were anger and amazement. The stupidity of his being fired is incredible. As fas as I am concerned, if all Santas acted as he did, my belief in there being a Santa Claus would be completely restored. Until a kid is too old to sit on Santa's lap, he is too young to have a gun. I think Santa should have been awarded the Congressional Medal of Honor complete with an antler cluster.

As far as the permissive father is concerned, I wonder what his reaction will be when his beloved son decides he might like a nuclear warhead? Or a laboratory kit that will make a batch of anthrax?

My reactions to the Christmas tree story were delight and enjoyment. That is all I can say. There is no reason to embellish a happy ending.

My reactions to the letter story were a somber happiness and a lot of questions. It is sad when a child has to shoulder adult responsibilities. I am happy that things worked our for the family but I can't help wondering where was the father of this boy? I wonder why the personnel representative of Russer Foods wasn't doing his/her job? I wonder why nobody was helping or counseling the victim of these injustices, the boy's mother?

So, on the quiet day after Christmas morning, these three stories kept nagging at me and I had to release their pressure by letting them trickle out of my pen. I really am at a loss to explain why they gripped me so hard. (Now that you have heard them you may be at a loss also.) Perhaps senility is setting in, perhaps it was being alone on December 26th, or perhaps it is because of the small flash of humanity each story told. Three burning embers flicked out of the bonfire of life.

Whatever, I have cleared my head of them and I can now proceed to tell you of my life as a dump truck driver.

The Anniversary Fiasco

Vandenberg Air Force Base, in California, is about 3,000 miles west of Boston, Massachusetts. This geographical fact was difficult for The Human Resources Department of GTE to take into account when they administered company Standard Operating Procedures. Why they did have problems I do not know, but during the time it took them to get their act together, they alternately amused and annoyed me. I sometimes wondered from what planet GTE beamed up their Human Resource personnel.

In 1983, GTE was having a lot of trouble fulfilling their contract on the MX missile. GTE was falling behind its contractual requirements to design, build, and deliver a new computer and the computer program for this new missile system. While our software and hardware was designed and developed at our Boston locations, the testing of MX was being done at Vandenberg. The Air Force was very displeased with our performance, and they said as much, in no uncertain terms. In an attempt to climb out of the dog house and to check out our equipment faster, GTE decided to enlarge the test team at Vandenberg. It was under those conditions that I was asked if I would consider transferring to California for two years and supervise the testing.

Vandenberg is located north of Santa Barbara and not only is the climate marvelous, but the Air Force Base itself is one of the most beautiful areas along the California coast. Because so many missiles are launched from Vandenberg, the forty miles of shoreline that belong to the base have never been developed. The view, along the shore, is absolutely breathtaking. I had always enjoyed going to Vandenberg on company business so I liked the idea of relocating. When I asked Virginia about the move, she was all in favor of leaving our New England winters behind. With her consent, I accepted the offer, we sold our home, and headed for California.

About a year after I was at Vandenberg, the GTE site manager was fired. I knew nothing about it before it happened; I was busy fighting my own fires. As a matter of fact, he and I rarely met as he was not the slightest bit interested in technical details. He was not much interested in anything except golf and the nineteenth hole at the country club. He was much more a figurehead than a worker bee. I had heard that he treated everyone who worked for him with disdain. To me, he seemed no better or no worse than any of the other retired colonels GTE hired as site managers. I never really bothered with him as he was not in my direct chain of command.

He tracked me down at the test site that afternoon and told me he had been fired. What could I say? I really knew nothing about the situation. I did feel sorry for him though because I was sympathetic to anyone who had been fired. I had lived through being laid off myself and I honestly do not recommend that experience to anybody.

I do know that some manager flew out from Boston, met with him in his office with the door shut, laid him off, and then turned right around and flew back to Boston. I found out later, that when he drank, he would make derogatory statements about his bosses and GTE. Now that could be, because I had never known of any manager, before this incident, flying 3,000 miles and back just to fire someone. Usually they use the phone after their secretary dials the number for them.

At any rate, about a month after that, I got a call from my boss saying that he wanted my opinion about me taking over the duties of both positions. I thought that over for a day or two and decided that doing both jobs would make my technical responsibilities easier to perform. That is how I became the GTE Site Manager as well as the Test Supervisor.

The fact is that I enjoyed all the problems associated with my job; I had a good time. It must be remembered though that I went to California at the request of GTE, and I was there, longer than anticipated, at their request. Almost everyone in our division, with the exception of Human Resources, knew where I was and what I was doing.

I had been at Vandenberg almost three and a half years when I received an Inter Office Memo from Human Resources. The IOM was a week and a half late because Human Resources had mailed it to a company address where I had been located years ago. The IOM had then been returned to our mailroom where it had been forwarded to me in California.

Late or not, I was glad to read it. The IOM informed me that in six months my twenty fifth anniversary with GTE, would be celebrated. They thanked me for my loyal service and informed me of the ground rules for the anniversary celebration. I was to have a luncheon, the menu I would choose later, for twenty five selected friends, relatives, or coworkers, whose names I would select later, at one of the cafeterias, which I would choose later, in one of the GTE facilities in the Boston area. In addition, at this luncheon, I would be presented a gift, which I would choose later, by my immediate supervisor. All I had to do to start the anniversary celebration rolling was to mail the enclosed form back to the author of the IOM. The form asked for some personal information along with my latest company mailing address.

Now that is a very generous offer. My only concern was that it discussed the luncheon in terms of me being in the Boston area. I thought that once they realized that I was in California the rules would be different. So, I filled out the form and mailed it back to the Human Resources representative whose name was on the letter.

A month later, I received another IOM from Human Resources with a different mailing address than the first. It also was a week and a half late because it was also an out of date address and had to be rerouted. It was from a different Human Resources representative but the memo thanked me for my prompt response to the first IOM and it included a blank list of attendees for me to fill out and mail back as soon as possible.

This posed a problem. Virginia, who was in despair of me ever making twenty five years without being fired, was automatically the first. I could easily think of twenty four other people to attend, but some worked in the Needham complex, some worked in the Waltham complex, some worked in the Westboro complex, and some worked at Vandenberg. This was not going to make any sense until Human Resources got their facts straight and came up with a better plan.

I called the person who had sent me the blank list. After I explained that I was permanently located out of the Massachusetts area and that I would not be back before the anniversary, the Human Resources representative said he understood completely and would take care of it. It was no problem, but in the meantime, just as a formality, would I please fill out the list and mail it. I was a little hesitant, but I figured I still had about four months to correct anything that wasn't right, so I filled it out and mailed it back.

In another month, a third misaddressed IOM was delivered from H.R., from yet a third representative. This one contained a catalogue for me to select my gift and a form for me to fill out. I called this third rep, introduced myself, and asked why my mail wasn't being sent to the mailing address they had asked me for in their first IOM. She was very pleasant, and, as she chatted with me, I could hear her keystroking her computer. She told me that they had my corrected address but that computers sometimes take time to get updated. She said that I was not to worry as there was no problem and would I please fill out the gift form and return it. I told her I would.

Another month brought the fourth misaddressed IOM. They must have been running out of representatives because it was from the person who had sent me the first IOM. This one wanted me to select the meal I wanted, from a list of enclosed menus, and to mail my selection back to as soon as possible.

By this time, I was getting a little owly. I called him up and I told him that I was concerned that everyone was filling out the forms but that no one was paying attention to the facts. When he asked what I meant, I asked him how was I to attend my twenty fifth anniversary luncheon when I was not in the same area where the lunch was being held. He told me that there was no problem, that it would be taken care of, and that all I had to do was fill out the menu form and mail it back to him. I did not believe him, but I still felt that I had the upper hand, so I selected the meal I wished to be served and sent the form back to him.

And damned if I did not get a fifth misaddressed IOM from my competent Human Resources department. This time they sent a calendar and asked me to select the specific date of my luncheon. Enough was enough; I was annoyed. I decided no more Mr. Nice Guy.

I just put the notice to one side.

About three weeks went by when I received a phone call from one of the Human Resources reps. "Mr. Carp," he began, "We have not received your selected date for your anniversary celebration."

"That is correct. I have not mailed it," I replied.

"We do need it as soon as possible. You will mail it today won't you?" he asked.

I said, "No."

"Why not, Mr. Carp?" he again asked.

"I will not mail it until I get the tickets," I replied.

"What tickets are you talking about?"

"Why the airline tickets for my wife and me to attend my twenty fifth anniversary celebration," I told him.

His reply was not too friendly. "That's impossible, Mr. Carp. Human Resources can't issue you tickets to fly across country. That is out of the question."

"That's OK. Until I get the tickets for us to attend my party, you don't get the date I selected. Make sure you tell that to your supervisor."

He must have because I got a call an hour later from a Mr. Pierpont who identified himself as the Human Resources Supervisor. Then he asked, "Just exactly what is this nonsense about airline tickets?"

I decided to try to be pleasant. "Mr. Pierpont, let me ask you a question. Human Resources is planning to celebrate my twenty fifth anniversary, isn't it?"

"Of course, that is our Standard Operating Procedure," he replied.

I continued, "And since I am the guest of honor, I should be there, isn't that correct?"

"Why of course, why would you ask such a dumb question?" I could picture Pierpont just smirking as he said that.

"Well, sir, if my party is in Boston and I am in California, how the hell does Human Resources expect me to attend?" I snapped.

"Mr. Carp, there is no need to swear. Our Standard Operating Procedures do not cover inter state anniversary parties. Why are you in California anyhow?" Pierpont wanted to know. "Why don't you come back for the celebration?"

I laughed, "Now we are back to my plane tickets. It appears to me that either you are going to have to change your Standard

Operating Procedures or have my party without me." I said that as a joke. Mr. Pierpont did not think that was funny.

"I will thank you not to tell me how to do my job. Those SOP's are corporate wide and can not be changed and will not be changed. I guarantee you that you will be hearing from us again." And he hung up.

I had absolutely no doubt that I would be hearing from someone. But this was so stupid and so asinine that I couldn't believe my good luck. I was atwitter with anticipation; I could hardly wait for the next episode to begin.

Three days later, I was at my desk when the phone rang. I picked it up and said, "GTE."

I heard a familiar voice ask, "Is Jay Carp there, please?" Although he was on a speaker phone, I recognized the voice immediately. It was Dick Diamond Vice President of our GTE division.

"Good morning, Dick. This is Jay." Dick Diamond had been a vice president for many, many years. He was a low key, sensible man. I couldn't have been more surprised, and pleased, that Human Resources had dragged him into this affair.

"Good morning, Jay. Of course, as you can hear I am on my speaker phone. I have an office full of Human Resource people listening to our conversation. Why is it that about once a year, I have to handle some kind of a problem in which you are involved?"

I tried to gloss over that question, "It isn't really that often is it Dick?"

He laughed. "Well, never mind, the frequency isn't important. But what the hell is going on with your twenty fifth anniversary? Mr. Pierpont is here and he tells me you are trying to get free airline tickets out of his office and that you want him to break all the company rules. Would you please tell me what the problem is?"

"It is easy enough to explain, Dick," I answered. "Human Resources is planning my anniversary as if I were in the Boston area. I am in

California and can't come back. Either they will have to change their plans, or they will have to have the party without me.

"If you remember when we were Sylvania, and not GTE, Personnel used to allow anyone celebrating his twenty fifth anniversary to go to any restaurant, and they would pay part of the tab. Why can't Human Resources do that when the person can't get back to the plant for the in-house luncheon?"

I could hear talking in the background. After a while Dick came back on and said, "Mr. Pierpont says that that is a violation of SOP's"

"Dick, it is a damn poor SOP if it doesn't apply to the very people it was designed for. I frankly don't give a damn what Human Resources does. I will have my twenty five years with GTE whether I have an anniversary party or not. Tell Pierpont to forget the whole thing and just ship my gift to Vandenberg. I am sorry that you had to get involved in this stupid affair."

"Now Jay, just cool down," Dick said. "I still run this organization. Believe me, I will take care of this now that I know what is going on. Oh, and by the way, congratulations on your twenty fifth, and I certainly hope not to hear from you during the next year."

"Thank you Dick," I said, and we hung up.

He was as good as his word. In a day or two my supervisor called me to say that when he came out for a missile launch which was scheduled in about five weeks, he was bringing a sum of money, given to him by Human Resources, for my twenty fifth anniversary party. I never asked him how much that sum was because my party was merged in with the celebration of a successful MX launch party. I do know that the celebrations were big, and wet, and expensive. About forty of us ate the finest steaks and drank the most expensive wines and my boss made a speech and presented me with an attractive clock. He also put the entire tab on his expense account. I am positive that he exceeded the sum of money Human Resources shelled out.

I do not think Mr. Pierpont ever found out about that party. And, on my mantel in the family room, I have a clock that has a brass plate which reads:

JAY E. CARP
25 YEARS
7-8-87
GTE

The Army and Me

Shortly after my eighteenth birthday, I was drafted into the army. At the time I went in, Germany had been defeated and the war against Japan was still being waged. I was in a hurry to get through basic training because I wanted the war, which I had seen through newsreels and movies, to wait for me. I wanted to go into battle. To be precise, I wanted to drop into battle as a paratrooper. That was almost an obsession of mine at that period of my life.

My basic training took place at Fort Belvoir in Virginia. The cadre who instructed us were all decorated veterans. I can only remember two of them. Our platoon sergeant, who led us through our daily grind, was Sergeant Cook. He worked us hard, but he cared for us like a mother hen. He was especially considerate towards me when he found that I was going to apply for jump school and he helped me gather some of the information I needed.

Our first sergeant was named Donnelly and I will never forget him. He was an army veteran of twenty-four years and he looked like the stereotype of first sergeants. He was short, pot-bellied, no neck, and red faced. Our platoon hardly saw him, which was just as well, because every time he appeared we received a punishment of some kind. He inspected the barracks every Saturday and he would always find something that had not been cleaned or stored correctly. Sergeant Cook hinted that Donnelly would plant cigarette butts that he brought with him, if he couldn't find anything wrong. First Sergeant Donnelly could always be counted on to give us extra pushups, or sit ups, or double timing around the barracks with our rifle held horizontally behind our necks and our hands draped over the rifle.

I didn't mind basic training at all. After all, I had no responsibilities, I was fed, I was taken care of, and the physical exertion of pushing my body to its limits appealed to me. I began to consider making the army a life long career.

Midway through our training, First Sergeant Donnelly appeared at one of our Monday morning roll calls. "Men," he said, "Next Saturday's inspection will be held by our company commander, Captain Smith. I want you to be sharp because this is his first personal inspection and any gig is a reflection on me. So, every night this week, after we come back from the field, we will practice and get ready for this inspection. Remember that you are to stand at attention, you are to keep your eyes straight ahead, and you are not to talk. This will damn well be done right."

Captain Smith had been around since the start of our training, he just had not been closely involved with us until now. He had been in his office in the orderly room when I brought my request for jump school in to be processed. He wore the patch of the 101st Airborne along with paratrooper wings and a combat infantry badge. We talked for a while and he told me that he would try to expedite my request. I was impressed both with him and with his background.

The first sergeant was true to his word. Every night we stood at attention, shifted our rifles to port arms, and waited. A port arm has your rifle held close to your body by both hands and the barrel pointing left. Donnelly would come in front of you, grab your rifle as fast as he could, inspect it, and then throw it back at you. You had to grab it and return to port arms with as little movement as possible. All during this exercise, Donnelly would be yelling, "No talking, stand straight, keep your damn eyes forward."

By Saturday morning we were well rehearsed. The entire company was standing for inspection and, when Captain Smith reached our platoon, I could see him out of the corner of my eye. He finally made his way in front of me, behind him stood First Sergeant Donnelly. He looked at me from head to foot and said, "Soldier, you need a shave."

Still remaining at attention and still keeping my eyes forward, I barely opened my lips and responded, "Sir, that is the nicest thing anyone has said to me since I joined the army."

Captain Smith was surprised. He looked at me for a fraction of a second and then he burst out laughing. First Sergeant Donnelly jumped in front of the captain. His face was beet red and he was so mad that he was almost shaking. "You shit. You son of a bitch. I damn well told you that there was no talking in ranks."

Captain Smith stopped him immediately. "First Sergeant Donnelly, the first pass that is issued for leave I want to go to this man."

Donnelly glared at me and then looked at Captain Smith. We had both made an enemy. His only reply was a muttered, "Yes Sir."

I actually did get the first pass and it is possible that I also got the last pass. In between though, First Sergeant Donnelly made sure that I got KP every weekend. Not only that, the cooks at all the mess halls I reported to told me that they had been instructed to give me the dirtiest jobs in their kitchens. As a result, I cleaned a lot of grease traps.

Sometime during each day that I was on KP, First Sergeant Donnelly would come into the mess hall to check on me. He wouldn't speak to me, but, if I caught his eye, I would nod. That would usually terminate his visit.

I did not like First Sergeant Donnelly at all. I thought that he was a petty and mean little bastard. But I was not angry with him. After all, it was my own fault that I had broken the rules. No one had told me to open my big mouth, and, as a matter of fact, Donnelly had told me not to. So I couldn't blame my newly found profession of cleaning grease traps on him.

However, my run in with Donnelly did make me do something I had not done before. I began to analyze whether I really wanted to commit myself to an army career. Jumping out of airplanes would be no problem for me; obeying orders without speaking up might be. Even back then I was starting to feel that I had a right to disagree with the world if I wanted. I decided that this subject needed some serious thought on my part.

The Art of Business Judo

For over a year, my boss, Walter Xavier Collinsworth repeatedly said that he would like to visit the radar site that was operating at Thule Air Force Base in Greenland. He also said that he did not want to stay there any length of time. He was just curious to see how GTE's equipment, and the men that we had trained to operate that equipment, were surviving in that wild, savage climate.

Walter led our team which consisted of four instructors and two laboratory technicians. Our job was to teach RCA technicians and engineers how to maintain and troubleshoot the equipment that GTE had designed and built. Teaching another electronic company's personnel happened because GTE had won the contract to manufacture some of the radar equipment, but RCA had won the contract to operate the equipment. The radar site in Thule was part of the Ballistic Missile Early Warning System (BMEWS) that was designed to detect any attempt by Russia to launch a nuclear attack.

We were three-quarters of the way through our last class of students when, one day, Walt called a staff meeting. Since we were all anxious about what our next job assignments were, we assumed that the meeting was to tell us what our options would be when the class ended.

Walt entered the conference room a few minutes late. Collinsworth was a stocky man of medium height, with deep blue eyes and very curly hair. He always wore either a suit or a sport jacket and he always had on a bow tie. The only time that the rest of us dressed up was when we were teaching in the classroom; when we were not in front of the students, we adopted the burlap bag dress code.

He was one of my first supervisors at GTE, and I learned a tremendous amount about managing from observing him. He was not a person to take short cuts on anything he did and he demanded the best from everyone who worked for him. His most marvelous attribute was that he was both very hard nosed and extremely soft hearted. Walter was both a good man and a fair boss.

When he sat down we began to pepper him with questions about what was going to happen to our teaching team when we finished with our present students. At first, he seemed surprised by our questions; but after a while he began to chuckle. "No, no, no," he said, "This meeting was not to discuss where we will be placed after we finish this class. However, since you all seem concerned, let me recap what I know; and that really isn't much.

"As I have told you before, management has assured me that, even though our days as a team are numbered, all of us will be placed in other jobs. There may be one or two openings as instructors on some other projects within this Training Center. There are some small contracts already in house and there is talk that we are going to win a huge Minuteman Missile contract. I can only repeat that I have been told that each of us is much too valuable to GTE to be laid off. That is all I know.

"What I really want to tell you is that last week I was asked, by our field engineering group, to go to Thule on a short time assignment. One of the GTE field engineers can't stand being in such a remote place and he has decided to quit. They asked me to go there, on a temporary basis, until they find a replacement for him. Since I am finished teaching at the end of this week, I have decided to do it. I have always wanted to see Thule. However, I told them that I would stay no longer than five weeks in that frozen Garden of Eden."

His announcement surprised us and we sat quietly for a while. Bob Brown, one of the instructors, finally spoke in a loud voice. Bob was as tall and thin as a fishing rod, and when he was teaching, his voice carried and you could plainly hear him with the door shut. That was in complete contrast to Walt who purposely talked in a very low voice, forcing the students to lean forward and pay attention to what he was saying. Both men were good teachers; it was just that each had different ideas on effective methods.

"Damn, Walt," Bob said. "Every one in this room knows that there are no replacements. We would be training him if there were. All of us also know that GTE gets a lot of money for having a staff of consultants at Thule. They will be in no hurry to bring you home at the end of five weeks. You are being naïve if you think you can hold them to their promise once you get there."

Walter grinned as he replied, "Bob, you know that I trust management as little as everyone else in this room. But believe me, I will stay there no longer than the five weeks that I agreed to."

I couldn't be quiet any longer. I piped up, "Once you are up there, there will be replacement delays, there will be transportation delays, there will be communication delays. You will be held there longer than just five weeks. You will be stuck in the snow. What does Dorothy think of this?" Dorothy was Walt's wife.

He seemed to be enjoying this opposition.

He looked at me and said, "Dorothy says that as long as I am back in five weeks to go ahead. She knows that I am looking forward to seeing the site. Of course they will try anything and everything to get me to stay longer. I know that, but I guarantee that I still will be back after five weeks."

We argued with Walt but he was adamant. Finally, he looked at all of us and said, "Oh, ye of little faith. I tell you that I will be back in five weeks and you don't think that is at all possible. Let me say this to you. I will be back in this room no later than five weeks and two days from the time I leave for Thule. I will bet each of you a case of beer that I am correct. That means I buy five cases if I am wrong, or I get five cases if I am right. It is time to stop arguing and put up or shut up."

We took him up on his bet; we were sure we would win. Thule is accessible only through Air Force transportation, and our management selected our passenger lists and forwarded them to the Air Force. Voice communications had to come through Air Force channels; there was a commercial phone link but it was so noisy as to be almost useless. And we knew that unless one of us volunteered to take Walt's place, GTE had no other personnel available. After trying to talk him out of going, I took his bet and started to think of what brand of beer I would order for winning my bet.

And so Walt left for Thule. Five weeks to the day we sat around the office hoping that he would not show up; he didn't. The day after that Walt did not show up. The next day we were sitting in the conference room at lunchtime, eating and playing cards. When we were finished eating, we gathered the cards, and got ready to go back to work. We were absolutely gleeful, figuring that we had won our bet. We were also a little worried that Walt would be stranded in a place he did not want to be.

Just as we were getting ready to leave the room, Walt walked in grinning from ear to ear. I said, "Son of a bitch." I was not pleased that I had lost a case of beer but I was absolutely delighted to see him. "Damn, Walt, I did not expect to see you for a while. How the hell did you manage to do what you said you would do?"

After we pummeled him and welcomed him back, we all sat down and we wanted to know how he beat us out of five cases of beer. He laughed as he told us. "Listen, you guys have got to learn how to think like management; and that really isn't hard because management is absolutely predictable and not too bright.

"I knew before I left that they had no intention of trying to get me back in five weeks. They would be in absolutely no hurry to replace me once I got there. So, Dorothy and I sat down and concocted a plan, which would capture their attention. I call it business judo; figure out the fulcrum, get management off balance, and then slam them with everything you can.

"After I was in Thule for two and a half weeks, I called to discuss my return home, and I started to get exactly the runaround that you all had predicted. I was almost sure, before I left, that that was going to happen. So, I called Dorothy and told her to put plan x into action.

"The next day, she called GTE personnel; I told her to completely bypass my management chain. She told personnel that my father had had a slight stroke and that she thought that it was advisable to bring me home immediately. Of course they started to hem and haw, saying that they hoped that my father was not seriously ill and that they would look into the situation. We also expected a response like that.

"The next morning, we had our family physician call and speak to the same personnel rep that Dorothy had. We have been going to Dr. Albert for years; he not only is our doctor, he is a family friend. And there is some truth to Dorothy's story; she did not say exactly when this stroke took place. Our doctor not only reiterated the same story, he suggested that it would be very bad publicity for GTE if anything did happen to my father and they had not tried to get me home.

"Pretty soon, I was getting calls from the division manager asking me to try to stay the five weeks I promised them. I was back in exactly five weeks. As a matter of fact, I could have come in two days ago, but I wanted to spend some time with Dorothy and I wanted to let you suckers think that you had won."

It was worth a case of beer to get him back. A month and a half after his return, our training crew split up and went on to other programs. During that time, I talked with Walt at great length about his stay in Thule and, after discussing it with my wife, I became Walt's replacement in that frozen Garden of Eden.

The Car That Caught Fire

Words evoke thoughts and thoughts have a way of bridging memories. That happens to me sometimes and, when it does, I drift away from conversations for a while. I drifted last Thursday when Marajean read her story about a Lasalle automobile. Afterwards, the discussion turned to old cars and experiences with old cars. And that was when I remembered an incident involving my mother's automobile that took place when I was still in junior high school.

The house we lived in, in Malden, Massachusetts, was a large, single family home in an old, established neighborhood. Our street was lined with large trees and all the houses were single family dwellings on large lots. The street was located about a mile from Malden Square, the downtown section of this small city that was part of the Greater Boston complex.

Our house was a white wooden home with a side porch on the first floor and five large bedrooms on the second. It was the largest house that my father, mother, and I, along with my two brothers and my two sisters, had ever lived in. At the back of our lot, in one corner, was a two car garage. A long, cinder driveway ran from the street to the garage.

Late one summer afternoon, shortly before dusk, I was finishing my job of mowing the lawn, when my father came home from work. He backed his pickup truck the length of the driveway and stopped close to the front of the garage. He always backed his truck in because he left for work about midnight. He would drive into Boston to the wholesale product district, called Fanuel Hall, to buy fruits and vegetables for his produce store. If the truck didn't start my older brother and I would have to push to get it to jump start. It was an old truck so we were routed out of bed fairly often.

My father came up to where I was pushing the two wheeled mower and asked, "Jay, are you almost finished? It is almost one hundred degrees today and humidity is high. Maybe you ought to stop and finish tomorrow morning."

I replied, "Dad, I wondered why I felt so hot. But I only have a little more mowing to do and I would rather finish today then tomorrow. I've made plans to go bike riding with my friends tomorrow so I need to get all my work finished today and there really isn't that much left to do."

"Well, make sure you drink plenty of water. This is a bad heat wave we are going through."

With that my father went into the house to prepare for his next day of work. Because of his long work hours, his routine at home was quite simple. He would bathe, eat dinner, read the daily newspaper and then go to bed. Six days a week he saw little of his family. Sunday dinner was really the only time the whole family was together.

After my father went into the house, I finished mowing and was in the garage wiping down the hand mower when I heard a strange noise. It sounded like metal grinding on metal and it seemed to be getting louder so I went to the garage door.

Just then, my mother's car pulled into the driveway. She had been out running errands and I expected that she might have bags to carry so I moved towards the edge of the driveway. As she slowly drove close to my father's truck, the grinding sound got louder. Standing where I was, I could see that the two wheels on my side of the car were cherry red.

My mother jumped out of the car and she yelled to me, "There's something wrong with my car. I can't get it to go fast."

Then she saw the wheels and screamed, "The car's on fire." She left the driver's door open as she ran into the house.

My younger brother and sister came out of the house when they heard the commotion and the three of us kept circling the car at a respectful distance because the heat from the wheels could be felt two or three feet away. As I think back about it, my older brother and sister must not have been at home that day or else they would also have been standing there with us.

None of us had ever seen a car with its four wheels cherry red. I wondered if the tires were going to catch fire but nothing happened. The car looked like any other car except for its four glowing wheels. Shortly after that, I noticed my mother and father standing at the edge of the driveway looking at the car. As the five of us stared at the car, I heard the wail of a siren in the distance. At first it was faint, but it slowly began to get louder and louder. Soon, it became so loud that I knew it was somewhere in our neighborhood. I began to wonder if my mother had called the Malden Fire Department when, surely enough, a fire engine stopped in the street, right at the end of our driveway. Besides having its siren wailing, its lights were flashing. The fire engine had a three man crew. There was the driver and on the back step of the fire engine two firemen were standing and holding onto vertical rails. They were clothed in heavy fireproof suits and they had hoods of the same material draped over their heads. The hoods each had a rectangular window made up of opaque glass for them to look through.

As soon as the engine stopped, the two firemen put on fireproof gloves, and jumped off the truck. One carried an axe and one had a fire extinguisher. They started rumbling down the driveway, as fast as they could, in their heavy suits and clumsy rubber boots.

There was only one thing wrong. Although the car wheels were still very hot the cherry red color had disappeared. The four wheels were a gray metal color, too hot to touch, but not near their melting point. My father, who knew what was going to happen, turned and went back into the house.

As the firemen neared the car they slowed down and, when they were beside it, they put down the axe and the extinguisher. They both took their hoods off. Their hair was soaking wet, their faces were beet red, and sweat was pouring off of them. One of them looked at my mother and asked, "Lady, where's the car that's on fire?"

My mother replied, "Well, it was on fire when I drove it here."

Neither of them said a word but they both went over and examined the wheels by putting their palms near the rims. When the driver joined them they talked for a few minutes and then the driver walked over to my mother.

"Ma'am, it looks like your brakes locked up and your brake drums overheated. Fortunately, no fire occurred and no one got hurt.

"However, I do have a question to ask you. This heat is stifling and both of my buddies are melting in their fireproof suits. Would you give me permission to back my engine down your driveway, close to your car, so that my buddies and me can change into our regular uniforms in private? We won't be exposed, we just want a little privacy."

Of course, my mother gave her permission. She still didn't understand exactly how the fire got put out without any visual damage, but she was grateful that the fireman had responded to help her. In fact, while they stayed near the back of their vehicle and changed, my mother made a couple of gallons of fresh, cold lemonade which she served them, along with a couple of batches of cookies that she had baked the day before. We three kids, the three firemen, and my mother had kind of a picnic at the tail end of the fire engine. They must have stayed almost forty five minutes drinking lemonade, eating cookies, and relaxing at the end of a hot day.

The next morning, at breakfast, I asked my mother, "Momma, where did Dad go last night? How come he didn't join us for lemonade and cookies?"

She smiled at me and replied, "Jay, your father really needed to get to bed. He doesn't get enough sleep. Besides, he didn't want to be accused of sending in a false alarm to the fire department. That's why he didn't join us."

I thought that was a silly reason to miss a good time. Later that day, when a mechanic from the repair shop came to drive my mother's car and inspect the damage, he found that the hand brake had not been released.

Sometimes, my parents puzzled me.

The Car Thief

One morning in Spring I left my house early in the morning to go to work. As I walked down the back porch steps I stopped dead in my tracks. My car, which I had parked on the street about five feet from the end of the driveway, was not there. My wife's car, which was newer than mine, was in the driveway, but mine was gone. I was sure that I had parked it on the street last night, so I walked to the end of the driveway and I looked up the street and down the street; still no automobile in sight. My car had been stolen.

Not wanting to believe it, I went back into the house and tried to recall exactly where I had parked last night. I was finally convinced; it was not where I had left it. Reluctantly, I went into the bedroom and, sitting on the edge of the bed, I woke my wife up. Virginia looked at me and asked, "Jay, is there anything wrong?"

"I think so," I replied. "Did you drive hunkajunk last night?" Hunkajunk was the name I had given my car.

"No, why would I drive your car when I like my own much better. Has it been stolen?"

"Yes," I answered, "I am afraid that it has."

Virginia quickly got out of bed, put her bathrobe on, and looked out the kitchen window. Then she did what I had done; she walked down the driveway and looked up and down the street. When she came back in she said, "Oh my god, I can't believe it. Who would steal a car in this quiet neighborhood? I guess we have got to report this."

And so we began our ride on the legal Ferris wheel. We called Foxboro's finest and reported our car as stolen. They did believe us, but they never came to the house. We had to go to the police station loaded with statistics; year, make, model, and color of the car, license plate number, car registration, insurance policy number, vin number, and proof of ownership. After all the squares were filled in, the search could begin. They said that they would be on the lookout, and that the information we had supplied would be available to all law enforcement agencies in Massachusetts, and that they would be in touch with us when they learned anything. They were neither optimistic nor pessimistic about us recovering our car. In fact they seemed a little indifferent; car theft is a harmless crime compared to the other crimes they had to deal with.

We did not hear anything for about three months. One day I got a call from the Boston police that my car had been found and that it could be picked up at a car pound in East Boston. Ginny and I were jubilant, we were going to get hunkajunk back. When we arrived at the pound we went through another barrage of paperwork. Part of the reason for the paperwork was that the car had been abandoned in a No Parking zone and the police had ticketed it regularly for about two weeks before the pile of paperwork under the windshield wiper caused them to check the license plate number more carefully. The police wanted to be sure that the car was reported as stolen before each and every parking ticket. Otherwise, I would have to pay for the tickets plus penalties. Finally, when all the paperwork was finished, we were shown where our car was. It was a mess. Outside of the ignition being jimmied there was no physical damage to the car, but the vehicle had been trashed by the thieves and messed up by the police. They had dusted for prints and there was enough fingerprint powder in the car to make me think that the police were searching for a football team. Nevertheless, we were glad to have hunkajunk back. With some minor repair work and some major cleaning, hunkajunk rejoined us and the car theft was placed in the background.

Four months after we got the car back, I got a call from a court official, an assistant district attorney, in Boston. He told me that the person who had stolen my car was going on trial, in the district court in West Roxbury, in about a month. I was needed as a witness to testify that I had not given permission to have my car stolen. He gave me the docket case number, time, date, and instructions on how to get to the courthouse. He also stressed how important it was that I show up; after that he hung up. I marked the appointment on the calendar. There was no way in hell that I was not going to go and testify against my car thief.

The day before the trial date I received a phone call from a man who identified himself as detective Logan. He told me that he was the arresting officer of the person who was charged with stealing my car. He asked if I still planned on being at the courthouse. When I said that I was he sounded relieved. He informed me that my testimony would be absolutely necessary to convict the person who stole my car. I replied that, because I wanted the thief who stole my car convicted, I would be there.

While I drove to the courthouse I had visions of Perry Mason standing in a packed room, slowly and logically convicting the guilty party. Such was not the case. The vestibule of the courthouse could have been an airport; people were coming and going in all directions and there was a totally impersonal air about all of this activity. I had to line up at the counter to get information on where the trial that I was interested in was going to be held. As I entered the assigned courtroom, I heard the clerk announce the next trial by calling out the case docket number. At first I thought that this was my car thief going on trial, until I realized that the docket number called out was not the same as the one assigned to my case. Sitting down, I looked around at my surroundings.

The courtroom was a large, rectangular room with one of the smaller walls having the judge's bench in the center, with a door and two flags on either side of his bench. The rest of the room was taken up with banks of spectator benches facing towards the judge. What struck me most was all the noise and activity that was going on, even while trials were being conducted. People were constantly walking in and out of the courtroom and there were many small groups of two or three people whispering to each other. It seemed unruly and confused. And all during this time, the judge was presiding over case after case, making rulings, and handing down judgements as fast as packages of cigarettes coming off production lines.

In a while, the clerk called my case docket number and the judge asked, "Is the prosecution ready?"

A man stood up and faced the judge and said, "We are your honor."

"Is the defense ready?"

Two men stood up, one was an older man and one was a young lad about seventeen. The lad was of average height, thin, and his hair was slicked back. He was wearing a suit and tie; he looked somber and seemed uneasy at being there.

"Ha, my perpetrator, my car thief himself," I thought.

"We are your honor," the older man said.

The judge nodded to the prosecutor who got up and told the judge that on a certain night eight months ago, the defendant came to Foxboro and stole a car from one Jay Carp, who lived in Foxboro. The prosecutor then told the clerk to call Jay Carp to the stand.

I was called and sworn in, and then the prosecutor asked me, "Do you know the defendant sitting there?"

"No sir."

Have you ever seen him before?"

"No sir."

"Did you ever give him permission, written or oral, to use your car?"

"No sir."

"Did you ever give him the keys to your car?"

"No sir."

"You do not know this man and you never gave him permission to use your car, is that correct?"

"Yes sir."

"No further questions. The prosecution rests."

The defense attorney did not ask me any questions, and I was dismissed. Ten words and no fireworks, I began to wonder where Perry Mason and Della Street were. I left the witness stand and took a seat close to the judge's bench.

The judge looked at the defense attorney. The attorney patted the lad on the shoulder, stood up and inquired, "Permission to approach the bench?"

The judge beckoned him forward, and he came and stood in front of the judge; the prosecutor joined him. I figured that, since it was my car that was stolen, I wanted to hear what was being said, so I walked over to the judge's bench to listen to this hushed conversation.

"Your honor," the defense attorney said, "This is a good boy. He has been raised in a strong Catholic family and he has been both a choirboy and an altar boy. He has had no trouble in school and, until his father died in an automobile accident two years ago, he has never been in any trouble. The loss of his beloved father hit him hard and he started travelling with the wrong type of company. He sees his error and, if the court will dismiss the charges, he will try to get on the right path by going to live with his older brother in New Hampshire."

I stood there, looking at the defendant while his lawyer was speaking; he looked helpless and hopeless. I actually felt sorry for him.

The judge asked, "Anything else?"

The lawyer answered, "No your honor."

The judge said, "Stand Back."

After we returned to our seats, the judge shuffled his papers and then said, "Six months in the Walpole house of correction." He banged his gavel, and another case was announced.

I walked out of the courtroom with a strange feeling. I did not know if six months for car theft was a long sentence or not but I did feel badly for the kid who had first lost his father and then had lost his way. I decided to forget about it and get a cup of coffee before I left the courthouse.

I was sitting at a small table in the courtroom cafeteria when a man approached me. Stuck out his right hand, and said "I am detective Jack Logan. I am so glad that you came in to testify."

I invited him to sit, and when he did I asked him, "Is six months a stiff sentence for car theft?"

"Your car thief will be back on the street in less than two months. I just wanted to make sure that this crime goes on his adult rap sheet. He is now old enough to be prosecuted as an adult."

"Why do you say that? According to his defense attorney my car thief is a good kid who has been hanging around with the wrong people."

Detective Logan laughed. "Don't believe everything you hear in court. First of all, that lawyer is a court appointed defense attorney and he knows nothing at all about his client. He probably never met or talked to your car thief until an hour before the trial."

"Second, I was the beat cop in the neighborhood where this kid was raised. For ten years, before I became a detective, I saw him grow up. I know him; his lawyer does not. Believe me when I tell you that there is something wrong with him. Your car thief is a real nasty piece of work. Before he is much older, he will kill someone.

"His lawyer said that he was grieving over his father? I'll bet his lawyer doesn't know that he attacked his father twice, the second time he used a knife and his father was sewn together with almost thirty stitches. He has a juvenile rap sheet that is pages long. Do you know why he was in Foxboro when he stole your car? He was escaping from the Plymouth Home for Boys when he wandered down your street and took your auto.

"I'll tell you why I dislike your car thief so much. Three years ago I had a partner who was retiring after being a cop for over thirty years. He was fat, sloppy, and out of shape, but he was a good person and a good cop. His last two months of work they assigned him to work inside the station so that he wouldn't have to worry about getting shot before retirement. One day he was escorting prisoners who had just been arrested. One of them was your car thief. He was arrested because he had attacked two people with a baseball bat.

"My partner was walking behind him with his hand on his shoulder. Your car thief said he needed a drink of water so my partner steered him over to the water cooler. As he leaned over to take a drink of water, he suddenly grabbed my partner's gun and jammed it into his belly. For over an hour he had my partner, on his knees, pleading for his life. It was a bad scene; we were around them but we didn't dare do anything because we didn't want to scare this punk into pulling the trigger. Finally, someone brought his mother in and she took the gun away from him after reassuring him we would not harm him. I have no doubt that he will kill someday."

When I left the courthouse to drive home, my thoughts were deep and my feelings were sad. It was true that my car thief was going to go to prison, but was that really important? I could not help but think of that old cop, on his knees for over an hour, begging a psychopath not to kill him. I kept hoping that his retirement wasn't clouded by such a harrowing experience. And what about the psychopath himself? Detective Logan was probably correct that he would kill some innocent person someday. Could he have been reached when he was younger and his life turned into something other than it was? Those questions bothered me then and, when I think about them, they still do today.

I wish my car had never been stolen.

The Closet Capitalist

Iinherited Bill Zendi when I became the test supervisor at GTE's Minuteman sites. The day after I took the job there was a note from him asking me to leave him permanently on the second shift. Since the practice was to rotate shifts according to our testing schedule, his request would be hard to implement. On the other hand, there were so many problems associated with this new job that it might be mutually beneficial to leave him on second shift. I sent him a note to drop by my office and discuss his request.

When he arrived at my office, his physical appearance surprised me. Bill Zendi was almost six feet tall; he was bald, pudgy faced, and what remained of his hair was close cropped, brown with streaks of gray. His shirt was stained, and the bottom three buttons were missing, launched into orbit long ago by the pressure of his belly; which hung over his belt. In all the years I knew Bill, I never saw him in a shirt that didn't have missing buttons.

We talked for over an hour during which time he chain smoked incessantly. I told him what I would need from him to keep him on second shift permanently. He was not happy because he would have responsibilities. But he realized that to stay on the second shift he would have to contribute something. So he reluctantly agreed with what I wanted. He left, and although I had my doubts, I decided to wait and see how this arrangement worked.

As I became familiar with the job, I began to do things differently. When I came to work, I would use the back door by the loading dock, to enter. That way I could check the sites and see what was happening. I kept noticing the dumpster top was usually open and in one corner there would be a pile of rubble, broken drywall, smashed window frames, hunks of plaster and splintered wood. One morning it dawned on me that that debris had nothing to do with our building. Some person must be dumping it. "That's odd" I thought and promptly forgot about it.

I had been test supervisor for five months when the Air Force requested a long, complicated series of tests. When the tests began I changed my hours and came in at noon and stayed past midnight. On one of the nights as I left, I found the answer to a question I had never even asked. As I opened the back door, I saw Bill Zendi's VW Beetle, which had been backed up and parked by the dumpster, start up and drive off. I now knew who was doing the dumping.

A few nights later as Bill and I were eating supper by ourselves I asked him about putting all that debris into the dumpster. His response was unexpected. "You are not going to tell Norm Fenton are you?" He quickly asked me.

"Bill, I wouldn't give the colonel the correct time of day. I am asking because I am curious." I replied.

"Well, the truth is that stuff is from my apartment house. I don't have enough money to pay to have it hauled off. I took the seats out of the VW and I bring it over here three barrels at a time."

Bill Zendi owned an apartment house? I had to find out more. It turned out that Bill Zendi was a closet capitalist. It began when his second child, a son, was born to him and his wife Betty six years ago. His son had spinal bifida and Betty became worried about what would happen to them if Bill should pass away. She wanted Bill to take out a large insurance policy but because of his weight and his smoking he failed the physical. Betty was very upset and gave him an ultimatum; either get healthy and pass the physical or come up with some sort of financial security for their son.

Bill thought that the health routine would be the easiest. After a magnificent supper of Greek food, which Betty made, Bill decided to go on a diet and stop smoking. Any one with a full stomach can declare that he will go on a diet. But by ten o'clock that night he was back to baklava and butts. He decided to try the other alternative.

He found an apartment house in Cambridge that a bank had just repossessed. It was old, it needed repairs, and it was in bad shape. Bill said the only things that worked at all were the utility meters. However, it was available. He took out a second mortgage and got on a fiscal treadmill. For years he would get up at 6:30 AM, go to his apartment house and work until it was time to come to GTE. After he got off at midnight he would go home and sleep.

At his apartment, he began by first cleaning and painting the building. As an apartment became available, he would refurbish it, as much as he could afford and put it back on the market at a higher monthly rate. Since his apartment house was close to Harvard University, the one thing he did not have was an occupancy problem. The money he got for rent barely covered all of his expenses, but at least he was starting to build equity.

About the third year of his ownership, the roof began to leak. While he was on the roof for the leak he noticed he could see all of Harvard Square quite clearly; his apartment house was the tallest building in the neighborhood.

Bill called a company, Donnely Outdoor Advertising Company. It took him five or six calls to get their interest, but once he got them on his roof they became anxious to do business. They built a billboard on his roof and paid him a monthly fee to rent his roof. When the contractor was through erecting the billboard, Bill slipped him a little more money and got the roof repaired.

Next he went to his home town of Newton and tried to convince the board of adult education to let him teach a course to housewives on home repairs. This was a hard sell because the board was convinced that, in their affluent town, there would be absolutely no interest. To their surprise when they finally allowed Bill to teach, it became their most popular course.

After the test, I lost direct contact with Bill when he transferred out of the test group and got laid off. I heard that he eventually took a job at Raytheon before being recalled by GTE. After he returned, he told me while he was laid off, he worked as a substitute teacher in the Boston Public School System. He worked almost fulltime and still collected his unemployment check. I always wondered how he could do that, but I really didn't want to know. I figured he gave his wife's social security number to the Boston School System. That's the only way he could break the law and not get caught.

At his leisure, after he returned, he filled me in on his business career. Once his apartment house began to break even and make money, the banks in Cambridge started to call him. Every time a run down apartment house was repossessed he was asked to take it over. At one time, he found himself with eight apartment houses, all needing sweat equity. He eventually cut back to four apartment houses, figuring he could not perspire any more than that.

From the hard labor and the building expenses, Bill incorporated into his own company, with his wife as President, and went into business. He knew, by law, that all contracts let by the Commonwealth of Massachusetts, had to be advertised. So he started reading the weekly document that announced the future contracts. By staying within the small and minority business sections, he got a lot of little contracts and subcontracts.

After he felt comfortable in this new area, he moved to the small and minority contracts let by the Federal Government. The first one he received was a subcontract to install the hanging ceilings in the Kennedy Memorial Library in Boston.

Bill's favorite contract was one involving no physical labor that he won by making six or eight phone calls. The Federal Government wanted to buy fifty stoves and refrigerators for a coast guard station in Maine. After looking at the specifications, Bill realized they were the same kind of appliances he was putting into his apartments. So he called the discount store he did business with and told them the specifications he needed. The store assumed the appliances were for him and gave him a hefty discount. He also told them the date he would place the order, if he placed it. He got the store to commit to a firm delivery date for all the appliances at their Alston warehouse. He then called up a trucking firm and got prices and a delivery date between Alston and the coast guard station. He added up all the costs factored in his overhead and a handsome profit, and submitted his bid. When he was notified that his firm had won the contract he made the necessary phone calls, and then walked to the bank.

Eventually Bill had to quit GTE because his job was interfering with his making money. He told me he would always stay in the small and minority business sections so that the big contractors wouldn't gobble him up. I don't know how his business did, but after his death, Betty told me that the family had been left in very good financial circumstances.

To this day I have a picture of Bill Zendi, wearing a robe that finally fitted him, giving St. Peter a quotation for upgrading the pearly gates.

The Director of Engineering and His Gasoline Gauge

L ate in the fall of 1959, I was hired by a company named Sylvania to work as a technical writer. Around the same time, either shortly before or shortly thereafter, Sylvania was bought out by a large utility company, General Telephone which changed its name GTE, General Telephone and Electronics. I mention this only because the core of people that I worked with, the old timers within Sylvania, were, for the most part, a salty bunch of individuals. GTE, being a large business, favored standardization. In fact, if GTE could have developed a serum, they would have innoculated everyone in Sylvania against individualism. As it was, it took GTE almost ten years before they brought the Sylvanian rabble rousers into lock step with them.

A case in point was Walter Xavier Collinsworth, the man I began working for six months after I joined Sylvania. Walt was the lead instructor of a group of five, who were teaching the operation and maintenace of equipment that Sylvania was building for the Ballistic Missile Early Warning System. The other four instructors were electrical engineers with degrees. Walt's formal education had ended when he received a certificate of graduation from The Colonial

School of Radio. That was all the education he had time for, because, when he got out of the navy after World War II, he was married and had two children. He earned a living by stocking groceries at night, and worked at getting his certificate during the days. Both of his older brothers had earned PH.D.'s at Yale, but they were single and had no other responsibilities. Walt felt that he had too many mouths to feed for him to be able to just hang around campus and get an education.

It was Walt who recruited me as one of his instructors. He had a problem keeping instructors because the students, literally, wore the instructors out. The students were RCA personnel, hired to maintain the equipment in Alaska, Greenland, and Scotland. They had been guaranteed at least a sixty hour work week and a twenty percent pay bonus. They were also promised a raise based upon their final standing in class; so that each nickel could end up as hundreds of dollars when they finished their 18 month tour of work. They were sharks in class, devouring information, arguing with the instructors, and trying to fluster the instructors into making mistakes. Walt would lose at least two instructors each pass; he needed teachers with thick hides. I think that was why he became interested in me.

My security clearance and my access listings were just coming through, when Walt asked me to become one of his instructors. At first, I told him he was nuts; I was a mechanical engineer with very little training in electrical work and absolutely no experience in electronics. He told me that he knew all of that, but he thought that if I worked hard I could overcome all of those obstacles, and enjoy swimming in the shark infested waters of teaching the BMEWS equipment. He said it would be either sink or swim, and he was betting on me swimming. That kind of a challenge appealed to me, so I decided to try. For the first five months, I was more under, than above, the waterline. It was close, but I did manage to swim; I learned teaching and electronics the hard way. Eventually, Walt got himself a crew that could both teach, and survive, our hungry students.

About a year after I started teaching, I went to a meeting at a Sylvania plant in Mountain View, California. I was there two days when I got a message that the Director of Engineering of that group wanted to see me. His name was Werner Schmitt, and I had no idea what he might want. I reported to his office, and his secretary led me to him. He stood up, shook my hand, and introduced himself. He was just below average height, carried a little too much weight, and had a small red goatee, red moustache and long hair. He looked exactly like a young Colonel Sanders would have looked, if Colonel Sanders ever had been young.

He sat down, put his two hands behind his head, leaned back, and asked, "You are here from our Needham plant aren't you? Do you happen to know a dirty son-of-a-bitch back there by the name of Walt Collinsworth?"

I had met enough Sylvanians not to be startled by such an approach, but I certainly did not share his opinion of Walt and I decided to let him know that. "Yes," I replied, "I happen to work directly for him, and I think he is one hell of a good guy."

"Humph," Schmitt snorted. "Obviously he has worked his fake charm on you and you are not clever enough to see through him. Well, that is your problem. However, I do want you to take a message back to him.

"You tell that childish bastard that I am now Director of Engineering at Mountain View and that I am still driving the volkswagon beetle that he nearly wrecked." And with that, he promptly dismissed me from his office.

The quick meeting with Schmitt left a bad taste in my mouth. I did not know what he was talking about, and I really didn't care. He was rude and arrogant and he had rubbed me the wrong way. I did not like him or his mannerisms, so, I promptly forgot about him and went back about my business at Mountain View.

After I got back to Needham, and had submitted my expense and trip reports, I went into Walt's office and sat down. I said, "I met a good friend of yours while I was in California."

Walt looked at me, and could tell I was not going to say anything else. He said to me, "OK, let's hear it. Who did you meet?"

"I met the Director of Engineering of Sylvania's Mountain View facility, Mr. Werner Schmitt."

Walt laughed, "Are you telling me that he is the Director of Engineering? Holy Nelly. Well if you did meet him, you know that he is no friend of mine."

I laughed also, and said to him, "You are right about that. 'Childish son of a bitch' and 'dirty bastard' were two of the things he said about you in the forty seconds he allowed me to talk to him. Whatever made him so fond of you?"

"Director of Engineering?" Walt laughed again, and continued, "Jay, when you reach puberty and grow up, I will tell you about Werner Schmitt and me. But right now, you and I have important things to do. I will tell you, I promise, but this is not the appropriate time."

Over the next two years, we worked together and I was able to observe him, and his method of doing business, very closely. I have never met a more honest, fair, and decent person than Walt Collinsworth. Years later, I realized that I had picked up some of his mannerisms in dealing with people and situations. That made me feel that I was doing a good job.

Walt and I were eating supper in a restaurant in Trenton, New Jersey one evening. We had been to see our customer, RCA, and we would be heading back to Needham the next morning. Out of a clear blue sky Walt asked, "Are you ready to hear about Werner Schmitt?"

"Hell yes," I quickly replied.

"Well, I hope you're not disappointed by the story. I was with Sylvania a few years when I ended up at Waltham with the Applied Research Laboratory. This lab was very interesting. They had working groups of four or five engineers who stayed together as a team. Each group would be given some problems, or some ideas, and they would wrestle with them to find answers or solutions. There may, or may not, have been any useful application; you never knew until you were finished. There were many, many duds, but every once in a while something important and interesting was discovered. Essentially, the lab was a practical think tank.

"My group was made up of three graduate engineers and myself. As a matter of fact, I was the only person in the lab who did not have at least one degree and it is still a mystery to me how I ended up in that job. Anyhow, my group was close knit; we not only worked well together, we were also compatible with each other. It was a stimulating and an enjoyable assignment.

"We had been together a long time, when Werner Schmitt was introduced to us, and we were told he was now part of our group. We didn't mind at all and he was made welcome by us, at least, at first he was made welcome. That lasted as long as it took Werner to reveal himself as a pompous horse's ass.

"Two things you should know about Werner Schmitt. One is that he is a damn good engineer. The other is that he is so arrogant and so sure of himself that he is obnoxious. Within four months of his arrival, the flavor of our group had changed. Not that we stopped doing our work; as a matter of fact, it might have even gotten better for a while, as we all tried to best Werner. But the fact remained that our camaraderie was shattered. We did our jobs, we worked with him, and we suffered from his continuous verbal abuse. He seemed to single me out particularly for his ridicule. I often thought that it was because Werner, an MIT graduate, had to treat me, a Colonial Radio certificate holder, as his equal. That is exactly the type of thing that would gall Werner. At any rate, work was not fun any more when Werner joined our group.

"One of the things that made life bearable was that he never came in on time; he was always a half hour late. It was not that he didn't put his time in, he would stay over and work late into the night if he had to. It was just that he got a slow start in the morning. That allowed our group to hold meetings without him being present. We called these our mini-meetings and mostly we talked about what we were going to do with him, and how to handle ourselves when he began ridiculing us.

"One day, Werner came in and announced to us that he was going to buy a new car, a Volkswagon beetle. We didn't say anything at the time, but at our mini-meeting the next day, we were pretty vocal.

"One guy said, 'He is going to be unsufferable as he tells us of the virtues of his Volkswagon.' Everyone agreed with him; they all thought that when Werner got his new car, we would be awash in engineering information that proved that he had made the correct choice.

"I asked, 'Has anyone thought of this as an opportunity?'

They all looked at me, surprised, and asked me what I meant, and I continued, 'I am not sure myself, yet. But I am thinking.'

"When Werner arrived, he again began to talk about the car that he was going to buy. I decided to do some exploring. I asked him, 'Why did you pick a Volkswagon beetle to buy?'

"Collinsworth, if you could keep your emotions under control, and just base your selection on facts, like I can, you would come to the same conclusions. Pound for pound, and dollar for dollar, the Volkswagon beetle is the best car on the road today. That is because German engineering is so much superior to American engineering that there is just no contest. I am expecting great results."

"OK," I thought, "I'll just remember that."

"He got his car shortly thereafter, and our misery index rose considerably. He would top off his gas tank every damn day, and come charging into work and announce, "I have checked my gas gauge and my mileage is 32.631 miles per gallon" or, "I have checked my gas gauge and my mileage is 34.155 miles per gallon." We cringed as

Werner extolled German engineering and gave us his mileage reports. However, I began to get the germ of an idea.

"After two weeks of listening to him, I asked him, 'Werner, won't your mileage get even better as your engine gets broken in?'"

"Collinsworth," he replied, "that is a fallacy that American engineering perpetuates. The Germans design, and then build, their cars to exact dimensions and tolerances, so there is no break in period. These cars will last for years and the mileage will always remain the same. If they had taught good design techniques at your school, you would know these things."

"I thought, 'La de da, you son-of-a-bitch.' But I said nothing. He had given me the idea I was searching for. I figured I would fix his wagon, or, more specifically, his Volkswagon. The next morning, at our mini-meeting, the guys were commiserating with me when I said, 'Listen, forget that nonsense. I want you to keep Werner occupied today between 1:30 and 2:00. I don't care how; ask him if German engineering is as good as American engineering, or ask him why MIT is a better school than Colonial Radio. I don't care what you do, just keep him busy. And don't ask me why yet. Just do it.' They promised that they would.

"By 1:30 that afternoon, I was out in the parking lot and had found where Werner had parked his Volkswagon. I drove my car over, opened my trunk, took out a gas can, and added gas to his tank. The next morning, Werner came in looking a bit unsettled.

He said, 'I have just checked my gas gauge and I am getting 73.867 miles per gallon. That doesn't sound correct, but the figures are precise.' My cohorts looked at me; I just shrugged my shoulders.

"I played this same cat and mouse game every day for about two weeks. When he got over his initial surprise, he almost started coming to work at the same time we did, so he could brag about his gas gauge telling him that he got 69.123 miles per gallon, or 77.459 miles per gallon. I wanted to hear his explanation so I asked him, 'Werner, didn't you say that the gas consumption would remain constant because of the high quality of German engineering?'"

He replied, "Well, I might have said something like that, but, obviously, there is some adjustment period necessary. And, do not forget, I am driving so much better, that I am bound to have an effect on gas mileage. I shift carefully, I brake carefully, I accelerate carefully. A good driver, like me, can have an enormous impact on gas consumption.

"That did it. I decide to burst his bubble. I now started to siphon gas out of his car daily. For the first time in almost two months he would come into work and never mentioned the gas consumption of his Volkswagon. After the third day, I asked him what his miles per gallon was and he replied, very sulkily, '13.812 miles per gallon.' By the middle of the following week, he would come in, call the car dealership on the phone, and literally shout and demand that they fix his automobile so that his good mileage would return. We once again began enjoying our mini-meetings.

"However, I knew I had to tell him the truth. Otherwise, I would be just as nasty as he was. So, the next morning, when he got to work, our little group sat down with him and I said, 'Werner, your gas mileage fluctuations are because I have been adding, and then siphoning gas out of your gas tank these last five weeks. Your initial readings of about 32 miles to the gallon are the only true readings you have had.' I did not apologize for what I had done because I was not sorry.

"At first, he would not believe me. When it dawned on him that he had been tricked by people he was contemptuous of, he was furious. He sat in his chair, silent for a moment, and then he looked at all of and said, 'You are all a bunch of childish bastards. Never have I seen such a group of jealous kids. I am so superior to you, that the only way you can try to catch up to me is with childish, stupid pranks. Which, incidentally, I was fully aware of; you really did not fool me. I have not told you before, but I am transferring out of here. I do not wish to be associated with anyone who thinks that going to Colonial Radio School is a technical education. May you all rot in Hell.' Werner Schmitt got up and left, and that was the last I heard of him until you met him in Mountain View.

"I will cheerfully admit that it was a childish, stupid prank. But it got rid of him and work was fun again. What would you have done if you had the same problem?"

The Engineers and the Stickers

When I returned to Massachusetts, after working sixteen months at the Grand Forks Air Force Base, some of my coworkers were glad to see me and a few were not. Either way, I was happy to be back because it had been a difficult assignment and I was looking forward to an easier job. I had been the leader of a group of five technicians and engineers sent by General Telephone and Electronics to work directly with the Strategic Air Command. Our job was to help them understand the Minuteman Missile System and to work with them as they kept the missiles ready for launching. Eighteen-hour workdays inside those silos, under the North Dakota prairie, were much more common than I really wanted. I was ready for a job that was less taxing; or so I thought.

My first week back was spent in briefings and meetings with groups of upper echelon executives in GTE. They wanted to know how the equipment we had designed and built, was working. This new missile wing was having problems keeping the missiles in what the Air Force called, "Strategic Alert", but the problems were not related to our equipment. However, I had a difficult time explaining to these executives, that, at the working level where I had been, the Air Force did not care which company built what equipment. All that SAC knew was that the system had too much down time and it was due to the equipment for which the government had paid millions of dollars. I tried to liken it to buying a very expensive automobile that had a defective carburetor; the new owner didn't give a damn who built the carburetor, he considered his new auto as a lemon. My upper echelon darlings couldn't conceive of an attitude like that, even when I told them these worker bees were worn out after putting in twelve hour days, in thirty below zero weather, for months on end. By Friday, I was glad to get back where I belonged; the basement of this ivory tower.

I was assigned as a test engineer to the Ground Integration Test Program (GITP). This was a test group that was set up to check out all the equipment used in the missile system. GTE had three test sites with identical equipment installed in the missile systems in North Dakota and in Montana. These sites were linked together to simulate an entire missile squadron. Our mission was threefold. The first was to examine any field problems that the Air Force encountered and couldn't understand. The second was to check out, by form, fit, and function, any modifications before they were installed in the field. The third was to check out the entire missile system against its design criteria. The Air Force was adamant in wanting to know whether their specifications were correct, and if the system was functioning according to specifications.

The specifications were contained in six huge volumes called "SYSTEMS REQUIREMENT ANALYSIS." Testing was a massive undertaking that would last five years. GTE had over sixty engineers and technicians running test three shifts a day, seven days a week. Every major subcontractor, Boeing, Autonetics, General Electric, and TRW, along with the Air Force and several government agencies, had representatives permanently represented at GITP.

After I had been there about a month, my boss, George Hoover, and his boss, Ben Hank, called me into Ben's office. I hadn't done anything naughty that I knew of, so I was curious about what they wanted. George started the conversation by asking, "Well, what do you think of this operation?"

"Since you asked, I will tell you. I think that this place is run sloppily. The paperwork needs to be strengthened to prove what the tests set out to prove."

Ben spoke up, "You think it is the paperwork, do you? Don't you think that it could be the people running the tests?"

"It could be, but it isn't. The test engineers run from outstanding to barely adequate. A breakdown in one or two tests could be because of the individual test engineer. But almost all of our tests are subject to second-guessing by the entire Minuteman community. That shows, to me, that the problems are above the test engineers."

"You are probably correct. Our customer is not pleased or impressed with our efforts. Boeing has asked the Air Force to change our contract and put them in charge of running tests. What do you think of that?"

"To hell with Boeing, I don't like them, though, I will give them their due. They have learned something that we have not; they reverence paperwork. They may be slow and cumbersome, and not as quick to react as we are, but they leave a paper trail. They know where they have been, and they document their every step. We don't; and it will continue to hurt us until we learn that paper is as important a product as our equipment or our testing."

Ben Hank leaned back in his chair and spoke to George Hoover. "See, I was right. We will be able to turn this around."

Then he looked at me. "The Air Force does not want Boeing to run this site, yet. We told them that we are going to reorganize. We have decided to change the way we run tests. We are going to make two people responsible for all the activities on the test sites. We are going to have a Maintenance Supervisor, who will be responsible for every piece of operational equipment. He will make sure that maintenance schedules are performed, that equipment is operating correctly, and when it fails, to fix it. He will work with the Test Supervisor, who will be responsible for all phases of testing. For this system to work, these two will have to work hand in hand. Every problem, every glitch, will have to be assessed between these two, and there can be no posturing between the two of you. Would you be interested in being the Test Supervisor?"

I had to chew on that a while. When tests are running smoothly, there are no problems. But when something does not happen as expected, is it really a problem? The paperwork could be wrong, the equipment could be malfunctioning, or they both could be correct and the equipment could be designed incorrectly. And if there is a problem, how is it to be solved? Neither the Maintenance Supervisor nor the Test Supervisor could shirk his responsibilities or try to usurp the other's responsibilities. If we couldn't get along, the split of responsibilities would not work.

I asked, "Who is to be the Maintenance Supervisor?"

Ben answered, "Tom Kerby. He has already accepted if you will take the job as Test Supervisor."

I grinned. I had known, and worked with, Tom for three years. He was honest, patient, and intelligent and he had a good sense of humor; I knew that we two could work together very closely without any personality clashes.

I said, "I accept."

The following week we started the new system. The first thing that I did was to speak to all the test engineers that were presently running tests. I told them that there were new ground rules. The paperwork for each step of the test needed had to be stamped by our quality control before the next step was to be run. To complete all the massive amount of paperwork before the shift ended, testing was to stop an hour before the end of the shift. This would allow the test engineer time to straighten out the massive amounts of paperwork. There were no objections from the test engineers, but my bosses caught hell from the GTE voices on high when they heard what I was doing.

Ben Hank did not come to see me but he sent George Hoover to ask me if cutting down testing time was necessary. I told him "Yes." That ended that. Within a month the benefit of emphasizing the paperwork was apparent in our test results and our customer began to gain confidence in our operation.

That left me with one problem that was not visible to anyone but me. That was the individual test engineer's logbook. It was a log that each engineer was to fill in with his own test observations. For example, shift changeover meetings were to be annotated in the engineering logbook. Other pertinent information, such as power outages, abnormal running conditions, or cockpit errors, was supposed to be logged by the test engineer. This information, while non-deliverable to the customer, was absolutely invaluable to Tom and me when we tried to sort out what happened during testing.

Because the test engineers had so much paperwork that they were responsible for, their test logs were almost barren. I cajoled, joked, threatened, remonstrated, pleaded, all to no avail. No one took the time to write enough information in their log-books. I was totally frustrated.

One Saturday in early fall, I went into Boston on an errand and my wife, Virginia, asked me to pick up some school supplies for a project one of my daughters was making for her class. The store I went to was Hammond's; they specialized in all kinds of school supplies. As I wandered around I noticed some sheets of stickers that teachers pasted on their student's papers. They were bright and colorful; orange pumpkins, sheaves of corn, red and yellow leaves, and witches on brooms. When I saw them I laughed, and then I bought sheets and sheets of stickers.

I took them to work and locked them in one of my security

cabinets without saying a word to anyone. It took over three weeks of searching before I found one test engineer's log-book that even came close to having any information. When I finally located one, I put a sticker on the page, and, without saying anything, I gave the logbook back to its owner. In about an hour he rushed into my office, opened his logbook and wanted to know what the sticker meant. I told him that it was for excellence in writing.

From that moment on, I had no more trouble with engineering logbooks. Each engineer wanted a sticker and they began to take infinite care in detailing their writing. They would analyze each other's logbooks to see what brought stickers and what did not. They would boast about how many stickers they received for each test they ran. For a while, I was concerned whether my test engineers were becoming more interested in their logbooks than in running tests.

Of course, the euphoria eventually died down. Stickers on well-written logbooks became routine and expected. On the other hand, the logbook entries were raised to a higher standard then they had ever been before; and this standard never wavered.

There is a message about human nature in this sticker episode, but, to this day, I am not exactly sure what the message is.

The Sound of Music

This is not about Julie Andrews gracefully gliding across the Austrian Alps singing lovely ballads. This is about music that can, fortunately or unfortunately, be heard at any traffic light in the United States. This is about what I heard.

Last week, as I was approaching the intersection of Main Street and the Ann Arbor-Saline Road, the light went from green to amber. At first, I was going to go through the intersection because red lights annoy me. However, I realized that the light would change before I even entered the intersection, so I reluctantly stopped.

Even if I am not in a hurry or have no destination in mind, I have the feeling that a red light is causing me to lose time. I am not pleased to be kept waiting for a light to change, especially if there is no traffic going through the intersection. I fight this childish impulse every time I have to stop for a traffic light but I do get impatient. I haven't run a red light in years but I do get the urge to do it.

For the first five or ten seconds my van was the only car waiting for the green light. As I sat there, telling the light to change, I began to hear a heavy drum beat and a car squealed its tires as it pulled up beside me. Its windows were down and its high-fi system was blasting so loudly that I thought that my van was vibrating. Pouring out of the car was a steady roll of staccato drumbeats and some one sing song-ing words. Rap music at its loudest and strongest.

I looked at the car and saw that there was a driver and someone on the passenger side of the front seat. Both were young men and both were black. The driver had both of his hands on the steering wheel and he was drumming his fingers. The passenger had both hands in front of him as if he were playing the piano and both men were bob-bing their heads in time to the music. I don't know how they could stand to have their music so loud. I was five feet away and it was hurt-ing my ears.

I tried to listen to the words as the lyrics were being chanted. Almost the only word that I could hear clearly and understood was the word, "fuck." It was the heart and soul of the lyrics and it was re-peated over and over with hardly another word. It was used as a verb, a noun, an adjective, an adverb, and it was used as punctuation. I was not the slightest bit shocked that the "f" word was being blared out so loudly. Nowadays, everyone from the poor to the Pope, has heard the word, and understands its meaning. However, there once was a time when we were more circumspect with its use in public. I was much more uncomfortable with the loudness than the lyrics; the volume was giving me a headache.

Just as I thought that it could get no worse, a car stopped behind me with its own broadcasting station that was playing the same kind of rap music. And it was even louder than the car beside me. I looked in the mirror and saw a young white woman driving the car. One of her hands was on the wheel and drumming with the music, the other hand was holding a cell phone up to her ear. I gathered that she was talking to someone but I wondered if either party could hear anything.

The rap from both cars was too much for me. I could only sit there and hope that the light would change before the decibels of deafness affected me permanently. Finally, the light did turn green and the concert mercifully ended.

That evening, after my ears stopped ringing and my headache cleared, I began to think about my musical ordeal. A friend of mine had told me that rap music was like all other forms of art in the sense that it reflected the lives of the people who express themselves using this art form. Rap music supposedly is a new and different art form that sprang from the indigent and the disadvantaged. He said that spirituals and blues had started the same way, from the bottom up. He is probably right, but I definitely have more of an objection to rap than I have to spirituals and blues.

I have no problem with a person, or a group, expressing themselves. Anyone who has something to say should be able to say it any way they wish. Whether I agree with them or even like what they say is immaterial, they certainly have the same right of expression that I do. However, if those who are doing the saying want those who are doing the listening to understand them, those who are doing the saying have an obligation to make their message clear. The rappers must resonate with their audience, not rebuff them. Otherwise, the message will not get through.

And therein lies my personal difficulty with rap music. It has not gotten through to me. Up until now I have rejected even listening to it. And some of the problem has been mine. Rap requires attention but the noise and the "f" word have stopped me right at the outset. And that is too bad because, if rap deals with the seamy side of society, we should listen. Everyone has an obligation to fight injustice and discrimination.

However, a large part of the problem is not mine, it lies with the rappers themselves. They are more interested in confrontation and shock than they are in stating their case. They fling the gauntlet down almost defying you to listen. For me, that doesn't work. I think they shoot themselves in the foot. Using the "f" word doesn't repulse me as much as it limits their ability to express themselves. Would the Gettysburg Address appeal to anyone at all if every other word were the "f" word?

Until rappers tone down their volume and express themselves better, their message will be lost on me. That is too bad because they probably do have a lot to say that is worthwhile. I am not being an elitist or a snob but, right now, I consider rap music as nothing more than the national anthem for road rage.

Hopefully, both sides will be more accommodating in the future and problems can be discussed without fear of hearing losses.

The Summer Camp Rebellion

Young children are like summer clouds. Even as you study them, they change in front of your very eyes. Their boundaries are never still. They are restless and switch moods frequently, either radiating sunshine or pouring rain. Children and clouds are fascinating and interesting, but never set your watch by either; they are both as exact and as accurate as a reading of tea leaves.

In the spring of 1964, my three daughters were young children. Cynthia was seven years old, Julie was six, and Elizabeth was three. We were living in a small house in East Foxboro and, as near as I can recall, our family life was normal.

One evening, after I had helped get the girls ready for bed, by bathing, reading, and tucking them in, Virginia and I were sitting in the back yard. We were watching the sun set and drinking a beer.

Virginia said, "Jay, Father Jackson called me this afternoon."

Ginny was referring to Frank Jackson, the rector of St. Marks Episcopalian church. He preferred to be called "Frank" by his parishioners, because Foxboro was a small town, but Ginny liked her religion to be much more formal, so she called him "Father." Both of them had enjoyed correcting each other's form of address since we had moved to Foxboro in 1959.

"And what did he call you for?" I asked.

"Well, he got a call from the diocese office in Boston. They are getting ready to open Camp Lincoln Hill for the summer, and they need a registered nurse to be at the camp full time. He called and asked if I would be interested in the job."

Lincoln Hill was a camp, run by the Episcopalian Church, which was located in Foxboro. It was primarily for inner city girls to get out of the sweltering metropolitan area in summertime. The camp was open all summer, but each individual camp session was two weeks long. That was to give as many girls as possible a taste of what summer was like, outside of the city. Not many local kids went to Lincoln Hill, but the archdiocese did try to hire Foxboro residents to fill all the jobs in the camp. It was a good will gesture towards the town.

"What did you tell Frank?" I asked.

Ginny looked at me, but did not comment at my use of his first name. "I told Father Jackson that my R.N. registration was valid and current, and that I might be interested, but that I would have to talk with you. I asked him how soon he had to have an answer."

"And what did he say to that?"

She replied, "He said that he was not sure, but, since the archdiocese was not known for speed, I would probably have plenty of time. He gave me the name and the phone number of the person that he had talked to and suggested that I contact him directly."

"Are you going to?"

"I already have. I called the number Father Jackson gave me and talked a long time with Father Jeffrey Benson. He was quite interesting. He has a problem; the woman who has been camp nurse for over twenty years has retired and moved to Florida. So, he needs someone, and he was quite anxious for me to come in and meet him. I told him that I had three young girls and I gave him their ages. He said that I could enroll Cynthia and Julie in camp and keep Elizabeth with me, in the dispensary. I told him that I had a current nursing registration, but that I hadn't worked in over five years; he said that was no problem. I told him that I would have to check with you, and he asked me to call him back as soon as I could. He sounded a little desperate.

"What do you think of the idea of me working this summer?"

I took a swig of beer, and then said to Ginny, "It really isn't what I think so much as it is what you would be interested in doing. Do you like the idea?"

She replied, "Yes, I do. It would be good for the girls, they have not been to a camp. The work would probably not be difficult, but I would be at the camp almost full time from late June until August. The pay won't be much, especially with the girls going to the camp, but, actually, it sounds like fun. Could you put up with us being gone all summer?"

"Listen, Ginny," I said, "If I could last almost a year up in Thule without you guys supervising me, I can easily manage one summer in Foxboro. Once you get there, you will have to stay all summer. That is quite a commitment."

"Yes, I know, but it sounds interesting to me. To be with young girls all summer would be enjoyable. Of course it will depend on Cynthia and Julie. If they would like to go to camp, I would consider the job."

I thought for a while, then said, "Ginny, if we just ask them, 'Would you like to go to camp?', they will automatically say, 'Yes.' I doubt if they even know what summer camp is. Instead of saying anything to them, why don't we take them over and show them Lincoln Hill. You should go tour it anyhow, before you make up your mind. We can look around, you can explain what happens at summer camp, and then we can ask if they would enjoy doing that this summer?"

Ginny agreed. So, the following Saturday morning, we drove the three miles from our house over to the camp and walked through the grounds. We did not tell the girls where we were going or why. They were used to that because we went somewhere almost every weekend and wherever we went, I would tell them that we were going on a "Secret Mission", as in Mission Impossible. They liked the suspense associated with our "Secret Missions."

When we got to the camp there were a few workmen taking winter shutters off the doors and windows, otherwise, the place was deserted. The buildings were crude, one story structures. Each building had walls, roofs, doors, windows, electricity, plumbing only; no insulation, no finished material.

The dormitories slept twenty girls each, ten closely packed iron cots on either side of the room; there was a footlocker at the end of each bed. The mess hall was the largest structure, big enough to feed about one hundred at one time, and with a small stage at one end for shows and summer events. The quarters were primitive, but adequate, for a summer camp.

The biggest surprise was the swimming pool. It was an Olympic sized pool, that must have been recently installed. It was tiled, fenced in, and there were lights for swimming at night; it would have been attractive anywhere. At Lincoln Hill, it was almost exotic.

We toured the entire camp grounds, pointing out things to each other as we saw them, and answering any questions the girls asked. The dispensary building had a small desk, with one of the few phones in the camp on the desk, and three or four small bedrooms for overnight patients. There was one room slightly larger than the others; we presumed that would be Ginny's bedroom.

After our tour we went and got ice cream. We still had not said anything to the girls about why we had gone to Lincoln Hill; that would come later, after Ginny and I talked.

That evening, when we finally had the girls in bed, we compared notes, and discussed whether Ginny should take the job or not. She was excited, especially about the girls spending their summer at a camp, something Ginny had not done when she was a little girl. The next step would be to talk with the girls.

The next morning we did, and of course, it was not a hard sell. Cynthia and Julie each said that they would just love to live in those houses we visited while their mother was the camp nurse. We repeated this conversation several times, in the next few days, to make sure that their wishes were consistent.

By the end of the week, Ginny called Father Benson and accepted the job. She had to make a couple of trips to Joy Street, in downtown Boston, to iron out a few details, and sign some papers, and then she was officially the Camp Lincoln Hill nurse. All that was left was to wait the few weeks until the camp opened.

Registration of the first group of campers was to take place on an early Saturday morning in late June. Since that would be the day I would start my bachelor summer, I decided to take the family out to dinner the Friday night before camp started. I made a reservation at a fancy German restaurant in Franklin, a town near Foxboro. The restaurant had been written up in the Boston Globe as being very good and very expensive. That was the reason I selected it; I planned on sending the Carp family off to summer camp in style.

I came home from work early to help with packing clothes, to help with getting the girls dressed for our night out, and to just visit with the family. When we finished our tasks, we got in the car and drove to the restaurant.

The restaurant was set far back from the road and was in what once had been an old house. It had been enlarged so that the dining area was big, but the setting was still very attractive. We were seated at a table that overlooked a huge expanse of lawn and gardens, and behind the bar was a mural of the Alps. We all felt good.

Ginny and I ordered Bavarian beer for each of us and Shirley Temple cocktails for the girls. Then we looked at the menu to try to figure out what to order for everyone. After we sorted out what we wanted, and had placed our orders, a trio of musicians strolled over to our table. One had an accordion, one had a guitar, and one had a violin. They were each dressed in a Tyrolean hat, each had a different patterned shirt with flowers embroidered on it, and short leather pants with leather suspenders.

As they came up to our table, my first impression was that they were all old, very old. So old in fact, that I thought they had been passengers on the Ark; I discarded that idea immediately because I know Noah allowed only pairs on board. My next thought was just as uncharitable, that they were retirees from the Lawrence Welk orchestra.

Whatever my naughty thoughts were, the three of them were very nice to us; they fussed over the girls and told us our daughters were beautiful. They did look pretty in their taffeta dresses and their hair in Shirley Temple curls.

They stood by our table and played for the whole dining room. They played a medley of tunes from "The Sound of Music" and the guitarist sang a few of the songs. They were excellent musicians and the singer had a strong, clear, sweet voice. It was while he was singing "Edelweiss" that the trouble started.

I happened to glance over at Cynthia and I could see that she was beginning to cry. I caught Ginny's eye, and cocked my head towards Cynthia. Ginny leaned over to her and Cynthia started to bawl, and bawl loudly. At first, the musicians did not notice; but when her volume began to exceed theirs, they became concerned. Ginny took Cynthia on her lap and cradled and rocked her and Cynthia's bawling subsided to tears and snuffles. The musicians stopped playing and asked us if they had done anything wrong. Ginny assured them, that whatever the problem was, it had nothing to do with them. They began to play again, but, in a short time, they strolled away from our table.

Ginny gently rocked Cynthia and quieted her down. She talked to her as if nothing had happened. Ginny was just getting ready to question her about her outburst, when our food was served. Ginny and I had huge steaming platters of sauerbraten and spaetzle; the girls had fried chicken and mashed potatoes done American style.

I tasted my food. It was delicious. Before Ginny had a chance to even pick up her fork, Cynthia started to cry again. Ginny hugged her and said, "Cynthia, tell Mommy what is wrong."

Cynthia sobbed, "I don't want to go away to summer camp. I want to stay home and I want Mommy to stay home with me." Then, she continued to cry.

I was absolutely stunned. I was also sure that Ginny was totally surprised. This was the very first time either of us had heard anything except that both girls were looking forward to going to summer camp. Cynthia's outburst was completely unexpected. To this day, I do not know whether Cynthia had harbored real doubts or if it was the fact that tomorrow she was actually was going to leave her house for camp. Whatever caused her anxiety, she was scared and frightened.

Virginia said to her, "Cynthia, you have nothing to cry about. I am going to be at summer camp with you."

"That's not the same thing as being at home with you, and me, and Julie, and Elizabeth," Cynthia sobbed.

Julie may have been having the same thoughts, because, just then, she decided it was time for her to get in on the act. She put her fork down, looked at Virginia, and said, "This food doesn't taste good." She also began to cry.

Not to be outdone, Elizabeth elected to join her sisters in the crying contest. That made quite a tableau. A table full of freshly served food, three sobbing little sisters, and a mother and father distraught and beside themselves. Within the space of three or four minutes, the waiter, the manager, and one of the chefs, had visited our table to see if they could offer assistance.

We thanked each one and told them that there was nothing that they could do. In an attempt to get the girls to eat I took a bite of my food. What had been tasty German cooking before, now had all the flavor of marinated mulch.

Virginia looked at me and said, "This is ridiculous. Let's pay the bill and get the hell out of here."

I couldn't have agreed more, so I signaled for the waiter, who walked over quickly with the bill already in his hand. I couldn't blame him for being ready to see us leave, we must have been a terrible distraction to everyone else in the room. However, when I read the bill I almost joined my daughters in weeping and sobbing. It was certainly not the fault of the restaurant that we had eaten almost nothing, but I was being charged an awfully high price just for sniffing supper. I felt they should have offered us doggie bags as they waved goodbye. Neither Ginny nor I wanted to wait around though, so we did not pursue it.

After paying the bill, we walked to the car without saying a word. The girls got in back, Ginny and I got in front. No one spoke. Each of us was alone in our own teepee of silence, contemplating our sour night out. I was a cauldron of boiling emotions. I was concerned about summer camp, I was displeased that my hospitality had been abused, I was upset about the cost of the evening, and I was angry at the girls. I felt like immediately driving up to the locked gates of Camp Lincoln Hill and dropping them off.

Instead, I drove home.

We put the girls to bed and they went to sleep immediately. Ginny and I poured ourselves stiff drinks, walked into the back yard, and sat watching the night sky. Seeing two shooting stars relaxed me, the cold drink revived me, and reason began to replace my anger.

I asked Ginny, "Did you get to eat anything?"

"Two breadsticks just before the storm," was her reply.

"Well, the three bites of Sauerbraten that I had were tasty. I am sorry that you did not get to eat," I said.

"Jay," Ginny replied, "I truly appreciate what you meant this evening to be. I will remember the sentiment more than the two bread-sticks. Thank you."

So we held hands and sat motionless, watching the night sky show us that life does have some beauty. After a while, Ginny stirred, and said, "Listen Jay, those girls are going to Lincoln Hill with me in the morning. That camp is totally dependent upon my showing up. It would be a crime to delay the camp opening for those inner city girls, just because of Cynthia and Julie. They will have to accompany Elizabeth and me."

"Would it be any better not to take them tomorrow? I could bring them over Sunday, if you thought it might make a difference," I said.

"No, I don't want them to have time to think about it. I don't know what upset Cynthia tonight, but I am sure that if she will just let herself, she will enjoy herself this summer. So, we will get them all up late in the morning, just before it's time to leave, and just go. Forget tonight, Lincoln Hill is waiting for the four female Carps."

In the morning, we did exactly what Ginny said to do. The girls were quiet as they got ready, but there were no tears. I accompanied them to camp, and watched as Cynthia joined the "Wrens" and Julie joined the "Hornets."

The first week and a half was touch and go. Julie did pretty well, but Cynthia ended up sleeping at the dispensary every evening, for almost ten days. After their fears subsided, they both adjusted and enjoyed the rest of the summer; Ginny and Elizabeth did also.

That was thirty five years ago, and the memories have faded into the past. I would probably have totally forgotten about summer camp except for the fact that my children, like the summer clouds they once were, rained all over me one night.

The Testosterone of Patriotism

What are we doing and why are we doing it?

I used to occasionally ask myself these questions after the cowardly, unprovoked attack of 9/11. However, since the invasion of Iraq, those questions have become a constant mantra for me. I think of them continuously because I believe that the policies of our present administration are not only destroying Iraq they are also, layer by layer, dismantling America's freedoms and our way of life.

The toxic waste, the stench, and the arrogance emanating from the Washington, DC cesspool has fragmented and poisoned our country. Anyone who questions or disagrees with our undefined goals is labeled "unpatriotic". And both parties, the Democrats and the Republicans alike, are guilty of narrow-minded slander. With their eyes toward the upcoming elections, they waste our time by daubing septic waste on their opponents while, at the same time, peeing on each other's shoes.

The major problem facing our country is that once the politicians have unleashed the dogs of war, our most sacred treasure, our young men and women, become death's fodder. And once the testosterone of patriotism is triggered, emotions engulf and inflame everyone and rational discussion becomes impossible. Our political leaders, in both parties, purposely take advantage of this fervor to insist that those who disagree with their policies are aiding the enemy.

Concerning Iraq, underneath the fervor of patriotism is the fact that the present administration has not been honest in explaining either its motives or its goals. If we are really at war, why don't we mobilize the country and ask everyone to make sacrifices? Why are we putting the entire burden on our armed forces, our brave and trusting younger generation who do their jobs with no questions asked? Why did we go into Iraq when the mastermind of 9/11 was, and still is, in Afghanistan?

Now that we are there, what are we doing? Does anyone really believe that the average Iraqi citizen is now better off that before we invaded? And why do we have a huge "shadow army" of mercenaries who are responsible to no one, shoot at everyone, and cost the taxpayers billions of dollars?

And while the present administration is completely dedicated to spreading democracy overseas, at home we are coming apart at the seams.

More and more of our people are falling from the middle class into the poverty level. Millions of Americans are finding the cost of health insurance too much for them to pay, so they have none. Our infrastructure is crumbling in front of our eyes. And education, the highway of opportunity for our youngsters, is almost unaffordable for the poor and the disappearing middle class. I am sure that our founding fathers would have considered our own needs first before deciding what we should do for the rest of the world.

Despite the fact that our country is under siege from a group of insane fanatics, we do not need to panic. We are the strongest country in the world and we are dedicated to diversity, respect, and the rule of law. We are blessed with climates of all kind, people of all races, fruitful farmlands, and abundant natural resources. There is much to rejoice about and be thankful for and we need not fear for our future if we keep to our traditions and to our purpose. Even though our enemy, al-Qaeda, is a different type of evil than we have ever faced, it is no stronger than any other evil that we have fought. We can defeat al-Qaeda by being resolute and maintaining our principles.

At present, because of our confusion, there are more questions than there are answers and we can't change what we have done. What we need to do is look at our future using the same guidelines we have used in the past. I would suggest that we forget our fears and our party affiliations, pause, and then talk quietly and honestly about what America, as a country, and we, as individuals, need to do to strengthen our resolve.

We absolutely need to emphasize what unites us; not what divides us. For example, we could temper our "Not in My Back Yard" attitude and we could again exercise the art of compromise as our forefathers did. If we forget fear, pay less attention to party affiliations, and work as a people, we can overcome any obstacle. We have done so from the time our country was founded and we should be able to do it again. The only way we can lose our noble experiment of democracy is if we allow ourselves to lose it.

As we were the recipients of liberty and freedom from our forefathers, so should we pass these ideals on to our progeny? For the sake of our country, our troops, our children, and the generations to come, let us do what is right for our future.

I am willing. Come join me and lets talk.

The Top of the World

PART I: ARRIVAL

In the early 1960's I flew to Thule, Greenland, in an Air Force transport plane and landed in the dark with the temperature hovering at -60° below zero. I was the only civilian on board the crowded military transport. The one person to meet me, after I dashed from the plane into the terminal, was Alessandro Genet, the Sylvania site manager. He was short and plump with a red face and a bald spot on the top of his head; he spoke with a heavy French accent. While we waited for my luggage, Genet told me a little about Thule and a lot about himself. I was too cold to be interested in either. We went from the terminal to the barracks in an Air Force truck driven by an enlisted man; that was the only form of transportation on the base. Genet accompanied me to my room in an Air Force barracks, gave me the key to unlock my door, and left.

Greenland belongs to Denmark and, at the time I went to Thule, the settlement was divided into three sections. One was the United States Air Force Base on an inlet at the edge of the frozen shoreline. The second was a small Danish community located on the other side of the inlet away from the base. This community is called Dundas

Village and was made up of Danish scientists, meteorologists, and their spouses and families. Dundas Village was strictly off limits to all but Danish nationals. The third, and newest, was the Air Force radar site on a high bluff about six miles from the Air Force Base. That radar station was the reason that I went to Thule. It was completely operated by civilians.

Because I was an engineer, I was given a two-man room, rather than the four-man room that technicians were assigned. And, since there were no other Sylvania engineers at Thule at the time, I had the small room to myself. Down the hall was the common latrine for every room on each floor. After I entered my room and looked around, I began unpacking the clothes I brought with me and wishing I had stayed home in Foxboro, Massachusetts.

There was a reason that this new radar site was occupying a small portion of Denmark. The Russians had the capability of launching a mass nuclear attack against the United States and, if the Russians ever did launch a preemptive strike, we needed to know immediately so that we could launch a retaliatory strike. That was the theory known as (MAD) Mutually Assured Destruction.

At that time, the United States was building three radar stations, in Alaska, England, and Greenland, to monitor the only path these missiles would take from Russia to America. These mamouth radar stations are called BMEWS—the Ballistic Missile Early Warning System.

My company, Sylvania, won the contract to build a special purpose computer to interpret the radar signals that bounced back to the radar station from intercepted targets. Our equipment was sophisticated and an important link in the equipment that made up the BMEWS system.

Although Sylvania designed and built the equipment, we had no contract to maintain it. The Air Force selected RCA to run the entire radar site. RCA hired technicians and engineers for the job and sub-contracted Sylvania to teach their personnel our equipment and procedures. I had taught these RCA men the theory of operation and the maintenance of our equipment for over a year. I had volunteered to come to Thule to replace my boss, Walt Collinsworth, who had just left to return to what he called, "The Real World." My job in Thule was to be the Sylvania contact engineer. I would updated blueprints, keep track of engineering change notices, order spare parts and equipment and occasionally, when asked, give technical advice.

The three BMEWS sites used two types of radars. There was the detection radar with its three antennas for initially detecting possible targets. Each individual antenna was massive and stood out on top of the high bluff. Each was larger than a football field, measuring 165 feet tall and 400 feet long. After processing, the detection data was fed to a tracking radar, a fully steerable tracking dish, a saucer 85 feet in diameter. The saucer was installed in a large radome and would track any target the detection radar located. Thule had dual IBM computers for processing missile trajectories and impact predictions. This information was sent to Higher Headquarters to warn of missile attacks. The full BMEWS radar network became operational in the early 1960s.

Genet had told me that I would be working the midnight shift and to leave in time to eat before taking a bus to the BMEWS complex, called J-Site. An hour before the buses left, I put on my Air Force-issued parka and gloves and walked over to the mess hall designated for civilians. This mess hall was open twenty-four hours a day, and the food was excellent. There were no restrictions on when anyone could eat or how much he could put on his plate. The mailroom, located within the cafeteria, was also kept open twenty-four hours a day. Every attempt was made to keep the civilian morale high and the attrition rate low. About forty minutes before the shift began, five Air Force buses arrived in front of the mess hall. The civilians boarded the buses and, at a prearranged time, we left for J-Site.

The bus drivers were all Danish men, as were the cooks, the

janitors, the kitchen help, and whatever support staff was needed to care for the civilian workers. By treaty, these jobs had to be done by Danish nationals. They were mostly young farm boys who were interested in making money, just as their American counterparts were. Most of them didn't speak English, or claimed they didn't, and there wasn't much fraternization between the Americans and the Danes. Each nationality lived within its own ethnic enclave which were both separate entities from the Air Force Base activities.

The buses departed in a convoy with the drivers in constant radio contact with each other and with traffic control on the base. The weather could change so quickly and so badly that radio communications had to be constantly maintained. We headed up the bluff for J-Site located about six miles away from the base. Spaced along the bumpy, narrow, dirt road were many emergency shelters connected to the base by heavy electrical power cables. If a storm engulfed the convoy, the buses would stop at the closest emergency shelter and everyone would get inside where there was water, food, and warmth.

When the buses arrived at J-Site, all the passengers were let off at one stop. It was a shed where trams picked up and carried passengers, inside a covered passageway, to their various buildings and workstations along the huge radar complex.

I was shown the Sylvania office, a small room with four partitioned cubicles. I picked one that had two government-issued desks sitting back to back. One was locked. The other was open and empty, so I took it. The rest of the shift I spent getting familiar with the surroundings and talking with the RCA crew on duty. I enjoyed seeing them again; most of them had been in my classes in West Roxbury, a few hadn't.

The next morning, as the shift was ending, my office phone rang. It was Genet in his heavy French accent asking me to come to his office. Over and above his accent, his voice sounded odd. I held the phone away from my ear because he was speaking loudly, and then it dawned on me why his voice sounded as it did. I could hear him without the phone. Genet's cubicle was next door.

I walked over and sat in the visitor's chair. I noticed a folded towel on one of the front corners of his desk. As I watched, Genet unlocked the desk and took out six pencils. He aligned the first one carefully so that it was parallel with the left edge of his desk. The other five had to be equidistant from each other, the erasers facing the same direction and in a line with every other eraser. When his pencils had finally minded him, Genet took out six pens and dressed the right side of his desk as obsessively as the left. After he was satisfied with his pencils and pens, he took out two rulers to align near the front of the desk. All in all, it took him almost ten minutes. And, the entire time he was setting up his desk, in his heavy French accent, he swore at the fools, the knaves, the bastards, and the sons-of-bitches that he was forced to work with.

When Genet finished getting ready for work, he said, "Welcome to my work crew. Let me tell you about Alessandro Genet. I've been at Thule longer than any other civilian in BMEWS, and everyone is jealous of me. They're jealous of my record, they're jealous of the money I'm making, and they're jealous that I'm fluent in three languages."

I thought, I surely hope you're not including English in those three as I can barely understand you.

"These people from RCA can't be trusted and even my bosses in Sylvania don't give me the credit I deserve. That's OK, because as soon as I make the amount of money I've decided on, the whole goddamn world can kiss Alessandro Genet's ass.

"I'll bet that your boss, Collinsworth, who I once thought was an honest man, has told you lies about me. Am I right?"

I again thought to myself, Genet, you're a bigger asshole than anyone has even given you credit for. You would be wise to hold your opinions to yourself. There is no more honest and patient a person than Walt Collinsworth.

Instead, I said, "Alessandro, he didn't say very much about you, and I don't think he lied."

"Well, it really doesn't make any difference because Alessandro Genet will do his job correctly until he leaves Thule."

The next evening, my coworkers asked me if I'd noticed the towel on Genet's desk. They told me to peek under it and, when I did, I saw that the towel covered up some dents and scratches. Then, they explained what had happened. The RCA crew knew about Genet's obsession with his pens and pencils, but no one cared until one day, Genet caught one of the RCA men breaking a site rule. Even though it was none of his business and had nothing to do with the Sylvania equipment, Genet turned him in and he was fired. To get even, one night they epoxied his wooden nameplate to the desk at an angle to the edge.

Genet was furious when he saw it the next day. Every morning when he arrived for work, he would try to square the nameplate to the front of the desk and he would swear at it. Every time he left his desk and returned, he would try to straighten it and swear at it. His name plate completely obsessed him. Finally, he showed up at work with a hammer and a chisel, chipped the nameplate off the desk, and covered the damage with a hand towel.

After a few days, my impression was that everyone at Thule was crazy and compressed. Crazy in the sense that insignificant ideas and things became very important to each individual and compressed in the sense that all major feelings and emotions were kept in tight check. I quickly realized that compression was the only mechanism a human could adopt to survive such brutal living conditions.

All sense of reality had disappeared. That's because most people are raised in a temperate climate where there is a balance of daylight and darkness each twenty four-hour period. When we go outside, we see trees, flowers, grass, and vegetation of every type. There are often pets or wildlife nearby. More importantly we have love, understanding, and human warmth from family, loved ones, and friends. These gifts are taken for granted because we've never been without them.

At Thule, everyone was stripped of human support. It was a forbidding place 2,000 miles due north of Boston and close to the North Pole. The environmental clock is totally reset from what it is in the "Real World." All summer, each day has twenty-four hours of light, and all winter, each night has twenty-four hours of darkness. The summer high is 50° above zero and the winter low is -85° below zero with winds over 100 miles per hour. There is no vegetation of any kind, and only an occasional Arctic rabbit or Arctic fox are ever seen. The landscape of dirt and snow, the living conditions, and the weather are all harsh and depressing.

But the worst part of Thule was not having direct contact with family and friends. The commercial telephone lines were almost useless. When they were working and were clear, which wasn't too often, there was a long line of men waiting to use them; a four or five-hour wait wasn't unusual. Everyone was anxious about the people we had left behind. If you didn't keep tight control on your feelings, you could easily get lost. I wanted to survive, so I also became crazy and compressed. Because of the extreme living and working conditions, drinking was the main Thule pastime.

. . . .

Two or three times a week Genet talked on the phone with Sylvania back in Needham, Massachusetts. He didn't use the old commercial lines since the Air Force had a new, underwater cable line installed for military and business use only. Genet reserved a conference room that had a speakerphone and he had all the Sylvania people attend his telecoms. I couldn't figure out why Genet needed anyone there. He would get very upset if anyone else spoke for any length of time. The phone lines were not secure, so the phone conversations had to be unclassified. As a result, only business trivia was passed back and forth.

No matter what was discussed, Genet would get excited, and after a few minutes, he would get angry and tell the people in Needham that they were not appreciative enough of what he was doing for the world, in general, and Sylvania, in particular. After he hung up he would continue to berate Needham, and the whole world, for not recognizing his contributions. Frankly, I could never figure out what his contributions were.

After two or three of these "meetings" I decided I didn't want to sit in on them any more. Genet's ranting and raving embarrassed me, and I was annoyed at his paranoia. I knew if I just stopped attending the telecoms, Genet would be furious and that thought kind of pleased me. However, before I decided to walk out, two incidents occurred that stirred me into action.

The first began when a field engineer, who was known by Sylvania management to be an alcoholic, was sent to Thule. Despite his addiction, they thought they could keep him under control and fulfill the contract, which was lucrative for Sylvania. Management warned him that he would be fired if he drank and then, in their infinite wisdom, management shipped him to a place where he couldn't possibly stay sober.

Genet had nothing to do with that decision but his handling of the situation was shameful. Before the field engineer, Bill Flint, left for Thule, Sylvania sent Genet a letter detailing Flint's past and outlining what steps would be taken to keep him sober. Genet was cautioned to keep this matter private, but he immediately let all six of the Sylvania people at Thule read the letter. In his telecoms, which I still reluctantly attended, he would talk about "the drunk" who was coming to Thule.

When Flint did arrive, his routine was simple. He was required to go to the RCA doctor every day and take two pills. After he had been there for a week, Flint did what everyone initially did; he went out and got drunk. And the pills did exactly what they were supposed to do; they made him extremely sick. The headache, nausea, cramps, and vomiting he had to endure were almost unbearable. When he sobered up, he became almost afraid to drink liquor.

After a couple of weeks, though, he learned to scam the system. He would throw the pills under his tongue, swallow some water, and show the doctor his empty mouth. The minute he left the doctor's office, he would spit the pills into a snow bank.

One night, I was examining some data when I heard a bloodcurdling scream from the work area. After a second high-pitched scream, I walked over to where they'd come from. I saw Flint sitting rigidly in his chair, his feet were flat on the floor and his hands were locked on the armrests. He was crying and staring at a wall clock, which read four o'clock.

Someone asked, "Bill, what's wrong?"

Flint screamed, "What's wrong? What's wrong? I'll tell you what's wrong. Look at that goddamn clock. That's what's wrong. It's 4 AM in Philadelphia and someone is eating my girlfriend and it ain't me."

He jumped up and ran out of the room. After he got back to the base, he avoided being caught and he went on a three-day drinking binge. He was put aboard an Air Force plane strapped to a gurney and suffering from delirium tremens.

The only person who expressed no sorrow or compassion for Flint was Genet. He complained about the extra paperwork that he now had to fill out and how Flint had hurt his image as a manager. Genet's attitude rankled me.

Shortly after Flint left, instead of meeting Genet in the telecom room as I usually did, I walked into his office and saw him going through his mail. Suddenly, Genet picked up a set of blueprints that were bundled together by thick rubber bands and threw them into the wastebasket.

When he saw me looking at him, he explained, "These were sent to Thule by mistake. Needham mails me duplicates quite often. They're really meant to go to the Alaska site."

I was appalled. "Why not return them to Needham and tell them that they were misdirected?" I asked.

"No," Genet said. "I don't want Alaska to complete its library before I do. Fuck them. I'll bet they're throwing my blueprints away. Besides, it's not my fault that those dumb bastards in Needham can't mail things to the proper locations."

I didn't say a word, but I'd had enough. I declared war on Genet. Actually, the battle was over within the hour.

Immediately after the telecom, I said, "Allesandro, I've been listening to these telecoms long enough to realize that there are communication problems, and I think I've finally figured out what's wrong."

Genet looked at me suspiciously and asked, "And what's wrong?"

"Well, to begin with, down at Needham are a bunch of idiots who don't listen to whatever words are being said in English," I said.

Genet got all excited. "Yes, yes, you're absolutely correct. That is what I've been telling all of you."

"But wait, Allessandro, that is only half the problem," I said. "Here at Thule, we have a mean, piss ant, little idiot who doesn't speak a word of English."

Genet sat up in his chair and glared at me. Then, without saying a word, he stood to the full dignity of his five-foot-five frame and stalked out of the room. I stuck my tongue out as he marched through the door. Genet never spoke to me again.

From that point on, I checked the mail and never told Genet when a duplicate set of anything arrived. I quietly brought the documents to the mailroom and had them sent back to Needham. Even better, I never again attended one of Genet's telecoms.

PART II: SURVIVAL

Thule, Greenland, was a harsh, unforgiving environment that either melted or molded a person. The basic elements of life that most people had taken for granted didn't exist there, and each person had to learn to cope for himself. The easiest way to survive the brutal conditions was to recognize the need for honesty and friendship with your fellow workers and to try to find humor in what must be endured.

When a new man arrived, it wasn't long before the bleakness, desolation, and loneliness combined into a depression that sank its hated fangs deeply into his consciousness. The bad feelings started in about one week if it were totally dark, and two weeks if it were totally light. His fellow workers would monitor him closely and, when he was completely depressed, they would take him to the NCO club and drown his sorrows. As they drank, everyone would exchange pictures of their loved ones and discuss personal and private issues, thus welcoming the newcomer to Thule. This would be his initiation into his work group, and it was this group that became his extended family.

My group developed an interesting variation to this ritual. I had found a colored photograph in a magazine of Totie Fields dressed in a tutu. Totie Fields was an overly plump comedienne, and I thought the picture was meant as a publicity stunt because in a semi-ballet pose, she looked more like a sumo wrestler in drag than a dancer. The picture was more surprising than sexual and it was wallet-sized, so I had it encased in plastic and I carried it with me.

Whenever a new man joined the group, the guys waited patiently until he was ready for the NCO club. They would take him there and treat him to whatever beverage was his pleasure. The members of the group who had been there the longest would show him pictures of their spouses and children and occasionally refer to my wife's picture.

As the evening wore on and the drinks flowed more freely, other men would show him their pictures and say, "But this isn't anything like Carp's wife," or, "Boy, you ought to see Carp's wife." They would get the new man to talk about his family and show his pictures. They would examine them and say, "Very very nice, but you really should see the picture of Carp's wife."

The refreshments and the hints would continue until the poor fish finally took the bait. At first, I would be coy, then the poor fish would insist, and I would waffle. Finally, the victim would demand to see a picture of my wife. The group had built him up to a fever pitch. It would be impolite to refuse his request.

I would hand him the picture of Totie Fields. Everyone watched to see what this poor, drunk victim would do and say. Usually, he would look, squint, and then look again, as if he couldn't see too well in the dim light. After staring at it for a while, the victim would hand the picture back to me.

What can one man say about another man's wife? Sometimes the victim gurgled; sometimes he shook his head. All of them finally, with great hesitation, would mumur, "Oh, she's beautiful."

At that point, everyone would laugh, pound the victim on the back, and tell him that it was a trick and that I was a bastard for carrying a picture like that. It was primitive, but it brought everyone together. For individuals struggling against adversities, being part of a group is necessary for survival.

. . . .

At Thule, mail delivery was the most important event of each man's day. Before a man would leave for J-site, he would check his mailbox, and after his shift, he would again check for mail. Even if he knew he wasn't going to get any, his hopes would take him to his mailbox. And, when he did receive a letter, he would sit at a table and draw a cloak of invisible privacy around himself and his letter, apart from the rest of the world. Eating and drinking sustained one's body; mail sustained one's sanity.

I wrote to my wife, Ginny, every other day from work and, in turn, received a letter from her on the same schedule. We had agreed that I would come home immediately if she ever asked. However, she was resolute, and every time I inquired, she told me to keep my agreement with Sylvania of staying a year at Thule. The money was too good to pass up.

I recognized that without structure and discipline at Thule, I could easily go off the deep end. I tried to get to the base gym every other day and work out strenuously. I scrupulously avoided all of the pornographic material and smut that was plentiful and available. Instead, I went to the base library and did a lot of reading. To counter all of this goodness I would go to either the Officer's Club or the Non Commissioned Officer's Club almost every weekend with my group.

After I'd been at Thule for five months, I got a roommate. I was told that Calvin Thomas, an instructor who taught programming back at the West Roxbury training center, was arriving on site. That surprised me because he hadn't worked on BMEWS equipment and I wasn't sure that Thomas had any idea what he was getting into.

Thomas was a Harvard graduate with a degree in sociology. He was brilliant and witty, very talkative, extremely opinionated, and he ran on nervous energy. He had a good sense of humor that was malicious most of the time. When we were at the training center, I'd avoided Thomas as much as I could. I thought he was one of the most egotistical people I'd ever met. When we were first introduced, Thomas told me that he had graduated summa cum laude and that he considered himself the smartest person he had ever met. He also said that he became a programmer because it paid so much more money than he had been making. His nervousness, along with his egotism, discouraged me from ever getting close to him. And now we were going to be roommates.

I met Thomas's plane when it landed. His batteries hadn't run down since I'd last seen him; he still seemed quick and nervous. On the way to the barracks, his chatter was nonstop. "I'm going to stay here for two full years and climb to the top of this money tree. Since all my food and shelter are provided courtesy of RCA, I'm going to bank every penny that I make and then I'll go to Denmark and join my wife, Inge. She's a Danish national and she just moved back to Copenhagen with her mother and father. By the way, I speak perfect Danish.

"After I make all this money, we'll live in Denmark and I'll write novels that will make me famous and earn me even more money. I've planned everything. You'll be able to tell all your friends that you once had a very famous roommate."

I didn't say anything. I just listened. When we got to the room, Thomas looked around and asked, "Is this the best you could do?"

I told him the Air Force only had one size. He sniffed and then said, "Well, it really doesn't matter. All I've got to do is sleep here for two years and I'll be rich, rich, rich."

When I asked him which group he was going to be working with, Thomas replied, "Probably the data takeoff area, but it doesn't make much difference. There isn't anything I can't master very quickly."

Thomas started on the day shift while I stayed on nights. I asked him if he wanted to meet for breakfasts, but after two days, he stopped showing up.

My first hint that there might be trouble came a week later. I was in the mess hall sitting alone and reading a letter from Ginny when the mess hall manager, Lenny Giustinani, came over and sat down at my table. It was considered a breach of manners to interrupt a man while he was reading mail. However, Giustinani and I were good friends, so I gathered that he had something important to say. I put my letter down.

"Jay, I hate to interrupt you, but maybe you should talk to your roommate. He's breathing a scab on his nose. He told the group he works with that he knows more about programming than all of them combined, and he doesn't spend any time with them. He sits only with the Danes and speaks only Danish."

"Listen," I said, "he probably does know more than all of them put together, and he's married to a Danish girl. So why shouldn't he sit and speak Danish?"

"That's not my point," Guistinani continued. "Whether he's right or wrong doesn't make a bit of difference to me. My cooks tell me they don't trust him because he insults his fellow Americans, and the RCA guys can't stand him because he acts superior to them. What he's doing is upsetting my entire kitchen staff and that bothers me. I need them calm if I'm to do a good job. This isn't a good situation."

"OK, Larry," I said. "You're right. It sounds like he is causing problems. I don't think he understands the trouble he's causing or the trouble he's getting into. I'll try to talk with him, that is, providing he'll speak in English."

I left messages for Thomas in both our room and at J-site saying that I wanted to talk with him. Thomas avoided all contact with me; he didn't even come back to the room.

Three days later, as I was coming down the hall after taking a shower, Ingmar, the Dane who cleaned the latrine on our floor approached me. I liked Ingmar. He was a young man who wanted to go to college in Copenhagen and had taken this job to earn money. I occasionally helped him with his English pronunciation. He had a heavy accent, and his grammar was more à la carte than consistent. He seemed nervous as he asked, "Mr. Jay, may I speak?"

"Sure, Ingmar, come on in." After I opened the door to my room, Ingmar looked up and down the corridor and then walked in.

He was flustered. "Mr. Jay, your roommate, is he an OK man?"

"You mean Calvin Thomas?"

Ingmar nodded his head.

"Are you asking if he's queer?" I asked.

Ingmar looked puzzled.

I thought a second. "Do you mean does he like men instead of women?" Ingmar smiled; that's what he meant.

I laughed, "No, Ingmar, he does not like men instead of women. What made you think that he did?"

Ingmar said, "It not right that he don't stay with his own and speak his own language. He speaks our language very odd, he gets drunk in our barracks, and he says terrible things about his own kind. We wonder if he says terrible about us in his other language."

I doubted that Thomas was bad mouthing anything Danish, but I couldn't say because I hadn't spoken to him since he went native. However, I decided to find out. I left my shift early to see Thomas and find out what was going on.

I was sitting in the mess hall when he came through the chow line. He came over to my table and sat down. "I guess I should have told you that I was sleeping in the Danish barracks," Thomas said.

"I guess you should have," I said.

"I've been on a binge."

"I heard."

"Listen, Jay," Thomas said. "Since I sobered up, I've been studying you and all these other stolid peasants. I've finally figured out how you dull people manage to stand this place. Now that I know, I'm going to act exactly the way you do. I'm going to last two years and make a lot of money."

I didn't believe he could do it. Thomas had been at Thule about three weeks and he had alienated everyone. The Americans didn't like him and the Danes didn't trust him. He was intelligent, but he was also a damn fool. I would have preferred to have nothing to do with Thomas, but I felt obligated to try to help him, so I shifted my hours slightly to make myself available to talk to him.

Much to my surprise, Thomas welcomed the chance to tell me what he thought of everyone at Thule, including me. One morning, he came back from the latrine and said, "Those damn hillbillies are playing their hillbilly music too loud. You probably haven't noticed, but there is absolutely no culture around here. I'll bet none of these hillbillies have ever heard of Bach or Beethoven. All I hear in the dorm is that damn hillbilly music. Every one on this floor is a damn hillbilly."

In another few days, he told me, "I saw those goddamn hillbillies that play that goddamn hillbilly music too loud. They sure are unsavory looking."

A few more days passed, and then Thomas said, "Those fucking hillbillies who play their fucking hillbilly music look like fucking rabbits."

The final stage would come when, after a while, he would say, "You all look like fucking rabbits," and then he would go on a three-day drinking binge.

After he sobered up, he again swore that he was going to act like the stolid peasants around him. Within a week, he went through the hillbilly and rabbit routine again, and headed for the NCO Club. Less than a month later, Thomas was on a plane to Denmark and I never saw or heard from him again. I often wonder what happened to him.

I was never able to brag about having a famous roommate.

PART III REVIVAL

Nothing can make a human happier than to rediscover something precious that has been lost and mourned. I was elated to get back to the "Real World" after more than eleven months in Thule.

After I'd finished my ten-month commitment, I notified Sylvania that I wanted to come home. Ginny had recently given birth to our third daughter and I was anxious to return to the "Real World" and see my family.

My going-away party was long and loud, and included a lot of alcohol. One of my former students asked for the picture of my "wife," so I left Totie Fields in good hands. I told the group that in honor of my going away, they should epoxy Genet's towel to his desk at an angle. During the celebration I was asked for my home address and phone number and I naïvely gave the information to the group without thinking anything about it. That was a mistake I regretted for many years after my return.

I returned to Foxboro and went on a three week vacation with my family. At first I couldn't get over the beauty of ordinary life. I reveled in talking with my three daughters even though the newest one couldn't reply. I would get up before dawn so I could hear the birds wake up. We went to Cape Cod and Cape Ann to see an ocean that was not a sheet of ice. We walked in woods and my family worried when I hugged trees and patted bushes. It was a relief not to have to worry about being caught outdoors and freezing to death.

When my vacation was over, I went back to work and was given my choice of several projects to work on. I chose one that I thought would help the troops fighting in Vietnam. Like the war itself, the project I chose turned out to be a bad choice, but that's grist for a different mill.

It took about two months after I returned to the "Real World" before I began to realize the mistake I'd made in giving out my address and phone number. I got home from work one evening and Ginny said, "You've had two phone calls from a Darrel Perkins in Austin, Texas."

I asked, "Did he say what he wanted?"

"No. He didn't say. All he would say is that he's anxious to talk to you."

Just then the phone rang. I picked it up and a voice with a heavy Texas drawl asked, "Mister Jay Carp, please?"

"Yes, this is he."

"Good evening, sir, this is Darrel Perkins talking. I've your application right here in front of me and it looks very good sir, very good. As soon as you send me your check for $800, we can start you in business."

"Application? $800? I'm sorry, Mr. Perkins, but I have no idea about any application or any business. What are you talking about?" I asked, confused.

Perkins replied in his deep drawl, "You wrote me about starting a hearing aid business in Foxboro, Massachusetts. That's what you said in your letter."

"No sir, I didn't," I said. "This is the first I've heard of any application. It certainly didn't come from me." As an afterthought, I asked, "What else does it say in the letter?"

"Well, it says you are in some place called Thule but you'll be home soon and for me to contact you in about a month," he replied. "The only other thing your letter said was that, because of the type of people you had to deal with, you wanted to change careers. You are making the right choice going into the hearing aid business."

I caught on immediately. My "friends" in Thule had invented a new game and I was in the crosshairs. I hadn't even known that the game had begun. I tried to explain to Perkins that we both had been victims of pranksters. Perkins said maybe we were, but while he had me on the phone, I really should go into business for myself. It took me quite a while to convince him that I wouldn't send him any money under any condition.

Two days later, I received a letter from Thule signed by nineteen of my group. They wanted to tell me the results of epoxying Genet's towel to his desk. When he saw the towel, Giorgio called RCA "bastards," Sylvania "bastards," the Air Force, "bastards," and Jay Carp, "bastard bastard." After a week of trying to straighten out the towel, he quit his job and flew back to France. They all thanked me and, in a postscript, they added that I would be hearing from everyone at Thule.

And they were right. Nineteen men with spare time, scissors, and dozens of different magazines to read meant disaster for me. They clipped every available coupon asking for free information to be mailed to the undersigned. Soon after I got the letter, I was swamped, inundated, and drowned in junk mail. The Missouri School of Butchery, Wig Wonders, Shoes for Sale, Valdosta Hair Cutting College, and the Rhode Island Truck Driving Institute were just a few of the hundreds of franchise names that began contacting me. Every day I would come home to find three or four pounds of junk mail waiting for me to sort through. The Foxboro post office was not pleased, the mail man was unhappy, Ginny was annoyed and I, as the recipient, got angry. Especially as the amount of junk mail increased and lasted so long. Years later, I met several of the people who initiated the junk mail campaign and they told me they had only clipped coupons for a month; after that they lost interest and went on to something else. I guess mailing lists and dandelions are both impossible to eradicate. There was no let up in the amount of junk mail I received.

Despite my bulging mail box my life returned to a normal pattern. The project I had selected was abruptly cancelled a year and a half after I started working on it. I was transferred to the Minuteman missile program and went to the same maintenance classes that the Air Force technicians were taking. After the class was over, my family and I moved to Grand Forks, North Dakota.

That proved to be my salvation because the United States Post Office does not forward junk mail; it only forwards first class mail. Even after being home almost two years, I was still flooded with junk mail. There was no way that either the post office or I could stop it. The move to Grand Forks was the antidote; the tide of junk mail disappeared. I could rejoice in only receiving bills.

The only lesson I learned was never give away your home address when a project ends and you are moving on. However, I often wonder if my friends ever clipped magazine coupons for our mutual good friend, Allesandro Giorgio.

'Tis the Season to Be Jolly— Isn't It?

This past Sunday I sat down to watch my beloved New England Patriots play the dreaded Dallas Cowboys. As I enjoyed the game, because the Patriots won, I saw an advertisement for a new movie soon to be released. One of the scenes in the ad showed a boy sitting on Santa's lap. Santa's moustache and beard, which were hanging about an inch below his chin, were obviously false.

Boy: "You're not the real Santa. You don't have any hair."

Santa: "I used to."

Boy: "What happened?"

Santa: "I loved a woman who was not clean."

The name of the movie is "Evil Santa," and I have absolutely no intention of seeing it.

Once upon a time, many years ago, the spirit that motivated the Christmas Season was treated with more reverence. The religious significance, which motivates the spirit of Christmas, was not obscured behind pop-up ads or tacky commercial enterprises. Not having Santa Claus hawking tasteless merchandise allowed the Christmas Season to fit very snugly into our calendar of events. In the past, the season would start the day after Thanksgiving and continue through until about mid January. The demarcation between Thanksgiving and Christmas was sharp and satisfying.

My good friend and neighbor for almost thirty years, Joseph Fertitta, loved the Christmas Season, and he would take vacation days from his work just to cook and bake for Christmas. He almost had to. He and his wife, Josephina, had seven children, and so much family came to visit them that I often wondered if anyone stayed at home in Boston and in Italy. The Fertitta's enjoyed a busy, but a simple, Christmas. What was important to them was family, friends, food, and peace on earth, good will to all.

It was during this period that I had my own cranberry bread company. My family, three daughters, my wife, Virginia, and I baked six or seven dozen loaves of cranberry bread each year for distribution to friends, business acquaintances, teachers, neighbors, and other unwary innocents. I got started because my wife, Virginia, did not like to cut the cranberries and I became the designated cranberry cutter. Over the years, our jobs shifted, and my daughters and I did the baking and Virginia did the wrapping and decorating. Baking cranberry bread, and then handing them out as gifts, was a Christmas tradition for our family.

The Christmas Season that pleased me the most occurred after my family and I went to Grand Forks, North Dakota. That was in the summer of 1963. Travelling to the missile sites located in the eastern half of North Dakota, I became aware of the appalling living conditions on the Indian Reservations. The survivors of their once proud culture were left neglected and on the edge of poverty.

As Christmas approached, Virginia and I began our yearly budgetary battle over how much money to spend on our daughters. We would always be miles apart when we started. I would say that she was a spendthrift and she would say that I was a skinflint, and, eventually, we would reach a compromise. A few days after our negotiations, Virginia and I went to the only indoor mall in Grand Forks. As we entered, we could see that two huge pine trees, one at each end of the mall, had just been put up. The trees were about twenty feet tall. The top third of the trees had Christmas lights and decorations, the middle third had no decorations, and the bottom third had little notes tied to the tree.

I walked over to the tree and looked at a note at random. It had a number on the back to identify the Indian child who had written it. "My name is Susie and I am seven. I would have a Merry Christmas if I could have warm gloves for me and my four-year-old sister and a warm scarf for my mother. Thank you and Merry Christmas." I took the note off the tree and showed it to Virginia, she read it and just shook her head. Then, she walked over to the tree, picked out a note, read it, and handed it to me. "My Christmas list would be a baseball mitt for me, a doll for my little sister, and some elastic stockings and a new coat for my mother."

We did not buy anything. We turned around, went home, and shared the notes with our daughters. The next evening, the five of us came back the mall and bought the items asked for along with ribbons, wrapping paper, boxes, and candy bars. On the way out, we took three more notes off the tree. We went home and wrapped the gifts, making sure that we put plenty of candy bars in each package. Up until Christmas Eve, we were taking notes off the tree and fulfilling small dreams.

My daughters got far fewer presents than they normally did but I don't believe they noticed or cared. That year, our Christmas was much simpler and more meaningful and even I had no bone to pick with Santa Claus.

Nowadays, we seem to be straying from the spirit of Christmas. This last October 24, a Friday and a full week before Halloween, I went to the Briarwood mall. Almost every store in the mall had Christmas gifts and decorations on display and available for purchase. At first, I was startled, because I thought it was an early start to commercial Christmas. After thinking about it, though, I won't be surprised when I see the Fourth of July parades showcasing Santa Claus in front of the marching troops. Christmas selling seems to have overtaken Christmas spirit.

Merchandizing is now aimed at having youngsters tell their parents what they need for Christmas. And the merchants make sure that there is no shortage of things to show the youngsters. In addition, for the affluent, there are Christmas baubles from the likes of Nieman Marcus. A few people can, and do, spend hundreds of thousands of dollars on his and her robots, jewel studded bras, or whatever items of conspicuous consumption catch their eye. This suggests to the overwhelming majority of ordinary households that they are missing out on the fun unless they buy at the same pace. Sooner or later, some corporation is going to commission the composition of new Christmas carols, like, "Spend 'til Season's End," or "The Credit Card Carol."

The most disturbing results of the tinseling of Christmas are the effects that it has upon younger parents and children. Coping with the ever-growing Christmas expenses is hard on families. This worry, along with the burdens of keeping up with the Jones' and the peer pressure exerted on their children, makes parents tense and nervous. Doctors say that ever-increasing numbers of people become depressed at Christmas and I believe it. The thought of Christmas now seems to bring almost as much dread to some people as it does delight to others.

I see this reflected in the families of my daughters. They spend a fortune buying their children whatever they ask for. By late in the afternoon of Christmas Day, most of my grandchildren are bored and their parents are burnt out. I have suggested to my daughters that being able to say no to their children is every bit as important as being able to say yes. They haven't quite gotten the message yet.

I can only hope that someday everyone will remember what is truly important about the Christmas Season. In an effort to refresh my own memories and show my daughters their early Christmas years, I have gathered our Christmas letters of years past which we put into Christmas cards, and had them bound. I have said nothing to my daughters and they will only find out when they unwrap this present on Christmas day. I will be interested in their reaction.

Our Trip to Havana

It was on the flight from Ft. Lauderdale to Cancun that I thought about visiting Cuba. According to the flight map in the airplane's magazine, we were skirting that bastion of communism located sixty miles away from Florida. I have always been curious about this nation of eleven million people that has threatened Washington D.C. for over forty years. In truth though, I had also been curious about the Russians when they posed a similar threat to us during the cold war.

I remembered that last year, when I had been in Cancun, I had heard that there were daily flights between Cancun and Havana. It got me thinking and I turned to Hazel, whose time-share unit was in Cancun, and asked her if she were interested in visiting Cuba. Hazel has been going to Cancun for over twenty years and she had never been to Cuba, so she was delighted with the possibility. After we checked into her time-share, I went to the travel agency down in the lobby to find out if there were any restrictions on Americans going to Cuba from Mexico.

According to the travel agent there were none. When we bought our tickets to fly to Havana, he would take our passports to the Mexican government and we would be issued Mexican visas. That was so that the Cuban government would not stamp our passports, which would, of course, be examined in Cuba. There would be no physical record of our trip on our passports. However, the travel agent did tell me to convert our money into Canadian dollars before we left Mexico, as it was illegal to use either Mexican or American money in Cuba.

The question then became when to go to Cuba. We had arrived on December 19th and we were coming back to Ann Arbor on the 31st, and we had already decided to visit Merida, a city on the other side of the Yucatan Peninsula. Looking at a calendar, I suggested that we fly to Havana on the 24th of December and celebrate Christmas in Cuba. We hoped that three days and two nights in Havana would at least give us a flavor of that city. With that in mind we bought tickets, made hotel reservations, and exchanged traveler's check for Canadian money. We looked forward not only to our trip but also to the chance to thumb our noses at George W. Bush. It wasn't much of a thumb but it was all that we could muster.

We passed through immigration at the Havana airport without difficulty and it was about a three quarter hour drive from the airport to our hotel. Even from our initial drive it was evident that Cuba was a very poor country. There was not much vehicular traffic on their main highways. We had noticed that as our plane came in for a landing and it was much more apparent as we drove. Almost all of the houses needed paint and repairs. Their corrugated roofs were rusty and everything looked dilapidated and run down. At first, I wondered if it weren't just the district we were passing through. Later on, I found that this was the general condition of most of the houses that people lived in.

As we got closer to downtown Havana I did see something that I had never seen before, a tractor trailer bus. The Cubans have taken the trailers and modified them to carry passengers. They have lowered the trailer body, between the tractor hitch and the back wheels, almost to the ground. This allows passengers to get on and off as they would on a regular bus. The roofline, instead of being straight, now has a square U shape where the lowered section is. The sides of these trailers have bus windows and every one of these busses that we saw was absolutely jammed with passengers.

We were driven to our hotel, Hotel Plaza, and we registered and went to our room. The travel agent had told us that the Plaza had been built in 1908 and that it was located in downtown Havana. What he neglected to mention was that it had not been updated from the day it opened. It was badly in need of repairs and refurbishment. The door into our room was almost ten feet tall, the room had a ceiling that was fifteen feet high, and there were heavy wooden shutters instead of windows. These older buildings were built so that air could freely circulate and cut down the oppressive heat. The room was small. It was sparsely furnished with two beds and two lamps, built in drawers, and a small television set that had three Spanish speaking stations. The ceiling was flaking and pieces of it were in the corners. The shutters were nailed tightly in place and could not be moved. This made the room dark and the only light was from the two lamps. Each lamp had a forty-watt bulb, certainly not enough light to blind us but enough, when they were both on, so that we could find our way around the room. At least the bathroom was adequate with plenty of hot water. It was very apparent that the Plaza had passed its prime sometime before Hazel and I arrived.

We unpacked and went back to the lobby to see what was available to us "gringos." When we got downstairs we examined the only Christmas decoration we had seen since we arrived. It was a potted tree, about fifteen feet tall, adorned with purple, orange, blue, red, and yellow balls. They were old and faded and the tree was sparse and lopsided, but that tree was the first indication we had seen that Christmas was coming. There had been no Christmas lights, no decorations, and no "Felice Navidad" signs such as there were in Mexico. I had forgotten that Christianity and Castro's communism clashed with each other.

We exchanged our Canadian Money for Cuban pesos and were given brand new notes. I also found out that there was a tour of Havana starting the next morning at 9:00 AM and lasting for four hours. When I asked if the tour would be scheduled, even on Christmas Day, I was told, politely but firmly, that tomorrow was another business day and that the tour would go on. In Cuba, I discovered that it was not the Grinch who stole Christmas. We bought our tickets and then walked through the front door, guarded by two doormen, to see Havana. The Plaza Hotel faced a huge esplanada, a long straight boulevard that had a very wide park down its center. To our right, across the street was a new building that housed a modern hotel. We walked by it and saw that, inside the lobby, was a modern, attractive, restaurant. We went to the center of the esplanada, and, since it was warm, we sat and people watched.

There were cars, trucks, and tractor-trailer busses but not nearly as many as a comparable city of two million would have in our country. The cars were old and there were not many new ones. There were a lot three-wheeled taxis that were round in shape and, at a distance, resembled large oranges because of their color. The driver rode in front leaning on handlebars while his two passengers sat on a small bench behind him. A tiny gasoline engine powered it. Other taxis were three-wheeled tricycles, which the driver peddled. Neither of these taxis had lights and, after dark, they were a danger. They would not slow down or veer away from pedestrians.

We returned to our hotel and decided to have dinner in the hotel restaurant. It was large dining room and every place at every table was set with dazzling white tablecloths, shining silverware, and fan folded napkins. It was also completely empty except for us. The food was excellent but eating by ourselves, in all that splendor with the waiters standing by, was eerie.

Thus ended Christmas Eve in Havana.

The next day, Christmas, we went for breakfast, which was

served on the top floor, away from the lobby restaurant. That was because a free breakfast was included with our room accommodation. It was a large buffet with ham, sausage, bacon, freshly baked bread, sweet rolls, omelets, fried eggs, soft boiled eggs, fruits, vegetables and fruit juices of all kinds. The orange juice was the sweetest I have ever tasted and they also had peach juice, which was refreshing. What surprised me was that they served cold slaw with breakfast. It was chopped finely and had pieces of yellow squash in it. It was different but very tasty.

After we ate, we had a couple of hours to kill until it was time to go on the tour and, eventually, we ended up going for coffee at the hotel across the street. Their lobby was fresh and modern and had the only other Christmas tree we saw while we were in Cuba. Their tree was larger than our tree and the decorations exuded much more Christmas spirit.

The tour was an eye opener. Our tour guide was a woman who spoke excellent English. Almost all of the other people on the tour were from Latin American countries so she spoke in Spanish first and then in English. We toured all of Havana with stops at the old squares, the ancient churches (which were closed), the suburbs, and all of the monuments to the Revolution that brought Fidel Castro to power. We stopped at a park for children, which had just been opened, named the Elan Gonzales Park.

Most everything we saw was in a state of disrepair. We drove down the street that fronts the Gulf of Mexico. Almost every building had boarded up windows, broken doors, and had vagrants living in them. The buildings had once been handsome but now they badly needed repairs. What struck me was that this was prime property, in a beautiful location, which, in any other capitol in the world, would be worth a fortune and would be kept in mint condition.

We toured some open-air markets, which were jammed with people and beggars, and we passed places that Hemingway had frequented when he lived in Havana. One of them was a restaurant that was close to our hotel.

Our guide's description of the Revolution that overturned Batista was passionate. For Cubans, their fight against tyranny is as important to them as the American Revolution is to us. Most Cubans have known no other leader than Castro and, in return for his dictatorship, he has instituted two good policies for the Cuban people. The literacy rate in Cuba is over ninety percent and there is free medical care for everyone.

Our tour lasted much longer than four hours. It was after 3:00 PM when we got back to our hotel. I did not want to face the glare of the forty-watt bulbs in our room so I suggested that we go get a drink across the street at the restaurant in the new hotel. As we sat there, we struck up a conversation with a couple at the next table. They were Americans and had just returned from touring Hemingway's cottage, located a few miles outside of Havana. They were very disappointed because the cottage is literally falling down and the Cuban government has no money to fix it up.

We talked among ourselves for a while and they happened to mention that they were going to the ballet this evening. We asked where the theatre was and they told us it was right across the esplanada from where we were. When we left the hotel, Hazel and I went to see if they had any tickets left for the evening performance.

The home of the Ballet Nacional de Cuba is a big granite building, a magnificent looking structure from the outside. We went inside to buy tickets. The price was twenty pesos for any seat in the house whether it is on the main floor or the highest balcony. The only seats not available to the public were those in a government box in the first balcony, which was always held for government officials. Castro would occasionally come to see a performance but his presence was never mentioned ahead of time. Our tour guide had told us that Cubans don't even know where he lives. Ever since Bobby Kennedy and the CIA tried to assassinate him, Castro had become even more secretive about his whereabouts.

While we were in the theatre, we paid for a guided tour of the building. Our tour guide was a pert, pretty young lady who was an actress in the Cuban National Theatre. She took us through all of the rehearsal rooms, small auditoriums, and finally, the large auditorium where the Ballet Company danced. Large sections of the building had mounds of plaster and debris heaped along the long corridors and neither the men's room nor the ladies room had running water. The government is restoring the building and only the large auditorium was immaculate with plush seats, bright colors, and a gilded ceiling. The restoration is slow because of the lack of funds.

After our tour, we went back to our hotel and got ready for our evening activities. When it started to get dark, we walked over to the restaurant we had seen on our tour. Every time we crossed the street we had to watch out for the rolling oranges and the tricycles because they loomed out of the dark and had no concern for pedestrians. I felt like a bowling pin standing in the middle of the lane with the ball rolling directly at me.

As we walked we noticed that the tall buildings had their large upper story windows open and groups of people were gathered at each window. Most of the windows had laundry hanging off their iron balconies and railings and the people were talking to each other and to their neighbors. It was a friendly atmosphere.

The restaurant was small and clean and the waiters wore black suits, white shirts and black ties. The service was slow. We were left to ourselves for a long time before we got menus and before they took our orders. However, we were in no hurry and the food more than made up for the delays. When the waiter brought the check he also gave Hazel a flower and me a cigar. I don't know whether that was to make up for the service or to guarantee a bigger tip, or both.

We walked back across the esplanada and noticed that the streets were mobbed with people casually strolling around or sitting and talking with one another. No one was in a hurry and it was a relaxed and pleasant scene. We got to the theatre just a few minutes before the lights were turned down. The auditorium was almost full and, from our seats close to the stage, we could see the couple we had met in the restaurant. They were sitting in the first balcony in a pair of box seats.

The Ballet Company performed four individual ballets. Three were modern ballet pieces danced to music of Spanish composers while the fourth was a classical ballet danced to an adagio of Mendelssohn. I was surprised to find that I enjoyed the modern ballet more than the classical. The young, lithe dancers were exuberant as they gracefully spun around the stage. At times, their gestures were so fluid that you couldn't believe what you were seeing. They were exciting to watch. The dancing was both sensuous and sensual. When the dancers finished each of the modern ballets, the audience stood up and applauded and whistled. I was glad to be part of the standing ovation. Those dancers were magnificent.

We walked back to the hotel in an aura of goodwill towards the dancers and the people of Cuba. It had been an interesting day.

The next morning we had another sumptuous breakfast, and then we packed for our return flight home. We had to check out of our rooms early and when we got to the desk I tried to exchange our Cuban pesos for Canadian dollars. I was told that this was not possible to do at a hotel desk. That left us with 200 Cuban pesos and four hours to pass until time to leave for the airport. I suggested that we take a cab ride to Morro Castle, which was about four miles from our hotel.

Hazel agreed so I went to the doorman and asked him to get us a cab and I told him our destination. He shook his head "Yes," and then ran off down the street. He came back a few minutes later and said that a cab would be here shortly. About five minutes later, our cab showed up. It was a 1953 Chevrolet Impala and the outside of the cab was in immaculate condition. There were no bumps, no dents, no rust, and the paint gleamed. When we got in, I could see that the inside has also been carefully taken care of. There were no rips or tears in the soft leather seats and everything was clean. However, the cab did have one problem. Every time it slowed down, the engine would emit black, sooty smoke and either idle roughly or stall. Because of the embargo, motor parts for old cars are impossible to get.

Our driver did not speak English but the doorman had told him our destination so he drove us over to the fort that guarded Havana's harbor. As we left the cab and walked over to the entrance we could see individual merchants setting up their vending tables in anticipation of the tourists. One of the vendors told us that Morro Castle wasn't open yet but to go ahead inside and look around. We walked through a long, vaulted corridor that had been built centuries before. The corridor was made out of rough stones and the floor was very uneven and slippery because of its rounded stones. When we emerged from the corridor we were where the old cannons had been mounted on the parapets and we had a magnificent view of the harbor and the city. The waves were dashing against the seawall and the spray was flying high into the air. We watched in awe until we started to get chilled. We headed for the entrance to the fort itself where there were five or six people standing around. I gathered they were Cubans who worked at the fort. One of the men said, "Go on in." So we did. We had gotten no further then thirty feet when a woman, in a brown uniform started running towards us screaming and waving her arms. When she reached us she yelled, "Get out. You have no right to be here. You are not allowed. We are not open. Go back and get in line."

When we returned to where the other people were standing she began to shout at them in Spanish. The man who had told us to go in came up and said, "I am sorry, Senor." I smiled and thanked him.

After all, it wasn't his fault that a dragon guarded Morrow Castle. We returned to our cab and were driven back to the hotel.

As we were going through customs and immigration at the airport we discovered a unique Cuban custom. No one is allowed to leave the country without first paying a thirty pesos departure tax. And it has to be in Cuban pesos, no other currency is accepted. Now we were down to less than 150 Cuban pesos.

While we were waiting for our plane, we struck up a conversation with a young American man who was also flying to Cancun. He was going there to meet his girlfriend. He was presently working in Havana doing some legal research for Fordham University where he was a senior in their law school. He had been in Cuba about a year and he would shortly be heading back to Fordham to complete his studies. He informed us that Cuba has two monetary systems, one for Cuban citizens and one for foreigners arriving in Cuba. He also told us that, because of the embargo, any ship that arrives in a Cuban port is automatically barred from American waters for six months. He made no personal comments but he did indicate that he hoped American policy would change.

When we returned to Cancun, I tried to convert our Cuban pesos into either Canadian dollars or Mexican pesos at the same bank that had exchanged our Canadian money. They weren't buying. Not even the time-share cashier would accept the Cuban money or apply it towards the bill. As a result, we returned to Ann Arbor richer in experiences but poorer by 150 Cuban pesos.

I do have some observations about the trip. None of them are earth shaking but all of them are personal. Here are my trivial observations.

One of the blessings of being a poor country is that there are not many people carrying cell phones. The Cubans enjoy talking to each other directly rather than by satellite.

Museums and shops are never open at the times listed. Only in the lobbies of the two hotels did I ever see a clock. The upside of this is that there probably aren't many people in Havana with stomach ulcers.

You can see the ethnic changes that have occurred over the centuries in any crowd in Cuba. The skin colors are black, tan, red, or white, with no one color being dominant.

Havana may have a water problem. On the first day of the trip, I saw a small tank truck similar to the trucks that deliver oil to single homes, double-parked near the hotel. I noticed that there were people standing beside it and drawing something from the tank. I walked over and saw that they were being given water. I didn't think anything about that until the next day when I saw another larger truck parked near the same spot. This truck was also a tank truck but it was much bigger, similar to the trucks that deliver to gas stations. There was a line of people, some had oil drums on dollies, getting water. After that I paid attention and, on our tour, I saw water trucks delivering water in various neighborhoods of Havana.

I asked the law student at the airport and he told me that sometimes, in the summer heat, the authorities have to bring in extra drinking and bathing water. I let it go at that because I didn't want to press the point that our conversation was in December, not summertime.

Cubans would come up to us and ask where we were from. When we answered, "Michigan," they would immediately say that they had relatives either in Miami or Detroit and then shake hands. They would strike up a conversation and, a few minutes later, try to sell something. I calculated that there must be eleven million Cubans in Miami and Detroit.

Here are my somber observations.

I feel sad that both governments stand between the Cuban and the American people.

I also believe that the Cuban people deserve better than Fidel Castro. He is a dictator and, like all dictators, he is cruel and vindictive. Do not forget that he has killed many innocent people. I believe that, even though he got rid of an oppressive regime, he has made a poor country even poorer.

I strongly believe that the policy of our government towards Cuba is a total and complete failure. Our government is illogical and it has never gotten over either the Cuban Missile crisis or the Bay of Pigs fiasco. In the past, we backed the likes of Batista, Pinochet, and Noriega and they were at least as brutal and as corrupt as Castro. Yet, we did business with them. But Washington will not forgive Castro for taunting it for forty years. We should open up trade and let the Cubans see what a free society can do for them. If morality is so important for Cuba, why don't we have an embargo on China and Saudi Arabia?

I only wish that, when Fidel Castro made his infamous visit to the United Nations headquarters in New York, he had stood up and simply said, "Let my people go."

The Big House

As I rapidly approach senility, I glance back and discover that the younger generations seem to be mired in disagreement and discontent. Considering what is happening in our lives today, that is an unfortunate, but not a completely unexpected, state of affairs.

The comfort zone for middle-class families and individuals has been dangerously compressed by the costs of gas and food, job losses and home repossessions. These deep personal problems are against a continual background of election tom-toms that beat out nothing but tommyrot. It is no wonder that civility seems to be heading the way of the kerosene lamp.

Under these conditions, the general impression always is that things are bad and nothing can be done. However, that is an attitude that is not correct. We humans have created most of our problems and we should be able to figure out most of our solutions. The trick is to overcome our individual lethargy and act in good conscience.

The method I use to face these large problems is to select the one that is the least emotional for me and ask it to dance. I waltz with it, cha-cha with it, tango with it. I am looking for new ways to approach old ideas and I reason that, once I make a breakthrough on a less thorny issue, I can work on a more disturbing problem.

I did this recently to a problem that has been provoking much controversy in the Ann Arbor area for a long time—the University of Michigan football stadium, otherwise known as THE BIG HOUSE. Much to my surprise, I found that there was one option that had never been discussed and that, if adopted, would forever cure all University of Michigan athletic revenue problems.

It is a very simple solution. The present plan calls for constructing the stadium upward; anyone driving along Main Street can see the steel skeleton rising high above the street. However, there may be an unexplored dimension. Along with high-rising the stadium, why not stretch it? Expand the north end of the stadium and lengthen the playing field from 100 yards to 200 yards.

Just picture how many thousands, no, tens of thousands, of new seats can be built in the newly created 120-yard extension between the present 40-yard lines. When combined with the "upward" expansion of the stadium, the new seating capacity will be enough to make every athletic director in the country salivate. And, rest assured, they will.

This approach immediately raises questions. Will the National Collegiate Athletic Association (NCAA) approve of something so new and so radical? How will the games be played until every stadium has 200-yard fields? If we build it, will they come? Initially, the NCAA will be adamantly opposed to any change to the size of the football field. They will be upset and dismayed and cite tradition and collegiate values as their only goals.

However, after the first flush of negative reactions, reason and finance will soon prevail.

First, let's look at tradition. The size of the football field is an arbitrary length decided upon over a century ago. Its dimensions started somewhere in the past in a school in Rugby, England. The game itself was not as wide open as it is today. There were no spread offenses and no passing so the field was only big enough for the smash-mouthed type of game that was played back then. Today, with passing plays of 30 to 40 yards, lengthening the field would make for interesting opportunities.

Remember that, not so long ago, tradition held that a football player played both offensively as well as defensively. Then, to make the game faster and more exciting, offensive, defensive and special teams were introduced. The idea of the iron-man in football became slightly skewed and it seems that tradition can readily be spun around by football turnstiles.

The athletes of long ago did not work out all year long. They were not as large, as fast, or as strong as are the present-day athletes. Nor were the games of yesteryear the subject of so much advanced publicity along with the huge crowds that today's football games enjoy. Considering all the changes that have taken place everywhere but on the football field, it is time for a change. Once Michigan demonstrates the idea of the 200-yard field, our jealous arch rivals will copy us as quickly as they can.

Of course the rules of today's games will have to be altered to fit the longer field, but the NCAA has always had a standing committee that reviewed the rules every year. With a little forethought, the transition should be smooth and orderly. Until the NCAA accepts "The Michigan Plan," the University of Michigan can still stage its home games on a regulation-sized field in its new, enlarged stadium. If large screen monitors are placed around the top of the new stadium, the views should be as good, if not better, than in the present stadium.

As to the question of, "If we build it, will they come?", there seems to be little doubt as to the answer. There probably never will be a shortage of people who will want to attend a football game. First, there are the football faithful who presently go to the stadium to see the games and participate in the electric atmosphere that now surrounds these events. Then, there will be the student body, which is getting larger every year, as well as the ever-expanding Alumni Association. The new stadium, with its improved facilities, more restrooms, gift shops and restaurants, will draw even more fans. Because of the huge increase in the number of seats, it may even be possible to reduce the price of individual tickets and still increase the revenue flow coming into the athletic department.

An enhanced stadium will be a financial boon not only to the university but also to the city and the state. However, care must be taken so that the weight and depth of the added influx of visitors doesn't overwhelm and crush Ann Arbor itself. If there are going to be any problems, they will be in the areas of coordination and cooperation among all the governments and agencies which must work together. A smooth-working governing network will ensure that the stadium will be prosperous for everyone.

Just picture the spectacle of more than 150,000 people singing "Hail To The Victors." That alone will get the BIG HOUSE into the Guinness World Records. Under those conditions it won't be long before every campus in the country is clamoring for an enlarged football stadium.

As my philosophy professor used to say, "GO BLUE!"